THE WATER RUPTURES

ELEMENTAL ACADEMY BOOK 3

D.K. HOLMBERG

ASH PUBLISHING

THE WIND GUSTED AROUND TOLAN, WHO STARED OUT INTO the distance. He and Ferrah stood upon the Shapers Path, once again walking to the edge of the city. They would soon depart Amitan, heading beyond the borders.

Tolan glanced over at Ferrah. Her fiery red hair appeared to glow in the sunlight, and she surveyed the area around them. There was more suspicion within her deep green eyes than there had been before. Ever since stopping Master Daniels and being near the Keystone, something had changed for Ferrah. Tolan didn't say anything about it, unsure if she wanted him to comment on it, but he could see it even if others could not.

She remained near one of the master shapers, an older man by the name of Master Krall, staying a step or so away from him. Tolan could feel the shaping she held and wondered if he was the only one aware of her shaping. When he had first come to the Academy, he had believed many of the other shapers could detect shaping the same way he could, but that turned out not to be the case.

An elbow caught him in the side, and Tolan glanced over to see Jonas looking at him. "You don't have to moon after her like that," Jonas said.

"I don't have to do what?"

"I see the way you're looking at her. Go up and talk to her."

"I'm not looking at her in any way."

"Not any way you should be looking at her. You're just staring at her. It's weird. Just go talk to her."

Tolan smiled tightly, pushing his friend away. "It's not like that with us."

"Only because you're afraid. I get the sense from her that she's waiting for you to approach her."

Ferrah and Tolan had both agreed they would not share with Jonas what had happened because it was likely he wouldn't really understand what had taken place. How could he, when he hadn't seen it? Now the Keystone had been moved, there wasn't any way to prove what they had experienced.

"Can you really believe they're allowing us to be a part of the Selection?"

Tolan glanced over at Master Marcella, a lovely dark-haired woman who was only a few years older than him. She was speaking to Master Sartan, her hands moving animatedly while she spoke.

"I didn't think students ever went on a Selection," Tolan whispered.

"They don't. Not usually. That's why this is strange."

"Why would they suddenly change?" He hadn't been able to get much information about why they would suddenly be permitted to travel with the Selection. It troubled him that it might be tied to what had happened at the Keystone—or any of the other strangeness that had happened since he'd come to Amitan to train at the Academy.

"I don't know if it has something to do with the increased movements of the Draasin Lord or not." Jonas flashed a grin. "Either way, it's good for us. Allows us to get out of the city a little bit. And this way, we get to do something other than focus on our training for a little while."

"If we don't keep our focus on our training, we'll never progress to finish the Academy," Tolan said.

"You have been spending too much time with Ferrah."

"What's that supposed to mean?"

"It means it's the sort of thing she would say. Aren't you excited to leave the city?"

"I am, but less excited about where they've asked me to go."

"Everybody is going back to their home towns. You're not the only one going someplace they aren't necessarily thrilled to be going." His gaze drifted over to Draln. The much larger man stood with his back straight, a wide grin spreading across his face, and he seemed to notice they were watching. He turned and grinned at them. "He's probably thrilled to be returning to Velminth. Last time we were there, he—"

"Don't forget both of you are different now you've been at the Academy."

Jonas sighed heavily. "I suppose you're right. It doesn't make it any easier."

"It's not like he has any more authority now he's at the Academy," Tolan said.

"In his mind, he does. Look at him. So smug. He's going to go back, his parents will probably fall all over him, and who knows who else. My parents will be probably more annoyed I've been gone than anything else."

"Why would they be annoyed?"

"They want me to train at the Academy, but my doing so also takes away their free labor. They probably had to hire on several others in order to accommodate me."

"I think I was lucky to have been Selected for the Academy. If I hadn't been, I wasn't sure what I was going to end up doing. With Master Daniels having been sent back to the city…" What was he doing, bringing that up? He shot a look over at Ferrah, who now seemed to be making a point of ignoring him. She was going to be traveling to Par, the farthest of any of them, and on a Shapers Path more treacherous than most. "Anyway, I was thinking I was going to end up working in the mines."

"What would that have been like?"

"I don't know. I've never been. Others without any shaping ability have needed to work in the mines. It's a place those who aren't able to secure an apprenticeship are forced to go." And it was the reason he'd felt rescued by Master Daniels when his parents had disappeared. He had been young then, but not so young as to be ignorant of the consequences. With their absence, he would have been forced to find work that wouldn't have been easy. Life in the mines was difficult, and he'd seen enough people who had returned to know just how difficult that was. Having Master Daniels apprentice him had saved him.

And yet, now it felt like a betrayal.

In the few months since the attack, he hadn't been able to shake what had happened. Master Daniels had attacked him. Tolan still wondered whether there was some connection to the Grand Inquisitor.

"Now you get to go back and show off," Jonas said.

He forced a smile. It didn't feel like he would be victorious in any way, and certainly not to show off. Part of him worried what would happen when he returned. When he'd left, he had not had a chance to talk to Tanner and let him know he was even leaving.

And now Tolan had progressed to the second level in the Academy, what would it be like if Tanner were somehow Selected?

Undoubtedly, it would be awkward. He didn't know what he would say to his friend, only that things wouldn't feel quite the same as they had before.

He wasn't the same. When he had known Tanner, his friend had been a wind shaper of some talent, but Tolan had no shaping ability on his own. In the year or so he'd been gone, he had developed a connection to fire, even if he required the furios to shape with it. His connection to the other elements had improved as well, though his connection to them remained different than others'. Tenuous. For the most part, it required he focus on the elementals, using that power to connect to the element bonds, and even then, he wasn't sure if he was really connecting to the element bonds or to the power of the elementals themselves.

"Are you ready?" Master Marcella asked as she approached.

Jonas grinned at her. "You have fun," he whispered, elbowing Tolan again and heading off.

Tolan turned away and nodded to Master Marcella. "I'm ready."

"I wasn't with you when you were Selected," Master Marcella said, starting off. Tolan kept pace with her, and the city below blurred past. At one point, they paused and, in the distance, Tolan caught sight of the spot he knew the park—and the Keystone—once had occupied. The Grand Master had moved it to protect it, and in the last two months, he had been unable to find it. Tolan had searched, wanting nothing more than to see if he could discover that massive bondar again, but there had been no evidence of it.

His training had become significant enough that he had felt compelled to focus on it rather than on his search for the Keystone. The time he'd spent in his classes had helped him continue to hone his connection to the elementals in the bonds, though he wasn't sure whether he was shaping correctly—only that he was now able to shape each of the elements, something he had not been able to do before spending any time with that massive bondar.

"Are most of the students returning with their Selectors?"

"Most are," Master Marcella said. "A few have gone off with others. I wasn't promoted at that time, not to the point where I was able to go off and serve in a Selection, so this is something of an honor for me."

"Have you ever participated in a Selection before?"

"I won't be doing this alone, if that's what you fear," she said, shooting him a stern look.

Tolan shook his head. He didn't want to start off on the wrong foot with Master Marcella. She might have tried to kill him once, but she did have a desire to have him reach the various element bonds, and she had been particularly pleased about the fact he had begun to reach some of the other bonds. He suspected she wanted to take credit for it, and he worried she would try to use the same shaping techniques she had with him if she were to work with other students.

"That's not what I fear at all. I just wondered whether you had been a part of a Selection before?"

"Nothing other than my own."

"What was yours like?"

"I suppose mine was like any other," she said.

The ground continued to speed past them, flashes of

color, greens and browns. Up this high, they were above most of the wind, though Tolan didn't know if that was merely the height of the Shapers Path or if some shaping prevented the wind from gusting around them. It wouldn't take much for them to be thrown free from this invisible platform. He had some control over his shaping, but possibly not enough to control a fall back to the ground and be able to survive.

"I thought the Inquisitors were involved in the Selections," he said.

"The Inquisitors are involved when it comes to the actual Selection. The time leading up to that is different. We will have some time on our own, so you will have a chance to reconnect with your hometown."

He nodded but said nothing. Like most of the master shapers, she knew he'd been unable to shape any of the elements when he first had come to the Academy, but he wasn't about to remind her of that fact. It wasn't something he was particularly excited to reminisce about, and she probably had no idea what it would be like to have been selected without having spent any time at one of the shaping schools within his home. He was different, and while he had been in Ephra, that difference had been tolerated. When he had come to the Academy, that difference had become quite a bit starker.

"We weren't all that far from your home when we went to the waste," she said.

"Ephra isn't far from the waste," Tolan said softly. Up this high, the sun shone brightly, giving warmth. Every so often, he would reach into the pocket of his cloak and run his finger along the runes of the furios. If only he had been able to figure out how to make a bondar for the other elements. He might be able to shape them in class, but that required his connection to the bondar in order to do so. He had managed with earth using a bondar during his display in the testing, but even with that, he still struggled to reach it consistently. The only element bond he seemed to reach with any fluidity and consistency was fire, and that was because of the furios. "Maybe a day or so, but not much more than that."

"What was it like living so close to it?" Master Marcella asked.

"I didn't really think all that much about it. Some believed us to be closer to the Draasin Lord, and—"

"The Draasin Lord doesn't cross the waste."

Tolan glanced over at her. "The disciples attacked in Amitan."

"You've been to the waste, Shaper Ethar. You've seen the power there. Nothing lives within the waste. If nothing lives there, then nothing could cross it. Even the most powerful Academy shapers struggle to travel very far into the waste."

He had seen that. Growing up, he'd always believed the Draasin Lord had been on the other side of the waste. The master shapers of Ephra had done nothing to alter that perception. Was there some reason they would want people to believe the Draasin Lord was on the other side of the waste?

"Why let people believe that?"

"If people knew the Draasin Lord and his followers were closer, they would be more afraid. The Academy shapers and the master shapers scattered throughout Terndahl are capable of stopping the disciples of the Draasin Lord." She looked over at him, fixing him with a bright-eyed stare. "Now you have progressed to the second level, you will be expected to be a greater part of the opposition. When your training is done, whether at the end of this level or in the future, you will be called upon to serve. All shapers who trained at the Academy are considered master shapers. Now you have progressed beyond the first level, you too will one day be called Master Ethar."

Tolan hadn't given that much thought before. It was true. Now he had passed through the first level—the one widely considered the most difficult— he would be considered a master. It meant that regardless of what else he did, he would always have a position within Terndahl. He would never be forced into the mines. He had a place. What did it matter if his connection to shaping was different than others?

As long as he was the only one to know about it, it probably didn't.

"Where is the Draasin Lord?"

She grunted. "If we knew that, we wouldn't let him and his followers continue causing trouble. Unfortunately, they've remained hidden and continue to attack such as you've seen."

They paused. From here, the Shapers Path veered off in several different directions. Master Marcella performed a shaping, sending it streaking away. For a moment, Tolan wondered what she was doing, but he realized she was using her shaping to guide her.

Could she really not know where they were going?

Perhaps not.

"How extensive are the Shapers Paths?"

"They have been added to over the years, and now they crisscross most of Terndahl. In places like Amitan and some of the other great cities, people with minimal abilities can reach the lower levels of the Shapers Path, but in most places, they require shapers with a reasonable ability. As you can imagine, there is some danger in coming to the Shapers Path."

As extensive as they were, he wondered if they all served the same purpose as the Shapers Path around Amitan. That one had served as something of a protective barrier, and it had helped conceal the Keystone. Would the other Shapers Paths be similar?

"Are there others as extensive as the one around Amitan?"

"Amitan, as the capital of Terndahl and the location of the Academy, is different than many other places."

"It's different, but are there others?"

She shrugged. "When I visited Par, they had fairly extensive Shapers Paths as well. Doman did too. A few other places."

Tolan tried to envision the various cities. Par was near

the edge of Terndahl, much like Ephra and Doman. Amitan was not, situated near the heart of the empire that occupied most of the free land. Though there were other nations beyond the borders of Terndahl, they were so far away as to be unreachable.

As they walked, wind gusted, and Master Marcella stopped, forming a shaping to push against it.

"That's odd," she said softly.

"What's odd?"

"Part of the shaping that binds the Shapers Path is one that settles all of the elements around it. There should be no wind blowing like that."

Another gust struck and she reacted, throwing up another shaping. The wind settled for a moment or two and then it picked up again, once more swirling with incredible force.

There was something within it that struck Tolan as strange.

Master Marcella forced him down but he looked up as she continued to shape, holding her hands outward, bracing herself against the wind. It pulled at her hair, sending it whipping around her. While she was a powerful shaper, the power of the wind was something more than she could stop.

It was elemental wind.

Tolan could feel it.

He closed his eyes, focusing on the elemental of wind, thinking through the various elementals he knew. There were dozens. Each could be responsible, but he thought about what he knew of wind and the wind elementals, trying to connect to one of them.

"Do you think this is a rogue elemental?" Tolan yelled against the wind.

"There should be no rogue elementals," Master Marcella said. She stood in place, her feet fixed, planted firmly on the Shapers Path, but with the wind gusting as it was, he wondered how long it would last before she were thrown free.

If she were cast off, she was powerful enough to catch herself, but with the wind blowing like this, it was possible she wouldn't be able to return.

It would leave Tolan by himself.

"Is this a shaping?" Even as he asked, he knew the answer. He didn't detect anything within it that suggested it was a shaping.

"There's no shaping energy within it."

If it wasn't shaped, and it wasn't natural—something Tolan had a hard time believing, especially as the Shapers Path was designed to prevent such things—that left only the elementals.

He had started to say something when another gust picked up and sent Master Marcella flying.

She was battered, thrown free from the Shapers Path, and Tolan spun, reaching for her. His hand grazed hers, but as he tried to close around her wrist, another gust kicked up and she went soaring away.

While Tolan watched, her eyes went wide. Shaping built from her, and he could see her trying to force her way back to him, back to the Path, but the wind continued to throw her farther and farther away.

Tolan remained crouched low on the Shapers Path.

The winds buffeted around him, and as he stayed low, he managed to avoid the worst, but not all of it. It tried to peel him free from the Shapers Path. The path was narrow but mostly solid. There was some texture to it that had to be shaped into it, and he dug his fingers into it, trying to grip and keep from being tossed free. As powerful as the wind was, he didn't like the odds of being able to survive the fall.

Another gust slammed into him.

If he were to survive this, he would have to counter the wind, but how?

Without the wind bondar, a withering, he would have no way of connecting to the wind effectively.

He again focused on what he could recall of the wind elementals. There were regional variations between the elementals, and he couldn't remember which ones had been more common in this part of the world. The time when the elementals had existed freely had changed the landscape, leaving it different and difficult to know what had once been here.

Rather than trying to focus on a single specific elemental, Tolan decided to pick a more powerful one. If nothing else, focusing on a powerful elemental might allow him a strength to counter what was happening.

With some of the other elementals, hyza and saa, he was able to use them, to speak to them and direct them.

He had even managed to do the same with jinnar and the draasin. Could he do the same with the wind?

He needed to do something, if only to keep from being tossed down to the ground below.

Another gust struck him, and he focused. The wind elemental that came to mind was one of the more powerful ones, known as ara. He maintained his focus on it. There was power within that connection, and as he focused, he envisioned what he recalled of it.

All he needed was to find that stirring deep within him. If he could do that, if he could draw out that connection, he wouldn't need the bondar.

Wind continued to slam into him, distracting his focus.

Every attempt to connect to the wind elemental failed. As much as he wanted to reach the elemental—even if it would help him—he couldn't.

Another blast of wind struck him and he went sliding, teetering near the edge of the Shapers Path.

Panic set in, sending his heart racing. Sweat beaded on his brow and his entire body tensed. He might be able to shape fire, but would there be anything that would be able to help him? He might need to hold onto any potential with fire in case he was tossed free from the Shapers Path. A burst of fire shaping might be required to keep him from landing too hard on the ground.

As the wind continued to batter him, he closed his eyes, focusing on the feeling he'd had when he had been in the park near the Keystone, the feeling he had known when he had his hand upon the bondar, the connection he'd had when he had called upon wind. He had done so before, and he needed to do it again.

There was no stirring from deep within him.

The wind battered him, and he slipped.

He fell off the edge of the Shapers Path. Somehow, he managed to grip the edge and he dangled, suspended in the air. The wind swirled around him, and all it would take was one more push and he would be tossed free, thrown down to the hard ground far below him. It was the kind of thing he would be unable to survive.

Please.

He sent it out as a plea to the wind, the same way he had when he'd been in the park, begging the elementals for help. When he had been there that time, he had been the one who had summoned the elementals, and so had a greater reason to believe he might be successful in convincing them to assist him.

Please. Don't hurt me.

He focused on the image of the elemental wind, and for a moment, he felt a fluttering, a stirring deep within him, but realized that had to be nothing more than the pressure of the wind trying to toss him down to the ground.

A gradual realization came to him that the wind was no longer pushing on him nearly as forcefully. Tolan cocked one eye open and then the other. He was still dangling, and so he pulled himself up, dragging himself onto the Shapers Path. The wind swirled around him, but with less force. As the moments passed, even that began to die off, and finally, it abated altogether.

He rolled onto his back, staring up at the sky, his heart still pounding and sweat still rolling down his forehead.

Thank you.

He had no idea if the elemental heard, but it seemed as if there came a soft sigh that faded slowly, disappearing into the sky.

2

Tolan lost track of time, losing any sense of how long he lay on his back, staring up at the sky, trying to regain a connection to himself. There was no additional wind, nothing that attempted to throw him free from the Shapers Path. After a while, Tolan finally sat up, looking around.

He was in the middle of the Shapers Path, and there was no gusting breeze, only the warmth shining down on him from above. The Shapers Path felt solid and he got to his feet, looking around, turning his attention to the ground below and straining to see if he could find any evidence of Master Marcella.

Where had she gone?

With the winds now having died down, Tolan and Master Marcella could continue on their way toward Ephra. If she didn't return, he had no intention of going on to Ephra on his own. It would be better to return to

Amitan, and from there he could check in with the Grand Master, report what had happened, and... What? Explain they had been attacked by a rogue elemental? Who would believe that? Even more than that, who would believe Tolan alone would have been able to stop the rogue elemental?

And he wasn't even sure that was what it was. All he knew was that they had been nearly been thrown free from the Shapers Path.

A shaping built and Tolan reached into his pocket for the furios, preparing for whatever might appear. If it was whoever had sent the elemental, he wanted to be ready.

Instead, Master Marcella appeared, landing on the Shapers Path with a flutter of wind. A small scratch had left dried blood on her cheek and her eyes had tension within them, but she looked otherwise unharmed.

"That was odd," she said softly.

"What do you think happened?" Tolan asked.

"I'm not sure. I haven't felt power like that in quite some time," she said.

"Not elementals?"

"There would be no elementals up here," she said.

She motioned for him to follow, so Tolan got to his feet and started after her. She walked a little more rigidly than she had before, and every so often, she would pause, a shaping building as if to check for anything taking place around them. Tolan understood her caution but doubted there would be anything she would be able to detect if it had come from the elementals. He had detected nothing that suggested a shaping had attacked them before.

"What if it was disciples of the Draasin Lord?" A memory of that attack came to him, a reminder of what he had seen when the disciples of the Draasin Lord had attacked in Amitan before. They were powerful, but they didn't simply abandon an attack the way this seemed to have been abandoned. He and Marcella pressed forward, continuing to force their way. If the disciples were involved, Tolan doubted they would have given up so easily.

"I found no evidence of the disciples," she said.

"You went looking?"

"I had to ensure this was just a natural wind," she said.

"Are there natural winds that powerful?"

"Have you ever stood upon the peak of any mountain?"

Tolan had. It was all part of his parents' plan for him to attempt to reach an ability to shape. Those were memories that stuck with him, their decision to bring him out of Ephra and to the top of the Maileen Mountains, their snowcapped peaks impressive. Even when he'd been there, Tolan hadn't been able to connect to earth any better than at any time prior. He had his ability to sense, no differently than he had when he was in Ephra itself.

It was similar to the way Marcella had attempted to connect him to water, though there had been no fear of death with what his parents had done. They hadn't tossed him from the mountain or buried him or any number of other awful things that might have been considered to try to bring him closer to the element. They had only brought him to help him reach the elementals, and it had failed.

Many parents throughout Terndahl went to great lengths to see whether their children had a connection to the elements. Having a connection would allow them to be brought into the shaping schools, and while all students attended the primary shaping schools, getting acquainted with shaping in general and any ability of sensing—something almost everyone had—very few were able to progress beyond that. There was prestige in joining the secondary shaping schools, places that had attempted to teach him in Ephra, but Tolan had never had much proficiency.

"I have."

"If you stood on the peak of the mountains, then you would have surely felt the wind."

"There was some wind when I was at the Maileen Mountains."

She glanced over at him. "The Maileen?"

He nodded. "Why?"

"Only that most would say that's a dangerous place, and certainly for someone who isn't a skilled shaper."

"It didn't seem so dangerous."

"Then perhaps it wasn't the Maileen."

Tolan was certain that was where his parents had brought him, but he had no recollection of any danger. In fact, his experience had been almost peaceful. There had been a welcoming sense, almost as if he had been supposed to be there.

"When you stand upon the mountaintop, and you feel the wind gusting around you, you recognize the power of the wind bond. There are several who recommend going to such places in order to connect to the wind. When you're there, if you can connect to that sense, if you can feel it in a way that is deeper than anywhere else, then perhaps you can grow to shape it."

"My parents brought me there to try to connect me to earth."

She nodded thoughtfully. "It might work. Earth is powerful there, as well. Imagine how much earth must be potent in such places in order to cause the mountains to swell up from the ground. Many argue that in places like that, you can be closer to all of the element bonds. Not only do you connect to earth and wind, but you are closer to the sun, and when you're high enough, there's snow on the peaks of the mountains, making it so even water would be reachable."

He hadn't considered that before, but it did make sense. And yet, when he had been on the peak of the mountain, he had detected nothing.

"You never thought to bring me to the mountains to try to reach my abilities," he said.

"I said some believe that, not me."

"And you believe the wind we just encountered was natural like that?"

She shrugged. "I searched for any sign of shaping, and there was none."

Tolan nodded. He hadn't needed to search for shaping to be able to agree with that. He had felt no shaping.

"And with no shaping, that means it was natural. We are deep enough within Terndahl that there would be no elementals released."

He decided not to argue with her. It would get him nowhere anyway and would possibly only irritate her if he did. It was better to just agree.

"How much farther do we have to go to reach Ephra?" he asked. He wanted to be ready when they reached Ephra, not wanting to be unprepared for returning to his homeland.

She pointed, and Tolan glanced down at the ground. He hadn't been paying attention to it, focusing more on the Shapers Path and trying not to fall, but now she did point, he realized they were approaching a city.

The last time that he had come this way, he had been with Jory, and heading away from the city. It was after his Selection, and he had gone with surprise and fear within him, not knowing what he might encounter. When they had come to the waste, they had avoided Ephra.

"Do you miss it?" Master Marcella asked.

Tolan debated whether to be honest or not. He defaulted to honesty. "I'm not sure how I feel."

"Is it because you struggled to shape?"

"Struggle would be implying I had any ability to shape," Tolan said. "I had no ability. One of my best friends did, and..." He stared at the city in the distance. The path didn't stretch all the way to Ephra, but from here he could make it out. Ephra was simple. From high above, it had nothing remarkable about it, not like places like Amitan. There, the towering spires of the Academy rose high into the air, giving a sense of majesty to everything. Ephra was rundown, an older city, and a place where he had been forced to live, but it had never been home—not really.

"He's the reason you went to the Selection."

Tolan nodded. Had it not been for Tanner, he would have never risked himself. There was no reason to have done so. He had no known shaping ability and therefore had no reason to think he would have any way of passing the Selection. As far as he knew, only those with shaping ability had ever passed the Selection.

"Do you think he will present himself again?"

He shrugged. "Considering everyone who present themselves for Selection has their minds shaped if they fail, he wouldn't remember having done so."

"It's how we ensure the integrity of the Selection."

"I've wondered about that. When I was Selected, they told me those who fail have their memories shaped so they don't remember, but I wonder what would happen if they wouldn't have their memories shaped. Would they be any more successful?"

When Marcella looked at him, he shrugged. "It's just that I wonder whether or not it makes a difference. It's not as if those who fail would stop studying and stop trying to learn. I imagine they still would continue to work, wanting to reach the Academy."

He knew Tanner would have, along with Velthan. In hindsight, Tolan was actually surprised that Velthan hadn't passed the Selection. He was the kind of person who Tolan would have expected to have been pushed forward, the kind of person he feared would be Selected, making life difficult. He already had someone like that at the Academy in Draln, and he didn't need another.

"The Selection process has been unchanged for centuries. We do it that way so we can ensure the greatest integrity of our students. Those who fail will continue to train at their shaping schools, and there is value in that. How could there not be, especially as we want them to continue training, to continue working, and to eventually either make their way to the Academy or remain within their city and serve."

They continued toward the city. As they neared, the outer buildings began to take shape. Most of the outer buildings were homes, and while they were once quite majestic, that was no longer the case. Over time, buildings had crumbled, and there weren't enough earth shapers to maintain those structures out here, this far into the Terndahl Empire. Those near the center of the city remained stronger, most stout structures, designed to withstand incredible forces of shaping, and Tolan knew the earth shapers had spent considerable time maintaining those buildings; otherwise, they would have fallen. Some of the central buildings, particularly the largest, had been there for centuries. Without continuous shaping maintaining them, they would have long ago fallen into disrepair, much in the same way many of the outer buildings had.

His old family home was one such building. After his parents' disappearance, Tolan hadn't gone back, and as far as he knew, no one had taken it over. He had moved into Master Daniels' shop and had stayed there while apprenticed.

"You never answered."

"I never answered what?"

"The question. You never said whether you were looking forward to returning."

"No," he said softly.

She studied him for a long moment before motioning for him to follow. They had reached the end of the Shapers Path. They were still a way outside of Ephra, far enough that they would have to walk the rest on the ground, but near enough that he still marveled at how quickly they had been able to travel between Ephra and Amitan. By foot or by horse, it would have taken days, or longer. On the Shapers Path, it was barely half a day, and Tolan suspected it could be even faster if they were to run. There was something about the pace they took that allowed for increased rate of travel upon the Shapers Path. The faster they walked, the greater the distance they traveled.

Squeezing the furios, Tolan jumped and focused on the ground, pushing up with a burst of flame that he summoned from his connection to hyza. There was no burst of the elemental, nothing that would reveal what he did, but he continued to fear that one of these days, he would accidentally reveal to someone of consequence the way he shaped. Master Marcella was definitely someone of consequence, and he worried what she might do or say if she realized how he shaped.

She followed, landing behind him, wind swirling around them.

"Do you have recommendations about where we should stay?"

"We get to choose?"

"Most of the time when we come to a town or village, we stay in one of the Academy-associated inns, but considering you have knowledge of this place, I wondered if perhaps there might be a better place."

Tolan shook his head. "I doubt you will find anything that will be any better than what the Academy has ties with." He didn't even need to know which place the Academy had connections to, not recalling it from the last Selection, but suspected it was someplace much nicer than what he would have known.

"You will stay there as well?"

"I don't have anyone else in the city to stay with," he said.

"I thought you grew up here. Don't you have a home?"

"I did. And I was apprenticed here, but…"

He cut off before saying too much. It wasn't so much that he feared she would uncover his connection to Master Daniels, though he didn't know if she was already aware of that. How much had the Grand Master shared with others? It was more that he didn't want to remind anyone of his connection to the Draasin Lord. He didn't have a connection himself, but there remained that tie from his parents, whether they had gone willingly or not. The more time he spent at the Academy, the more he questioned whether it had been willing or not.

If they had gone willingly, why wouldn't they have brought him? Unless they feared the Academy and its shapers coming after them and endangering him. And if they hadn't gone willingly, why them?

So many questions, and he had no answers. Perhaps he never would, which troubled him even more.

"I'm going to make arrangements, so you are free to meet me at the Winding Inn at sunset."

Tolan glanced the sky. That gave him far more time than he wanted, but at the same time, maybe it would be good to have some time to wander.

She headed toward the center of the city, and Tolan followed for a little while before veering off. The pull of some of these outer homes called to him, and he didn't know if it came from the fact he had no idea what Master Daniels had implied about his parents or whether it was simply the fact he'd been away from Ephra for the last year, making it so that he now wanted to see what his old home was like.

He meandered through familiar streets. Mostly, they were empty. Occasionally, he came across a few children, though he recognized none. Every so often, he would find older people hurrying, and in this outer section, they were often dressed in well-worn clothes.

At one point, an older man who Tolan thought was familiar glanced in his direction, and as he did, his eyes widened and he jerked his head around, veering off and heading into a different direction.

When it happened again with a different person, Tolan paused. Was he recognized?

That didn't make any sense. There would be no reason for people to turn away from him in such a way, even if he were recognized.

He glanced down at his clothing and understanding came to him. They were turning away because he was from the Academy.

There was no questioning his clothing. It was distinctive, the navy and gray marking him as one of the Academy. Most people wouldn't recognize the stripe of the student; they would only see the colors and know that he was a master shaper.

He debated taking off his cloak and bundling it up but decided against it. It might be better to wander alone, not be burdened by others wandering near him or questioning why he was here. With the Academy cloak and colors, he didn't have to worry about any others coming to close to him.

He could explore without anyone bothering him.

He made his way around the city, following streets that had long ago been ingrained into memory. His feet knew where they were going even if he didn't direct them. He was able to let his mind wander, and he went from thoughts of the strange wind elemental attack to the proximity to the waste, to thinking back to Master Daniels and the way that he had betrayed Tolan.

And then he came to stop before a home he had last looked upon over a year ago.

When he had lived in the home, he had felt it comfortable. It was in one of the outer sections of Ephra, far enough removed from the edge of the city that they didn't have to feel quite as if they were on the outskirts, but not so central that he felt as if they were in one of the more privileged sections. It had been as well-maintained as his parents had been able to make it. The stone crumbled in certain sections, but no more than any of the other neighboring homes. The windows were dirty, but the glass remained intact. The The relatively recent paint left a certain vibrancy to the home that others nearby didn't have. He approached the doorway slowly, resting his hand on it, feeling a familiar surge of comfort.

Tolan pushed the door open and stepped inside.

Dust covered everything. He had wondered if someone else might have taken over the home, especially if as it had been unoccupied for so long, but perhaps the fear of a connection to the Draasin Lord kept others away. There would be a superstition about it, and while Tolan hated that some would think that way, the fact there would be such a superstition had its benefits.

The furniture was all as he remembered. There were several chairs situated near the hearth, charred embers long ago burned away. As he took a step toward it, dust drifted toward him, cloying in his nostrils. Near the kitchen, the table and chairs were all arranged neatly as his mother would often situate them. She was always organized, and the pots hanging from hooks in the kitchen fit that organization. Everything looked as it had.

Tolan stepped back into one of the back rooms. His parents' room was unchanged, nothing more than a wardrobe and the bed which, like everyplace else, had a coating of dust. He resisted the urge to go over to the wardrobe and open it, not certain he could stand the sight of his parents' clothing. It would be a reminder of too much he had lost. He turned away, heading to his room, and that was more chaotic, less organized, his belongings having been hastily gathered, taken when he had gone with Master Daniels, and he had grabbed everything he thought he might need.

The only other room in the house was his father's workshop. Tolan stepped to the end of the hall and pushed the door open. It was larger than most of the other places, with an arched roof that gave even more sense of space. Like everything else, it was covered in dust. He went to his father's bench and ran his hand along the surface, wiping away the dust. The tools lining the wall called to him, but Tolan resisted the urge to pick any up.

A cabinet over the bench drew his eye. His father would often put partial projects inside, and he pulled it open but found it empty. Whatever had been here had long ago been taken. He was surprised the tools remained.

Tolan took a step back, his gaze drifting around the inside of the workshop, and he noticed something in the corner.

He made his way over to it and lifted it off the ground, holding it up. It was made of stone and it sparked a memory, the same memory that had come to him during the Selection. It was odd that particular memory should come to him now, especially as he couldn't recall ever having that memory before the Selection. His father had been working on something much like this piece, creating a sculpture or whatever this was. He stared at it, twisting it in his hands.

Tolan wiped it on his cloak and held it up. There wasn't enough light in the workshop to make out anything about it, but the ridges he had detected reminded him of the shape of the runes on the furios.

That was odd, wasn't it?

He slipped the item into his pocket and looked around the shop. There was nothing else for him here and he turned away, heading back into the house. He paused in the kitchen, wondering if there was anything here of his mother's that he could take as a reminder, the same way he now had this item of his father's as a reminder of him, but there wasn't. Instead, he decided to go back to their bedroom, forcing himself to look in the wardrobe.

When he pulled the doors open, dust came with it. He waited for it to settle, then pushed aside the hanging clothing. Three drawers occupied the back wall and Tolan pulled them out, noticing one was filled with jewelry. He reached inside, grabbing a necklace. He held it up, but in the dim light, he wasn't able to make out anything about it, and it certainly wasn't enough to remind him of her. She would wear jewelry, but never anything like this necklace.

There were several rings in the drawer, and he slipped those into his pocket, too. If nothing else, all of this belonged to him now. There was nothing else in there.

He pulled the next door open and found a stack of folded clothes. He sorted through it, but there was nothing other than what he had found initially.

The bottom drawer was much the same.

At least he had jewelry of his mother's. Even if it was jewelry he didn't recall her wearing, he would be able to think on it, remember her, and maybe feel connected to her in a way he hadn't in some time.

As he made his way out of the home, he closed the door behind him. Out in the brighter light, he pulled from his pocket the item from his father's workshop and held it up. In the sunlight, areas on the stone carving took on a clearer image. Where he thought he had felt ridges, he was now certain they were runes.

And he recognized them.

Earth.

Had his father known of the runes and rune magic?

He focused on earth, thinking of jinnar and squeezing the sculpture. As he did, it rumbled quickly.

More quickly than he would have been able to do on his own.

The fact he reached it so easily with the sculpture...

Could it be a bondar?

Tolan started to shape again, and once again, earth began to rumble.

He released it before calling to jinnar, fearing he drew too much attention to his shaping, yet feeling a strange thrill that worked through him, but also concern. If his father had knowledge of rune magic and how to make a bondar, could that be why they had been taken by the Draasin Lord?

The idea it had been left him unsettled. If that was the case, then his parents had been valuable to the Draasin Lord, and he could understand why they would have been targeted, grabbed.

Only... As Tolan thought about it, he remembered his father working over several years. If he had been making sculptures like this—if he had been making bondars—who had they been for?

3

TOLAN WANDERED THROUGH THE STREETS, HEADING AWAY from his home, his mind spinning. All those years his parents had been working together, crafting as he had thought, and only now he began to wonder if there had been more to it. Running his finger along the edge of the sculpture, he continued to feel the runes marked in it.

Why had they never told him?

But then, why would they have? He had no connection to the element bonds, and without that, having an ability to shape something like this, to create a bondar, would have been useless.

What were the chances that he would attempt to create a bondar, considering his parents had done the same?

It seemed surprising and, at the same time, fitting.

So many questions came to mind. Master Daniels must have known, which was probably why he had taken Tolan in all those years ago. And if he had known, who else would have?

Maybe his parents hadn't been quite as innocent as he had believed. He had thought they didn't serve the Draasin Lord, and he had argued against those who made the claim they did, but what if that wasn't true? What if they had served, and had gone willingly to continue to serve, making bondars for the Draasin Lord? Tolan had never really understood what value his parents would have had to someone like the Draasin Lord, but if they were able to make bondars, that would be incredibly valuable.

"Tolan?"

He blinked and looked up, half expecting to run into Master Marcella, but she would have called him Shaper Ethar, not Tolan.

He came face to face with Tanner.

Tanner Venan was tall and slender, carrying the build of many of the wind shapers. In the year they'd been apart, his face had grown slightly leaner, and a faint scruff of beard had begun to grow on his face. He was dressed in a jacket and pants, a nice cut to them indicating a certain degree of wealth, something Tanner had never known when Tolan had been in Ephra.

"What are you doing? What are you wearing?"

"Tanner." As he said his friend's name, tension built within him. All this time he'd been away, all he'd experienced, he had never considered how he would share it with Tanner.

There was a part of Tolan that had simply moved on after he had left Ephra. That part had never known how and what he would explain to those he had left behind. Unlike some, he didn't have any reason to return, and they wouldn't have known or wondered where he'd gone.

"I have so much to tell you about."

"That's... That's the cloak of the Academy!"

Tolan nodded. "I was Selected."

"You? But you can't shape!"

Tolan looked around. While there were people out, they were making a point to avoid them, moving off to either side of the street. Single-story buildings lined either side of the street, some shops while others were homes. The shops on the street weren't well labeled, though that was not uncommon in this part of the city. It was only then Tolan realized Tanner's dress seemed so out of place for the section of the city they found themselves in.

"Apparently, you don't need to have an ability to shape to be Selected."

"How?"

"It's a long story."

"One you don't intend to tell your friend?"

He took a deep breath, glancing up at the sky. There was still quite a bit of time before he was to meet Master Marcella, so he might as well share with Tanner. What else was he going to do? Now he had been to his home, there really wasn't anything else.

Other than visit Master Daniels' shop.

"Walk with me?" Tolan asked.

Tanner nodded and they started through the street, making their way toward the shop. As Master Daniels had been an earth shaper, he had been allowed to set up his shop in one of the nicer sections of the city. Tanner watched him, and Tolan felt a flush building within him, rising in his neck and working up toward his face. He took a deep breath, steadying himself. He had to remind himself he had been Selected and he belonged. And, surprisingly, had he not gone to the Academy, he would not have been able to have a hand in stopping many other things that had taken place.

"I went to the Selection a year ago to find you."

"To find me?"

"We'd gotten into an argument, and I went to support you."

"I never went to a Selection..." He turned toward him, a flash of irritation washing across his face. "They spirit-shaped me?"

Tolan nodded. "Everyone who doesn't get Selected gets spirit-shaped."

"But no one seems to have been chosen!"

"No one else was picked. It was just me."

"I don't understand."

"I can't say I understand any better. From what I can tell, it's not uncommon to not have any Selected. They're looking for those who have particular talents."

"Can you tell me anything about the Selection?"

Master Marcella and the Grand Master had been quite

explicit that they not reveal anything, and so Tolan shook his head. "I'm not sure me telling you anything would make it any more likely you'd succeed. The Selection is different for each person."

"I thought it was just a test of shaping."

"Apparently it's not. If it was a test of shaping, I never would have passed."

"Are you here because you never developed the ability to shape?"

Tolan sighed, reaching into his pocket and gripping the furios. He didn't like having to prove himself, especially to Tanner, but there was the residual memory others had of him and his inability to shape. If nothing else, he wanted to end that now, to have Tanner recognize he belonged at the Academy. It had taken Tolan a long time to come to terms with the fact that he belonged.

He focused on saa, letting his connection to the furios help him focus his connection to the elemental, and as he did, power began to build and the flame flickered above his open hand. Tolan held it in place, then began to spiral it, slower and slower until he squeezed, extinguishing the flame altogether.

Tanner's breath caught. "Fire?"

"Fire. Earth. Occasionally, wind and water."

Tanner's eyes widened. "All of the elements?"

"The Academy has ways of helping to ensure shapers can reach other elements," he said.

"What sort of ways?"

Tolan shrugged. Would it matter if he told Tanner about bondars? Probably not, and seeing as how the only bondars Tanner would get near would be the ones Tolan had in his pocket, the only time that would matter would be when Tanner attempted to shape.

"They are called bondars."

Tanner's face screwed up in a frown. "We have bondars. They aren't worth anything. I mean, they might be able to help some people connect, but they aren't that useful. I've tried, and I can't get them to do anything."

"I bet the bondars at the Academy are more potent than the bondars you would have access to."

As he said it, he realized that sounded somewhat conceited, but at the same time, it was true. The Academy had the original bondars. The shaping schools in places like Ephra likely had copies of copies.

"I still want to know how you were Selected. I just can't believe you would be the one chosen from here!"

"To be honest, I can't believe I was chosen, either." There was no harm in admitting that, especially as he still marveled at the fact he had been the one picked. More surprising, or perhaps maybe not more surprising, he now felt as if he *should* have been picked. Had he not, he would never have begun to understand how he could reach the elements.

Maybe the Selection was more accurate than he had given it credit for.

"Why did you return?" Tanner asked.

Tolan wasn't sure how to answer at first but realized it didn't make a difference if he told him the truth. The fact they were here for a Selection would get out to those who had the ability to participate.

"There's going to be a Selection," he said.

His eyes widened. "There is? Usually we would hear about it, wouldn't we?" He frowned, biting his lip. "I guess if we've been spirit-shaped in the past, we might not remember being notified."

"They might not know yet," Tolan said.

"I didn't realize students get to participate in the Selection."

"I don't think they normally get to, but this year is different."

"Why?"

"To be honest, I'm not entirely sure. All I know is the other students in the Academy have been sent out to participate in the Selection."

They reached the street with Master Daniels' shop, and Tolan hesitated. There was no reason he should hesitate, but Master Daniels had been a part of something he hadn't known about, and because of that, Tolan worried he might have some way of surveying what he was doing. If so, Tolan wanted to be careful not to draw Master Daniels' attention.

"He's not come back," Tanner said.

"I know," Tolan said.

"You know?"

"He was sent away, but…" He looked around, debating whether he would head into the shop or not before deciding to go in. Why wouldn't he? There was nothing for him to fear here.

"I know he was sent away, and I know he shouldn't be returning anytime soon. And if he does, those of us in the Academy need to know about it."

"Why? What did he do?"

"It's nothing," Tolan said.

Tanner studied him for a moment, a slight grin on his face. "You haven't changed so much that I can't tell when you're lying. Something happened, but it seems you don't want to tell me."

"I'm not sure I'm allowed to tell you," Tolan said.

"So, whatever this is happens to be Academy business?"

"For now," Tolan said.

Tanner smiled. "I still can't believe Tolan Ethar was Selected. I mean, when you disappeared, everyone thought you had run off to the mines, especially when Master Daniels disappeared at the same time. We knew he had gone off with people of the Academy, so we had thought you had disappeared." Tanner's smile faded. "I was disappointed. I thought you'd left without telling me."

"I did leave without telling you," he said.

"If you were Selected, at least I understand why."

"They don't. Even though I wanted to tell you, they wouldn't let me. I wanted you to know I supported you.

That was the reason I went to the Selection in the first place."

Tanner met his eyes for a moment and Tolan turned away, pushing open the door leading into Master Daniels' shop.

Much like in his home, the shop had a layer of dust coating everything. The air smelled stale and Tolan looked around at half-completed projects, a stack of wood in one corner, and the door leading back to the storeroom where he had once been asked to sort through the wood. With his weak ability for earth sensing, sorting through things had always taken him incredibly long compared to Master Daniels. And yet, Tolan had gladly done it, preferring that over the alternative.

"What are you hoping to find here?"

"Maybe answers," Tolan whispered.

He looked around, and as he did, he felt much the same way here as he had in his old home. This had been a place of safety for so long, a place where he had felt protected, and the fact Master Daniels had welcomed him had only strengthened that feeling over time. All of those feelings had been a lie.

And now he would see if there was anything Master Daniels had been keeping from him. If he had, Tolan was determined to know what. Maybe he would uncover some key to what he had been after in Amitan, or perhaps a connection between him and the Grand Inquisitor.

He continued to look around, but there was nothing here that suggested Master Daniels had been hiding anything. As much as he wanted to believe he would come up with something, it was possible he wouldn't. Master Daniels had hidden his intentions for a long time—long enough that Tolan hadn't known what he was doing even when he had been apprenticed to him. It was possible Master Daniels had expected someone to have come through here.

As Tolan was pulling open cupboards, Tanner watched him. "What are you thinking you might find?"

"I'm not entirely sure."

"You just wanted to look through his cupboards?"

"I wanted to see if there was anything that might explain him a little better to me."

"What are you looking to understand?"

Tolan glanced over, debating whether he should say anything before deciding not to. There was no point in sharing anything with Tanner, especially as it was unlikely he would be able to help at all.

"I just thought I would try and understand why Master Daniels was summoned back to Amitan."

"I seem to remember it had something to do with an elemental."

Tolan had wondered how much Tanner would remember. Considering the way the shaping spirit was used on him, he didn't know whether Tanner would recall anything at all, or if it was limited to a specific timeline. How tightly controlled was the shaping used upon them?

The fact Tanner remembered the elemental suggested it was more tightly controlled than he had expected.

"There was an elemental. Do you remember anything about it?"

"Only that it was terrifying." Tanner watched him for a moment, cocking his head to the side. "Did they teach you how to face elementals at the Academy?"

"Not in lessons I've been through so far."

"What sort of things are they teaching you?"

Tolan wondered if there was any harm in sharing with Tanner before deciding there must not be. "They have been teaching the way the element bonds and the elementals are all interrelated."

"How are they all interrelated?"

"More than you would expect. It has something to do with the way the elementals have been forced into the element bonds, and together with that, the power is considerable."

"Are you haven't learned how to defeat elementals?"

Tolan squeezed his lips together, frowning deeply. He shook his head. If Tanner wanted to know how to defeat the elementals, Tolan wasn't going to share anything with him.

He continued to go through the cabinets but found nothing more than woodworking implements in a drawer full of tools. There had been a time when he had thought he would be trained to use those tools, though now that time would never happen. When he had been working with Master Daniels, he had wanted nothing more than to have the opportunity to gain experience working with the tools, thinking that over time, Master Daniels would allow him to work with him. That had all been part of his plan. And there was nothing here that would help him understand what the master's plan might actually have been.

He glanced in the back room, looking for anything he might be able to find, but there was nothing. The stack of wood was unchanged from when he had been here before, a reminder of his old tasks.

Tolan straightened, wiping the dust off his hands. "There's nothing here that I can find," he said.

"If you would tell me what you were looking for, I might be able to help."

He smiled tightly. "Just something that would be a reminder of Master Daniels."

"A reminder? Like with his tools? He's been gone long enough that I don't think he'd mind if you took them."

"No. I don't need any of his tools. Besides, someone might come and take over his shop eventually and—"

"You don't think he's going to return?"

Tolan cursed himself silently. He needed to be more careful.

"Eventually, he'll probably return, but it's possible once he's done, he won't have any interest in returning to Ephra."

Tanner grunted. "I feel the same way. When I get a chance to go to the Academy, I don't intend to come back here. I hate being so close to the waste, fearing the elementals escaping and worrying about what they might do to me."

Tolan smiled to himself, and he wondered what Tanner might think if he knew that part of the training at the Academy involved coming back to the waste, taking that chance to sit on the other side of it, experience the absence of shaping.

Probably the same as most of the shapers who were in the Academy. Having a separation from their shaping ability was difficult for most. Even for Tolan, losing the ability to detect others shaping around him had been more difficult than what he had expected, letting him know just how much he had come to rely upon that ability.

"I need to meet my mentor, Tanner."

"What are they like?"

"She's young. Frustrating. And she only tried to kill me once."

Tanner started laughing, but when Tolan didn't join him, his eyes started to widen. "She tried to kill you?"

"Only when she thought it would help me reach water better. She dropped me in the ocean to see if I would be able to access it."

"Why would she think that would work?"

"Apparently the shapers of old used to think similar things, though I'm not sure they ever really did or whether it was simply something she was trying with me because of frustration." He trailed off toward the end, thinking the last mostly to himself. Regardless of Master Marcella's motivation, Tolan wasn't sure he ever would know what she intended with him. It was possible she really *did* think he would find a way to connect to water in the way she had attempted, though he had a hard time believing anyone would ever reach it through stress like that.

They stopped at the front of the shop and Tolan rested his hand on the doorjamb. As he looked around, he reached his hand in his pocket, pressing his fingers on the runes for the bondar his father must have made, and sent a soft—and quiet—summons to jinnar.

The earth elemental rumbled, although it came softly. Tolan focused, listening to see if there was anything similar within the woodsmith shop, but came up with nothing.

If there was going to be something here, maybe it wouldn't reverberate with jinnar, or perhaps there was nothing at all here anyway.

"I… I felt that."

Tolan glanced over. "You did?"

"Was that you?"

Tolan shrugged. "An earth shaping. I was looking to see if there were any residual items I could find here that might understand Master Daniels better."

"That was subtle work, Tolan. *Great Mother!* I still can't believe you have learned to shape."

"There are times I can't either," he said.

He stepped out of the shop and closed the door. It was growing darker, but it still wasn't dark, not yet. "I'm sure I'll see you at the Selection."

Tanner flashed a smile. "I'll be there."

"Good luck."

"With you there, I don't know that I'll need it."

Tolan smiled tightly, wondering if that was true or not. He doubted the Selectors would allow anyone to play favorites, and certainly not a student who had very little of his own ability to shape. He started off away from Tanner and paused at the end of the street, glancing back to look over at his old friend.

Tanner hurried off and a shaping built from him, soft and subtle, but without any real power to it. Tolan had been around enough shaping these days to know what a powerful shaping was, and he didn't detect anything like that from Tanner.

Maybe Tanner wasn't as strong a shaper as he had believed when he'd been in Ephra. When he had been here, he had always believed Tanner was skilled, but part of that came from the fact he had believed his friend to be a far more potent shaper than him. He was—or had been.

It was possible that at the Selection, Tanner wouldn't be chosen.

As he wound his way to the tavern and inn where Master Marcella and he were going to stay, he focused on what he noticed around him. Ephra was different than Amitan, but for many reasons. Partly it was because in Amitan, as the capital of the Terndahl Empire, it was busy. Not only the people who lived there, but others came and went through the city frequently. Merchants and other traders came through, adding to the commotion.

And then there was the sense of shaping. Within

Amitan, there was always someone shaping nearby, and the power that radiated from those shapers was significant. It was enough that he became numb to it. In Ephra, Tolan realized there was an absence of shaping. Having detected Tanner had been the first shaping he had noticed since reaching this place.

That surprised him, though it shouldn't. Very few people came to Ephra, so those who were here lived here, other than the occasional merchant who rolled through on their way to other places. And they weren't flush with shapers. Situated as they were at the edge of Terndahl, there simply wasn't the need for shaping. The only time Ephra had needed shapers had been when the threat of the Draasin Lord had been higher, raising the risk of potential attack.

Inside the tavern, he found Master Marcella talking to an older man with gray hair. He wore a maroon jacket and pants, and as Tolan approached, he recognized him.

He bowed his head respectfully. "Master Salman."

Master Salman glanced up at him, his eyes narrowing for a moment. "Tolan Ethar?" He glanced over at Master Marcella before looking back up at Tolan. "You've returned to the city?" He stared at him for a moment before it seemed as if his gaze locked onto Tolan's cloak, finally taking it in, recognizing Tolan wore a cloak that matched the one Master Marcella wore. "*You* were Selected."

Tolan nodded.

"Most believe you left the city after Master Daniels was chased away."

"That actually had been my plan," Tolan said.

"Then how did you get Selected?"

"It's a long story, but not all that interesting."

"On the contrary, I imagine it would be quite interesting. Anyone who is Selected to the Academy has a story to tell." He glanced over at Master Marcella. "Why have you brought a student with you for the Selection?"

"There have been a series of attacks in Amitan," Master Marcella said. "That is what I was beginning to tell you."

"You had only said there was one attack."

"You didn't give me the opportunity to finish," she said.

"How have there been so many attacks in Amitan? There has been no movement out here."

"Are you so sure?"

Master Salman shrugged. "Perhaps there has been. It's not as if I would have known. As isolated as we are, most of the time, we aren't involved in anything like that."

"Be thankful for that," Master Marcella said. "I was instructed to inform you the last attack on the city involved someone you were familiar with."

Master Salman's eyes narrowed. "Who?"

"Daniels."

Master Salman tensed, flicking his gaze at Tolan as he frowned. "Daniels? He wouldn't have been involved in any sort of attack."

"The Grand Master feels otherwise."

Master Marcella didn't glance up at Tolan, which led

him to believe she didn't know he had some familiarity with what had taken place.

And if she didn't know, he wasn't going to be the reason she learned. It was enough she knew of Master Daniels and his involvement. She didn't need to know Tolan had been a part of it, too.

"That's why you're here?"

"We're here for the Selection," she said.

"No. Him."

"What about him?"

"You think to discover if he knows anything about his whereabouts."

Master Marcella shook her head, smiling tightly. "Fortunately, Shaper Ethar does not know anything about the location of Daniels. He has been in Amitan for the last year. I believe he blessed Amitan at the same time as Daniels."

"Even more reason to question him," Master Salman said.

"I don't believe the Grand Master feels the same way. Regardless. We are here for the Selection, and I am here to warn you about your previous colleague. If you feel he is trustworthy, then I will leave it to your discretion."

Tolan opened his mouth as if to say something before biting it back. He couldn't reveal that he had seen Master Daniels working with disciples of the Draasin Lord. If he were to do that, he would reveal his role in things. It was better to play along and claim ignorance.

"When will the Selection take place?"

"When the Inquisitor arrives. You know the process," she said.

Master Salman sat back, grabbed his mug of ale, and studied Master Marcella. "I know the process, but do you?"

"What's that supposed to mean?"

"It means nothing more than that you are young."

"Perhaps I'm young, but I successfully graduated from the Academy and do have my share of ability."

"Clearly."

She frowned. "You can go."

Master Salman studied her for a long moment before grabbing his mug of ale and standing. Tolan nodded respectfully and waited for him to leave. Master Salman's gaze lingered on Tolan for a moment before turning away.

When he was gone, Tolan took a seat in the chair Master Salman had vacated. He looked over at Master Marcella. "What was that about?"

"It was nothing but posturing," she said.

"Posturing?"

She smiled tightly. "There are some who trained at the Academy who believe age and experience matter more than ability with each element bond."

"Isn't there a role for age and experience?"

"Of course, there is, but there's also a role for understanding that there are some who are born to power."

Tolan frowned as he regarded her. It wasn't the kind of thing he had expected her to say, and he hadn't known she felt that way about those without a connection to all of the element bonds. Would she have felt him somehow less if he had failed to reach another bond?

Then again, had he failed to reach another bond, he wouldn't have been able to continue on in the Academy. He would've been sent away, or perhaps offered a chance to continue to train, though only holding his singular ability.

"When do you think we'll begin the Selection?"

She clenched her jaw before turning her attention back to him. "It's the same as what I told Master Salman. We have to wait until the Inquisitor arrives."

"When do the shaping schools get notified?"

"Why?"

"Only because I ran into a friend of mine."

"A shaper friend of yours?"

"A wind shaper. I think some earth. I don't know what else he can shape."

"If he can reach wind and earth, then he already has potential."

"He wasn't Selected the last time."

"Then perhaps he is not a strong shaper."

"Does strength in shaping have anything to do with the Selection?"

"It's a part of it. Not all of it, but definitely a part."

As he sat back, leaning and looking over at Master Marcella, Tolan wondered which Inquisitor they would be assigned. The question didn't last long. The door to the tavern opened and Master Irina entered.

Tolan looked over at her but knew better than to say

anything. What was there for him to say? Would he question her openly about any connection to Master Daniels?

When she saw him, the corners of her eyes tightened. She took a seat and regarded Tolan for a long moment before turning to Master Marcella. "We will begin the Selection in the morning."

4

STANDING ON THIS SIDE OF THE ROW OF SHAPERS DURING A Selection felt considerably different than the last time he was here. When he had been here before, Tolan had been nervous, but it wasn't the kind of nervousness that came from any real fear of failure. There was no real thought he would succeed, so he hadn't worried about the possibility of failure. For that matter, he hadn't really wanted to succeed.

And now he watched from a different position, a place where a row of students, all longing for the opportunity to train at the Academy, stood before him.

The door opened at the back of the room and another entered.

Tolan stood motionless and when Velthan came closer, his eyes widened slightly when he took in Tolan. He mouthed the question, but Tolan could only stand and smile.

Others began to file in, one after another, including Tanner. There were several Tolan knew, though not nearly as many as he thought he would have. He couldn't help but wonder who would pass. Maybe none of them.

When the entire line of students was situated, Master Irina spoke up. Her voice was sharp, and it carried on a shaping of wind. Tolan could feel the way she manipulated the shaping, maintaining it, ensuring everyone within the room could hear her.

"You are all here with the intention of passing Selection. The process is arduous and involves three steps. You may all choose to abandon your pursuit now, and you will not be looked down upon. Many have come before the Selection committee and have decided their hearts weren't there. They have decided that perhaps this wasn't the time for them. Others have come and failed, and when you fail, you will have no memory of this."

A soft murmuring came over the line of students. It seemed they were all suddenly reminded of the fact they were spirit-shaped if they failed.

"Only a few of you will pass. That is the nature of the Selection, though there are times when none pass through and others when many pass through. The Selection is beyond the control of the Selector."

He found that surprising. Why wouldn't the Selector able to guide the Selection process?

Master Irina continued, taking away the questions. "For those of you who move on, arduous study awaits you at the Academy. You will be tested. Many will fail. Those who do not are destined to serve the Academy."

Tolan could feel Velthan's gaze upon him and he turned, meeting the other man's eyes. More than anything, he hoped Velthan failed. He simply wasn't a man he wanted to deal with at the Academy.

"If you would like to take your leave, this is your last opportunity. If you fail to do so now, the testing will begin, and for those of you who fail, you will no longer recall anything of the testing process."

Two people peeled off, and a shaping built from Master Irina. They headed out of the room, a glazed expression on their eyes, and he realized she had shaped them already.

The amount of power she had impressed him. Even more impressive was that he had somehow managed to not succumb to it.

"The testing begins now," Master Irina said.

As she said it, a powerful shaping built from her.

Tolan remembered his own experience with the first part of the Selection process and remembered all too well the memories that he had. What must these people be experiencing? What sort of memories were they having?

Tolan stood with his hands clasped in front of him, and after a while, a shaper fell, collapsing to the ground. Another one fell. And then another. Master Marcella motioned for him to help, and he grabbed the fallen, dragging them out of the room, where a pair of shapers from the Ephra school of shaping waited for them. He hurried back, heading toward the others, and continued to grab the fallen shapers.

After a while, there were no other shapers who had fallen, and Tolan returned to his place at the front of the room. He glanced over at Master Irina and recognized the shaping she held continued to build. Whatever she was doing was powerful, and it was potent enough she maintained it while watching the inside of the room, sweeping her gaze from one person to the next. Was she shaping each person?

Perhaps that was part of the testing. Maybe she was using some shaping in order to determine who was here.

He knew she was a powerful spirit shaper—she had to be, as the Grand Inquisitor—but she was holding onto a shaping, shifting it from one person to the next, and doing so without any evidence of strain.

Slowly, everyone in the room began to blink, opening their eyes. Tolan was not surprised to see Velthan and Tanner still in the room. How many times had they gone through a Selection and failed? Probably more than they were aware of.

Was there any way for those who had gone through a testing and failed to realize they had? Or were the memories forever gone, taken from them as part of the spirit shaping?

"The next step in the Selection will be difficult. You will find you are tested in ways you have never been before. You will look outside of yourself, and those of you who succeed will move on to the third and final part of the Selection."

There were still nearly twenty people in the room, more than Tolan remembered from his own Selection, enough that he wondered if perhaps there wouldn't be several moving on to the Academy.

He should be pleased by that, and yet, the idea there would be some who knew him left him unsettled. One of the things he had appreciated about his Selection was that no one had known him when he reached Amitan.

Another shaping built from Master Irina, and it swept over the shapers, moving from person to person, power radiating from her. As it did, several of the shapers began to fall again. Occasionally, they would twitch, and Master Marcella rushed forward, a shaping building from her.

A water shaping, Tolan realized.

There had always been rumors a Selection could be dangerous, and he had wondered how. If there was some way to get injured during a Selection, he was observing it.

He and Master Marcella continued to drag the fallen out of the room. He didn't know if there was a spirit shaping done on each person, but most had collapsed, so he wondered how much they would remember anyway.

Seven remained. All were standing. Tanner and Velthan were among them.

"And now we enter the last phase of the testing. For those of you who have survived this far, this last part of the testing is perhaps the most difficult."

She walked along the line and tapped each person on the forehead.

One by one, they fell.

They all remained motionless. Tolan wondered if perhaps that was all of it or if there was more to the shaping than that.

He glanced over at Master Marcella, but she was watching the Selection. This might be the first time she was seeing it from the other side as well.

As powerful as Master Marcella might be, he didn't think she had the ability to shape spirit, and so she would never be the primary Selector, not the way Master Irina and the other Inquisitors were. She was serving a role similar to what Jory had served when he had helped with the Selection.

"These five," Master Irina said, motioning to five of the students, including Velthan.

Tolan's stomach lurched as he realized Tanner wasn't among them.

It meant Tanner had failed the Selection.

Unfortunately for Tolan, Velthan had not.

How long would it take Tanner to realize Velthan was gone? He wasn't entirely sure how shaping worked for those who weren't Selected. Maybe they wouldn't remember anything, or maybe he'd remember coming to the Selection and not being chosen. Or perhaps he wouldn't remember he had once known Velthan. The other possibility—that memories of Velthan himself were wiped from his mind—seemed the most difficult. In order to do that, the spirit shapers would need to have incredible control, enough to remove specific memories. Tolan wasn't sure how well the spirit shapers were able to control their shaping, but that seemed beyond what he expected of them.

Tolan took his place next to Master Irina, who crouched next to Tanner. Her shaping built, letting Tolan know she was performing her spirit shaping on him.

"How much of this will he remember?"

"This is your friend?"

Tolan nodded.

"He will remember very little."

"What of the other shapers?"

"We don't conceal the fact some shapers are Selected. He will know that these five were chosen." She swept her gaze along the row of shapers. Other than Velthan, he didn't recognize any of the others. "There is value in having this many selected. They will believe it likely they will be chosen the next time."

"Why is that a good thing?"

"Because the Academy needs for shapers to strive to reach us. We need for others to recognize there is an opportunity for them to join our ranks. In order for them to do so, they have to feel their effort has merit. Trying and failing while you see others succeed is definitely valuable."

She nodded to him and Master Marcella, and they were prompted to lift Tanner. Tolan carried him back, looking down at his friend, wondering if he would see him again. He needed to be prepared for the possibility he would never see his friend again.

The last time he was here, he had been taken away quickly, with barely any opportunity to say any goodbyes. The same would happen this time. He wasn't sure which side of the Selection he would prefer to be on.

They returned and grabbed a young woman, hoisting her and carrying her out with the others. When he returned to the main room, the other five were starting to come around. Velthan and grinned when he saw Tolan.

"We passed?" he asked.

Master Irina nodded. "It was a good year for Selecting in Ephra," she said. "Most years, we have only one or two come from each place. In the case of Shaper Ethar, he was the only person. You will have only a brief period of time to say your goodbyes. Gather a few items and you will be escorted out of the city, where we will continue our journey."

Master Irina nodded at Master Marcella, who guided the others away but left Master Irina with Tolan.

"Come, Shaper Ethar. We will meet them at the Shapers Path."

"You're not going to help?"

"The other part of the selection process does not require my intervention. Master Marcella is perfectly capable of coordinating things from here."

They left the room and went back out on the street. Master Irina made her way through the city, reaching the edge and then hurrying outward. When they approached where the Shapers Path would be found overhead, she barely paused before shaping herself up and overhead, landing on top of the Path.

Tolan stuck his hand in his pocket, pausing as he reached for his furios and using it to summon a shaping, drawing power from it as he launched himself into the air. A part of him wanted to try using earth, but he decided against it, not knowing if he would have enough control. It would be better to wait and practice on his own to see if there was any way to grow more competent.

When he landed on the platform next to Master Irina, she studied him. "You have been particularly difficult for me to study."

"I don't know if I should be thankful or not."

"It tells me you have potential, Shaper Ethar."

"And by potential, you mean the ability to shape spirit?"

"It's possible. Many who have the ability to shape spirit develop that later in life, and those who do develop it later in life will often be stronger than those who are born to it."

"Are you trying to shape me now?" he asked, feeling her shaping building.

"Are you aware I'm shaping?"

There was no sense in denying it. "I can feel when you shape, though I can't tell what element bond you're reaching for."

"That is a unique gift to possess. There are many powerful shapers who never have such abilities. The fact you do, and without much control over your connection, tells me you have much potential."

Tolan studied her, debating how much he wanted to say to her. He had an opportunity, standing here with her, just the two of them, and wondered if perhaps he could find out what she knew.

Taking a deep breath, he decided it was best just to say it. "I presume the Grand Master told you about what happened with Master Daniels?"

She frowned, her lips pressed together tightly. "Unfortunately, he did."

"Unfortunately?"

"It's unfortunate he decided he needed to abuse his abilities in such a way."

"Did you know he was a spirit shaper?"

"Master Daniels was not a spirit shaper."

She said it with complete conviction, and while he wouldn't put it past her to lie to him, the way she said it, and the fact she seemed completely convinced, left him wondering if perhaps he had it wrong.

But then, there were other ways of reaching spirit. He had seen a spirit bondar, and while it took the ability to shape each of the other elements, that didn't seem to be Master Daniels' ability, either.

Unless he had hidden it.

He thought back to what had been in his parents' home. Bondars.

If Master Daniels had known of them, Tolan had to wonder if perhaps he had used them.

"Did you know I was there when Master Daniels attacked?"

"The Grand Master and I don't have any secrets, Shaper Ethar."

"None?"

"It would be dangerous for the Grand Master and the Grand Inquisitor to have secrets between themselves."

"Where have you been since the attack?"

"I've been trying to find answers," she said.

"About why Master Daniels decided to start working with the disciples of the Draasin Lord?"

She looked past his shoulder. "I'm not convinced he was working with the disciples."

Another shaping built, and Tolan realized the new Academy recruits were arriving. He was disappointed, wishing for more time to continue his conversation with Master Irina, but even if he did, there probably wasn't anything more he would be able to learn from her.

Other than the fact that Master Daniels had hidden his ability with spirit from her.

Either he had an ability on his own, or he was using a spirit bondar. Either way, it meant there might be others who didn't necessarily shape spirit on their own but were suddenly able to do so.

What would happen if he tried to use spirit in such a way? Would he be able to control a bondar well enough to be able to do so? He doubted it. He struggled with trying to summon a single element and couldn't imagine trying to summon more than one at a time.

As the recruits for the Academy arrived, Tolan stood next to Master Irina, watching them. They were all eager, similar to some of the other recruits he had met on the Shapers Path when he had been guided the Academy.

Velthan was the most boisterous. "I can't believe we're on the Shapers Path. I never thought we'd be granted access to it. Can you believe it, Kristin?"

He looked at a dark-haired woman standing next to him, and she smiled at him. "I can't believe I was Selected. And on my first try!"

Velthan's face soured. "We don't know if it was your first try or not. For all we know, this was our fifth or sixth try. I suspect this was my first, though."

Tolan smiled to himself and shook his head at them. Maybe he shouldn't, but it felt good to antagonize him, if only a little.

What if part of the reason he had been Selected was because a spirit shaping wouldn't work on him? Master Irina might not even share with him if that were the case or not. Was the Selection designed to detect those who had potential with spirit?

That seemed an odd reason for the Selection. There had to be a benefit in searching through Terndahl and finding those who had the ability to shape spirit. The Inquisitors had always been valuable to the empire, and without some way of finding them, there wouldn't be any additional way of adding to their ranks.

"How long do we have to go to reach Amitan?" one of the others asked.

"The journey is not so far, but you must be prepared for what you find there."

Tolan smiled to himself again. What would they think when they reached Amitan? They'd probably be as impressed as he had been. He had been amazed at just how much had been in the city, and just how powerful the shapings were.

Master Irina guided them along the Shapers Path. They walked quickly over the path and away from Ephra. As they did, Tolan glanced over his shoulder, looking back. A sense of a shaping built from within the city, though it was faint, weak, and it left him wondering whether it came from Tanner.

He squeezed his hand around the furios. While he felt as if he belonged at the Academy, it was something of a shame his friend wasn't able to join him there. Worse, Tanner probably wouldn't even remember Tolan had returned.

He glanced up at Master Irina as they walked, needing to know. "Will he remember I visited?"

"We couldn't take that risk," she said.

"When am I allowed to return?"

"When your time at the Academy is done."

5

THEY REACHED THE CITY LATE IN THE DAY. TOLAN AND Marcella stepped back and watched the group of new first-year students jump off the Shapers Path, into the courtyard outside the Academy. There they would meet with the Grand Master, beginning their journey.

Master Marcella looked over at him. "We should study together later. I would like to see how much you've learned over the last few weeks."

Tolan nodded. She jumped from the Shapers Path and departed, heading off into the city and disappearing quickly. Tolan waited a moment before descending from the Path, himself. The city was awash with energy, as it often was, and he watched as several carts rolled past him, He peeked through the bars on the windows, wondering if he could see inside.

When would Jonas and Ferrah return?

He and Marcella had only been gone for two days, so

he suspected they were among the earliest to return. Ferrah had the farthest to go, traveling all the way to Par, so her journey might be days or weeks just to reach Par, and that was not accounting for the Selection.

Rather than wandering the city, Tolan headed toward the library.

Since coming to the Academy, the library had become something of a second home to him. He felt comfortable there, and as he had spent quite a bit of time studying the elementals, he had found there were others who shared his interest. Master Minden always was willing to work with him, and because of that, Tolan had come as often as his schedule allowed. It had been at least two weeks since he had spent much time there because most of that time had been spent celebrating the promotion to the second level.

The library was quiet today.

Tolan made his way inside, looking around at the stacks of books stretching high overhead. He marveled at them the same way he often did. A particular shelf drew his attention today; there were some books on elementals there that he had yet to study.

He wandered along, his gaze drifting from book to book, taking in a variety of volumes he had not seen before. Most were old, many pre-dating anything he had read by a considerable amount. These weren't even the restricted sections of the library.

Master Jensen wandered between the tables, picking up books before returning them to the dais at the front of the library. The other librarian was Master Kelly, a youngish-looking man with sagging cheeks and ruddy skin. Tolan didn't know him as well as he knew some of the librarians but didn't feel intimidated by him the same way he did with Master Minden.

Tolan still had much research to do on the elementals, but now he had the earth bondar, he supposed he should try to understand more about them.

His father had obviously known some secret to making bondars. It was a secret Tolan had tried on his own to understand—and failed. There had to be something to the making of them.

"Shaper Ethar. Is there anything I can find for you today?"

Tolan turned to Master Jensen and forced a smile. He looked around the library, searching for anyone he might recognize, but most of the people here were all upper-level students. Soon the library would be occupied by the new first-year students, all looking to see what they might be able to uncover in their studies, the same way he and his friends had come searching for answers.

"I was wondering if there was anything about the Selection I might be able to read about." It wasn't what he was thinking about, but there certainly would be some value in reading about the Selection, as he had now seen it from the other side.

"The Selection? Normally, that information is kept until you have been raised to master shaper level, but…" Tolan waited, wondering if he would tell him no, but instead, Master Jensen only shook his head. He rubbed a knuckle against his forehead and smoothed back his thinning hair. "I suppose as the students have been brought out into the Selection, the Grand Master has decided you should be included now, so perhaps the details on the Selection process should not be quite so mysterious." He hurried away, heading toward the stairs leading up to one of the upper levels, and Tolan stood frozen.

Had he ever been given one of the books from the restricted section? He didn't think so, but that was certainly where Master Jensen was heading.

He didn't have to wait long. When Master Jensen returned, he carried three books, each slender volumes and all bound in some crackling black binding.

"These must not be taken from the library," he said.

"I wouldn't."

Master Jensen arched an eyebrow at him. "I understand you and Master Minden have an arrangement when it comes to certain works, but when we are dealing with the restricted volumes, I must remain adamant these remain here. You may read through them, and if you are finished, you can have them reserved for you up at the desk, but if you take them from the library, I will know."

Tolan nodded, and the intensity in Master Jensen's voice left him quite certain he did not want to upset the man.

Tolan took the books, surprised by how much they weighed considering how slender they were, and took a seat at one of the unoccupied tables. He stacked them in front of himself before pulling the top volume off and flipping open the binding. For a moment, he worried it would be written in a language he wasn't able to read. Many of the works within the library were written in some of the ancient languages. He didn't have enough experience with many of those ancient languages to be able to easily interpret them. Ferrah had an easier time, as she spoke—or at least read—the ancient Par language, something Tolan found incredibly complicated. There were a half dozen other languages written in many of the unrestricted books, and that said nothing about those that were restricted.

Surprisingly, this was written in the modern tongue. More than that, the ink was not nearly as faded as he would have expected. Some of that might've come from the way the book had been shaped, preserving the writing through the shaping of the ink onto the pages, but even when done, there were some of the older books that obviously had been shaped, trying to preserve the knowledge within, but that had not been successful.

It was an explanation on shaping. At first, Tolan thought that odd, but the more he continued to read through it, the more he understood the reason why the explanation on shaping was so important.

It described shaping itself.

Strangely, it wasn't so much of a description on how to contact the element bonds. There were quite a few volumes within the library that would go into what was required to reach the bonds. This instead talked about connecting to the elements in general terms, speaking to both the bonds and shaping and elementals as distinct things, but as he scanned the pages, he found a remark on the runes as well.

It was the first book he'd ever had the opportunity to read through that had directly referenced the runes. None of the others he'd been given access to had said anything about them, or if they had, any reference to it had been scrubbed from them over time.

For the most part, Tolan understood. Learning about the runes posed some dangers. He didn't understand all of what was involved in those dangers, but he did recognize the power from the runes, and the way they somehow sealed to the element bonds—and the elementals.

He glanced up at Master Jensen. He had asked about the Selection, but rather than giving him something that described the reasoning behind the Selection, he had given him something that described the connection to shaping in general.

Tolan continued to flip through the pages, skimming them. The entire volume spoke of shaping, and it did so almost on a philosophical basis. There was one part where he found himself dragged deeper into the writing, trying to understand what the author of this book was saying about the interrelatedness of power, when the soft sound of footsteps near him caught his attention.

Tolan glanced over his shoulder and saw Master Minden approaching. Her gaze took in the stack of books on the table, and he had no doubt she immediately knew what he was studying. There had to be thousands upon thousands of volumes in the library, and he suspected she knew each and every one of them.

She turned her milky gaze on him, somehow seeing through that film. "Shaper Ethar. You must have returned from your Selection."

"I did. I don't know I understand the process any more than I did when I was on the other side of it, but I thought..."

She approached the table, resting her gnarled hands on its surface. He'd seen her writing, documenting as most of the librarians did, either studying or making observations or analysis of things she had studied, and wondered how she managed to do so with her hands as destroyed by time as they were.

"You thought to understand the Selection process."

Tolan shrugged.

"There aren't many who have gone through the Selection process who have looked for an understanding of what they experienced."

"I'm sure most of the master shapers who go out as Selectors come back to understand what their role in the entire process was."

"You'd be surprised."

"What of the Inquisitors?"

"Most of the Inquisitors follow what they've been taught."

That surprised Tolan. He could see how they could learn the particular shaping required for the Selection, as he suspected the first two shapings were consistent, though the reactions to them might vary. It was the final shaping he thought to be the most significant. He had no idea what was involved in it, other than some shaping of spirit.

And if it was some way of sussing out whether people had a connection to spirit, maybe it was nothing more than searching for a reverberation with spirit.

"You should continue to question, Shaper Ethar. As you question, you will find the answers are often different than the ones you thought you were looking for."

He watched as she made her way toward the dais, where she spoke softly to Master Kelly.

Tolan turned his attention back to the stack of books and couldn't help but feel like he was something of a fraud even in this. He hadn't really wanted to understand anything. It had only been a desire to avoid other questions he had asked about the Selection, but now he had the books, he found himself reading through them and still not understanding anything more than what he had experienced. There might be knowledge of the process that he could glean, but even that was not entirely what he had expected.

Putting away the first book, Tolan grabbed the next one. This one was different than the last. It spoke of the type of person necessary for shaping ability. Even the first paragraph called that out, leaving Tolan staring at the page and the words written upon it.

. . .

We search for those who have the strength to connect to the elements. It is through that strength we can know the power the Great Mother has granted us. We search for those who have the courage to understand the elements. It is through that courage we will gain new insights. Finally, we search for those who are fearless. Only through fearlessness can we have the capacity to grow with the knowledge we obtain.

To Tolan, that sounded like three aspects to the Selection, though how did they fit with what he had gone through and with what he had now seen?

He stared at a page for a long moment, trying to decide what he thought the words meant. Maybe it was nothing more than a philosophizing over what was involved in becoming a shaper, but he couldn't shake the idea this reminded him of what went on during a Selection.

Tolan continued to flip through the pages, going one by one now. There was more of the same throughout this book, and as he looked, he didn't come up with anything more that would help him.

He pushed the book away, grabbing the third one. The first book Master Jensen had brought him had involved information about shaping in general. The second involved a theoretical approach. Would this one describe the actual shaping involved?

Tolan pulled it toward him and flipped open the page. A rune marked the first page.

His breath caught. He recognized the rune. It was one

for fire, and he had seen it often enough he had it memorized. It was one of the many runes on the furios. He
could reproduce this rune and, in particular, do it in his
mind.

Flipping the page, he found a flowing script. This was
different than the other two in that it was almost like a
journal, not the same as the others, and within the pages
of the journal were attempts at shaping. Whoever had
documented here described the way they had demonstrated various shaping techniques.

As he continued to flip through the pages, he came
across another rune. This one was for earth. His hand
went into his pocket, running his thumb across the
symbols he could feel there, the symbols suggesting his
father had known how to make bondars, and found they
were the same as he'd found on this page.

There was more information within these pages,
though all of it referred back to an understanding of earth
and trying to get a handle on how one would shape it.
Whoever had written this had an incredibly clear train of
thought when it came to the element bonds. Tolan
marveled at the understanding the person must have had.
Was this what he would gain over time? The master
shapers he had been working with all seemed to have a
high level of knowledge, but nothing quite like this.

As he continued to flip, he reached a symbol he knew
to be water. It was similar to those he had seen on the
water bondars. Much like the other two sections, he found

the description on reaching the element bond with water was the same...

None of this described shaping through the element bonds.

Tolan sat up, staring down at the book. Surprisingly, all of this described shaping, but it described shaping in a different way than how the master shapers he worked with described it. The ones he worked with described shaping as pulling something from deep within you, connecting to the element bond, and drawing upon that power. Whoever documented here described pulling upon the power within the shaper.

Tolan frowned, feeling as if he were close to reaching some sort of understanding. He had to be. How long had he searched for information about how he was different? If the shapers of old didn't connect to the element bonds, then how did they shape? Could they be more like him?

The idea they had, that there was a different sort of power than what he had been taught, left him excited.

When he reached wind, he flipped through the pages, searching for any sort of information that matched what he was finding on the others, but there was nothing different.

And then the last. Tolan had half expected the book to end, but it didn't.

Spirit.

The symbol wasn't one he had ever seen before, but it strangely seemed a combination of aspects from each of the other runes, markings he could piece together, and he could see how the marking for spirit came from it.

That was odd. Odder still was the fact the book continued to go on, sharing insights about the shaping of spirit, describing what was involved when one would reach spirit, and Tolan sat back, wondering if there might be some way to use it.

These shapers didn't require latching onto some element bond. The connection to spirit came from within them, not some ability to reach the nebulous bond.

Could he have that ability?

If he did, it would explain why he wasn't able to be spirit-shaped—at least not easily.

Tolan continued to flip through the pages, and he kept looking for something that would give him insight about what sort of shaping was involved in the Selection, but there was nothing. The only thing that came close was the second book, and in that one, it was only the first paragraph or so.

He flipped the book closed. Why were these restricted?

He understood why the last book might be restricted, especially if it described a way of shaping that did not involve the element bonds. The others seemed much less dangerous to have shared, and he couldn't understand why they would not be allowed out.

He rubbed his eyes, realizing he was far more tired than he had known. The journey back to the city had taken quite a bit out of him, and now he would begin his sessions for the second level, it was time to get some rest and prepare. Besides, he still had to settle back into the new quarters.

Tolan didn't want to give these books up quite yet, but if he attempted to take them from here, Master Jensen would find him. He would be angry. And it was possible Tolan would not be allowed to borrow anything like this ever again. Having the master librarians allowing him access to works like this was a privilege, and it was one he wasn't about to take lightly.

Tolan got to his feet and headed toward the front of the library, where he glanced up at Master Minden. For some reason, he wished it was Master Jensen, especially since he was the one who had allowed Tolan to borrow these works in the first place.

"Are you done for the day?" she asked.

"For now," Tolan said. "Master Jensen suggested I could keep these volumes here and continue to study."

She glanced down at them, nodding slowly. "They are an interesting choice for you to use. Do you think they've given you any insight?"

"I'm not really sure. I haven't had an opportunity to dig into them. Mostly, I was trying to see what Master Jensen thought I might gain from them."

"There is much we can learn from those who helped us understand shaping as we know it."

Tolan glanced down at the book she'd set on the desk. "How did these help the shapers understand shaping as we know it?"

"This one," she said, pointing to the book he felt was

nothing more than a basic description of shaping, "came from one of the founders of the Academy. The first Grand Master, Joseph Olian. Some have regarded him as dry, but he has a way of explaining things few today can even match. The knowledge within it is still considered basic, but considering it came from the first Grand Master, there is incredible value to it."

At least it explained why it was restricted. Considering its age—and knowing how old the Academy was—a book like that would be incredibly valuable.

"What about this one?" he asked, pointing to the second book he had gone through.

"Ah. That is an interesting choice, and one I am surprised Master Jensen allowed you to read." She glanced over to him, arching a brow, and he stirred, almost as if alerted to her talking about him.

"The work of the first Grand Inquisitor? I figured since the Grand Master has allowed students to attend the Selection, they should have every right to understand the process. Who better to learn from than the first Grand Inquisitor?" Master Jensen said.

It intrigued Tolan that the first Grand Inquisitor had such a philosophical approach to shaping. The Inquisitors had served a different role in the Academy over the years, and not one where he ever would have expected them to have been philosophical in the way he saw depicted in this book. Even more than before, he wanted to continue reading through it, see if there was anything he might be able to pick up from it.

"And what of this last one?"

"This last one is the most surprising."

"Why is that? I found it to be interesting."

"Did you? Why is that?" she asked.

He considered his answer before saying anything. The master librarians were master shapers in the same way all of the master shapers throughout the Academy were. They were powerful individuals, and they exerted incredible control over their domain. With access and the ability to restrict that access to the library at their disposal, Tolan didn't want to do or say anything that might upset one of them.

So far, he had been given quite a bit of freedom in the library. Some of that came from the fact it seemed Master Minden liked him—for whatever reason. Maybe that came from the fact he had helped stop the attack on the Convergence. He didn't want to lose that freedom. Not now he had begun to have a different type of question.

"There is a description of shaping in it that is different than what I have felt before."

He cursed himself almost immediately. He didn't need to reference what he had felt, only what he had read and experienced.

"And what have you felt, Shaper Ethar?" Master Minden asked.

"Nothing different than what we know from using the bondars," Tolan said hastily. "It's just... Well, it's just it doesn't seem as if this book references reaching for the element bonds. It speaks of shaping a different way, power coming from the shaper themselves."

He looked up, worried about meeting her eyes, but found her watching him with a thoughtful expression on her face. Why would that be?

Maybe he had said something more than he should have. Or maybe he had gotten his interpretation of it wrong. It wouldn't be impossible to believe he didn't have the interpretation of that book correct. As much as he wanted to try and understand it, he might not be able to know exactly what the shaper had intended when writing.

"You have identified something intriguing about that volume, and it's something very few outside of the master librarians have ever identified," she said. She glanced over at Master Jensen, frowning for a moment. Was she upset with him for sharing the book with Tolan? He should apologize and be on his way before he lost access to the library, but she turned her attention back to him, the weight of her gaze holding him steady. It was times like these when she looked at him with that intensity that he felt as if despite the milky film over her eyes, she was somehow able to see deeper into him than anyone else at the Academy. Almost as if she were shaping him. "The shapers who came before the Academy had a different understanding of the connection to their abilities. We refer to it by the same terms as they did, but that's mostly paying lip service to the similarity with what we do. Most who study these things suspect our ability is quite a bit different than what their ability once was."

"Were they more powerful?"

"The power of the element bond is nearly limitless, Shaper Ethar," Master Minden said. "With power like that, we don't ever need to fear losing our connection to shaping. We may grow tired, but the power we reach into, the power we can channel, does not. Those shapers," she said, nodding toward the book, "had limits to their own abilities. It is those very limits we don't have that make us so much more than they ever could be."

Tolan realized not only did this book have a description of a different sort of shaping, but it was much older than the Academy.

"Who wrote this?" He glanced from Master Minden to Master Jensen. "You said one was the first Grand Master and the other one is the first Grand Inquisitor, but who wrote this?"

Master Minden sniffed, glancing down at her notebook before looking up again. "That was written by one of my ancestors, Shaper Ethar."

"Yours?"

"My family is descended from powerful shapers, and we have been affiliated with the Academy for as long as it has been in existence. While the first Grand Master is one of the founders, my ancestors are another."

Tolan looked back at the book, thinking through the implications of what she said. If her ancestor was one of the other founders of the Academy, and if her ancestor had some way of reaching shaping that was different than the Academy taught, then was there some connection between the two?

He could see from the way she had devoted herself to her reading that she wasn't going to answer any more questions. He let out a heavy sigh and pushed the books toward her. "I would like to continue reading these if I have the permission of the master librarians."

"You may continue to study them here. They are restricted, which means only master shapers should be reading them, but as you seem to have Master Jensen's permission, I won't intervene."

She took the books and placed them into one of the drawers. When she shut it, she looked up, and for a moment, it seemed almost as if her eyes cleared, but then that faded.

Tolan hurried away, departing the library and heading back to what was now his quarters that he still shared with Jonas, Wallace, and Ferrah. He needed to organize it. Now he was a second-level student, it was time for him to work through his lessons.

6

It was late in the day on the fourth day after Tolan's return from Ephra when Ferrah finally returned to the Academy. It surprised Tolan she would arrive before Jonas, who was in Velminth. Velminth wasn't very far, much closer to Amitan than even Ephra had been. Par was quite a bit farther, and even if they had run along the Shapers Path, it would have taken quite a bit of time to have gone, established the Selection, and then return.

During the time they'd been gone, he'd been trying to settle into the second-level quarters. The room was not all that different from the last. There were four beds and a wardrobe at the end of the beds. These rooms were a little bit nicer than the first-level rooms, and they had a small table next to their bed for their belongings. A series of paintings hung along the walls suggested the various elements, though they weren't all that well done, and in the years since they were made, they had been around second-year students long enough that they had been damaged, some of the paint flaked off, one punctured, and something sprayed on the third. A thick carpet covered most of the floor, giving a little more warmth to the second-level rooms than there was in the first-level rooms. Shaped lights glowed in three sconces around the room, casting quite a bit of light around the entirety of the room. It took little more than a touch for these to be dimmed, and with Tolan here all by himself, he left them blazing brightly. He enjoyed the light.

When Ferrah entered their new room, she swept her gaze around it. Her belongings were still stacked in a corner, piled much like his had been when he had first returned. Jonas's belongings were also stacked, though he didn't have all that many. The only other person to have been here had been Wallace, and a part of Tolan had wondered whether he would continue rooming with them as they progressed or whether he would find another set of roommates. It wasn't that he and Wallace and the others didn't get along, it was more that Wallace didn't socialize with them quite as much.

"You're here," she said.

"I am," Tolan said, sitting up. He had been reviewing what he could find of the elementals, going through the books he still had borrowed from the library. They were volumes Master Minden had lent him, and he kept waiting for her to ask for them back, but she never did. Either she didn't care he had them, or she had forgotten.

Considering what he knew of Master Minden, he doubted she had forgotten. "How was your Selection?"

"Only one. How was yours?"

"There were five students. And from what I can tell, they have been obnoxious since reaching the Academy."

"Is one of them your friend?" she asked.

Tolan shook his head. "I came across him, but he didn't pass the testing this time either."

"This is the same friend you went into the Selection to observe?"

Tolan nodded. "The same. This time, I was standing on the other side of it, and it felt different."

"I know what you mean. There wasn't the same nervousness I felt the last time, and I have to admit it felt good to be there and show those who doubted me all those years I had already passed the first level and even more, the Grand Master had allowed us to come out to the Selection."

"That's not exactly what I was getting at, though that felt different, too. It's more that the connection between us was different."

She studied him for a moment before starting to smile. "Did you think it wouldn't?"

"I didn't expect to walk in and have him welcome me, but I haven't seen him in the better part of the year. When I was last there, Master Daniels had been sent back to Amitan, and as far as he knew, I was going to head off to the mines."

"Well, he had to have been relieved you didn't go off to the mines."

"I'm not sure if he was or not. I think Tanner always enjoyed that I wasn't able to shape. It was something he had that I didn't."

"What kind of friend is that?"

"One of the only friends I had when I was in Ephra."

"I'm sure you had other friends, Tolan. Everyone has friends, even those who don't know how to shape."

He glanced down at the book. It just so happened that he had been looking through the earth elementals, and as he had, he had been running his finger along the markings his father had made on the bondar. Every so often, he would pause and attempt a shaping, summoning the earth elemental through the bondar. It had become easier each time he did it, to the point where he now could summon only a low rumbling. Would it become as easy for him as fire was when he used the furios?

"I haven't really told you much about my parents," Tolan said without looking up.

"I figured they'd have to be shapers," she said.

"You would think so," he said.

"What is it?"

Tolan breathed out. "My parents disappeared when I was younger. It came during an attack on Ephra by disciples of the Draasin Lord. They were there... And then they were gone. Most within the city believed they were claimed by the Draasin Lord, though enough people wondered if perhaps they hadn't sided with him all along."

He looked over at her. Her face was pale. It wasn't quite the reaction he had expected, but he appreciated she seemed to understand the implications.

"They blamed you for that?" she asked.

"I was too young to be blamed. I was still a child, so most adults didn't think I had been corrupted by the Draasin Lord, regardless of what they thought about my parents. Children weren't quite so kind to me."

"What did they do?"

"Most taunted me, so when I had no ability to shape, it was something of a blessing. If I would've been forced to attend the shaping school in Ephra, I don't know if I would've been able to tolerate it. It was easier for me to just be different, but not so different I had to deal with everyone else."

"But you had some ability even before you came here. You were able to sense earth, and you passed the Selection."

"We both know my passing the Selection was surprising. I think it surprised even the Grand Inquisitor."

She glanced around at the mention of the Grand Inquisitor, her gaze falling on the door in the far corner. A shaping built from her, as if attempting to seal off the room, though even if she did, Tolan wasn't sure it would make a difference to the Grand Inquisitor. Ferrah still felt anger about the fact she had been spirit-shaped. She didn't seem to mind that she had just taken part in a Selection where other shapers had been spirit-shaped so they would forget what had happened to them, but having it done to her was something different altogether.

"That's the reason why, when Master Daniels took me in, I felt as if I had been given a reprieve."

"I didn't know."

"It's why his betrayal hurt so much more."

"And you never knew he was a spirit shaper?"

Her comment got him thinking again and reminded him of what had troubled him ever since visiting Ephra. "What if he wasn't a spirit shaper?"

"You saw what he was able to do. Nothing other than a spirit shaper would have been able to do it in quite that manner."

"And yet, Master Irina didn't know he was."

She studied him intensely for a moment. "You spoke to her?"

"She was a Selector in Ephra."

"Why?"

Tolan shrugged. "I don't really know, but she was the one sent there. She ran the Selection, and it went faster than before, at least from my recollection of it. And I don't know if she was the one to have gone because Master Marcella was a part of it also, and she had never taken part in a Selection."

"It could be," Ferrah said.

"Why do I get the sense you don't think that's the reason?"

"Think of what we've experienced out there so far, Tolan. First there is you, and as much as I care about you

—and I do—even you can't deny it's strange you would have been the one Selected. Then there's the attack at the waste. I haven't heard any of the master shapers talk about what happened there, and to be honest, I don't expect them to, but that also took place out near your homeland. And then there is the involvement of this Master Daniels in whatever plot that was. What if there's something taking place centered in that part of Terndahl?"

"I'm not really sure what it would be, but…" Tolan thought about the strange wind attack when he and Master Marcella had been making their way to Ephra. He hadn't really talked about it with anyone else, and with the way Master Marcella had dismissed the idea of an elemental attack, he had let himself forget about it, especially with everything else that had been going on. "There might have been another elemental attack on my way to Ephra." He told her about what had happened, including the way he had attempted to reach the elementals. Ferrah watched him, her frown deepening the longer he spoke.

"And Master Marcella didn't think it was an elemental attack?"

"It wasn't shaped."

"Are you sure?"

"I didn't feel any shaping, and she went searching for someone who might have attacked us and didn't find anything. I'm as certain as I can be."

"If it was an elemental attack, then why? Do you think there were rogue elementals? Or was this another action on behalf of the disciples? Could they have freed them?"

Tolan glanced down, looking at the book on the elementals. He didn't think they had been commanded to attack.

"I don't know. It felt different than the attack we had here."

"How was that?"

"That was frenzied, almost as if the elemental had been agitated." He wasn't sure why he was describing in that way, only that it fit. When they had been attacked by the rogue elementals in the Academy, they had both nearly died. "This was nothing more than a persistent and gusting wind. It was power, and it nearly threw me off the Shapers Path, but I didn't sense any malice within it."

"Tolan, you need to be careful with the way you're thinking about the elementals."

"Why?"

"You're starting to be sympathetic toward them."

"Why shouldn't we be sympathetic toward them?"

"Because they're dangerous. They're a part of the bond. I know you have your own unique way of reaching your shaping, but I still think you need to be careful with the elemental component. If nothing else, go to somebody we trust and share with them what you're doing. Even the Grand Master would be better than nothing."

"The challenge is finding someone who won't pass judgment on me." He didn't want someone to think he had dangerous sympathies, and he needed to be careful with who he might approach. They had seen the way those who had a tendency toward the elementals had been treated. Jory had attempted to free them to control them, wanting power the same way the Draasin Lord had wanted power. Master Daniels had wanted something similar, though the disciples had managed to rescue him before he and Ferrah had a chance to find out exactly what that was. If he went around making comments like that, what would others think of him?

The same sort of thing they had thought about his parents.

And now he wouldn't have his youth to protect him. He was too old and had been at the Academy for too long to be able to hide behind that.

"I guess what I was getting at is what if Master Daniels was using a bondar to control spirit?"

"There isn't a bondar that can control spirit," she said. "The one I was lent allowed me to combine the elements but didn't control spirit the way the Inquisitors do. What you're describing simply doesn't exist."

"But what if it did?"

"It would be powerful. Dangerous." Ferrah leaned forward, her eyes narrowing. "Tolan—why are you asking these things?"

"Because I think my—"

He didn't get a chance to finish. The door opened and Jonas hurried in, his cloak dirtied and his face showing signs of fatigue. He looked around the room and a powerful shaping of wind built from him, slamming around all three of them in a barrier.

"Is Wallace here?"

"Just us," Ferrah said, glancing from Tolan back to Jonas.

"Good." He sank onto the bed, looking up at the ceiling. "We were attacked the entire way back to Amitan."

"Attacked?" Tolan asked.

"Disciples, at least that's what Master Nevith thought. The attack came suddenly, attempting to tear us off the Shapers Path. There was enough shaking and trembling, it caused the path itself to buckle. We had to hurry along it to make it back to Amitan safely."

"The Path buckled?" Ferrah asked.

"I don't know how to describe it. It was there, and then it buckled. It sort of created a hill, but it was nothing like anything I've ever experienced before. I asked Master Nevith if he thought he could repair it, and he claimed he did, but we didn't stay behind for him to investigate further. He was worried because we were escorting our Selection back."

"Just one?"

"There were three."

"Why do you sound as if you're disappointed?" Ferrah asked.

"My year was unusual. Normally there's only a single person Selected from each year, and when it was both Draln and I, that was significant. With this, with three having now been Selected, I can't help but feel as if our being chosen wasn't nearly as impressive as it was before."

"There were five in Ephra," Tolan said.

"Five? That's a lot for Ephra. No offense, Tolan, but it's not exactly a hotbed of shaping."

"Master Irina made it sound as if the numbers were good."

"That *is* good. It's more than I would've expected for there to have been at the Selection. It's more than I think there has been at any Selection from a single place before."

Tolan started to think about what he knew of the composition of various classes and knew Ferrah was right. In their class, there were at most two people from any given place, and the most came from Velminth. It was rare enough that he understood there shouldn't be so many people from a single place getting Selected.

And five?

That was odd.

"What do you think it means?" Tolan asked.

Jonas glanced from him to Ferrah. "Why would it mean anything?"

"Think about it, Jonas. You're talking about a Selection where so many people have been plucked from a single place."

Jonas flopped his head back, shrugging. "I don't think that really matters. All that matters now is they are first-levels and we are second-levels."

"There are more of them than there are of our class," Ferrah said.

"You don't know that." Jonas kept his eyes closed, and he crossed his arms over his chest as if to sleep. "For all we know, there were none chosen from any of the other cities. We don't know what took place there. Maybe the Selection was such that only a few were chosen."

Tolan shook his head, but he wasn't going to argue with Jonas about this. "What more can you tell me about the attack?"

Jonas sat up and glanced from Tolan to Ferrah. "I already told you everything I can about the attack. When we were come upon by the disciples of the Draasin Lord, we had to run. I don't think I've ever moved so quickly along the Shapers Path as I have at that time. Even with it changing as it was, we ran."

Tolan glanced over at Ferrah, but she kept her gaze on Jonas. "Did you have any difficulty getting between here and Par?" Tolan asked.

Ferrah shook her head. "Nothing like what you experienced."

"Wait. You had trouble too?" Jonas asked, turning to Tolan.

Tolan told him about the wind attack and left out the part of how he had directed the elementals. He still wasn't sure how much of that to share with Jonas, and Ferrah's advice on keeping some of that to himself stuck with him. She was right, he shouldn't reveal too much about his connection to the elementals and he needed to be careful with making it seem as if he were too sympathetic to them.

"It's almost like they don't want us to have a Selection," Jonas said.

"What was that?" Ferrah asked.

THE WATER RUPTURES | 99

"I don't know. It's almost like they don't want to have a Selection. Maybe the disciples are afraid there are too many shapers preparing to oppose them," he said. He rolled over and raised up to rest his head on his arm, glancing from Tolan to Ferrah. "What if they're afraid of numbers?"

"They've never been afraid of the Academy before. To the point where they came and attacked."

Jonas rolled back, staring upward. "There is that. It was just a thought."

"What was your Selection like?" Tolan asked, looking at Jonas.

"Nothing all that extraordinary. We got to Velminth, and it took a few days for the Inquisitor to arrive. We had the Grand Inquisitor, if you could believe that."

"You did?" Tolan asked.

Jonas rolled his head toward him and cocked an eye open. "Why?"

"Because I had the Grand Inquisitor in Ephra."

Jonas shrugged. "We don't know how many Inquisitors there are, so I don't really know how uncommon it is for the Grand Inquisitor to be a part of the Selection."

"When I went through the Selection in Ephra a year ago, most people thought it was unusual for the Grand Inquisitor to have a role in it," Tolan said.

"I think you two are trying to find some sort of excitement that doesn't exist," Jomas said.

"Or maybe we're finding the excitement that does exist," Ferrah said. Jonas waved his hand at them. "Don't you think we should look into how many were Selected from various cities?" Ferrah asked.

"Only if you want to continue chasing this down, but I'm not entirely sure we need to," Jonas said.

Ferrah leaned back, studying Jonas for a moment before turning her attention to Tolan. He could see the uncertainty in her gaze, and it was more than just with Jonas's response.

"What did Wallace experience?" Jonas asked.

"Wallace hasn't returned, yet," Tolan said.

"Not yet? I thought my trip was the last to make it back to the city."

"Apparently not. Ferrah just got back, much like you."

"How is it you took no longer than I took and you're already back?" Jonas asked.

"Par isn't as far as either of you seem to think. With the connection to the Shapers Path, we have the ability to get there pretty quickly."

"How quickly?" Jonas asked.

"It only takes the better part of two days."

Jonas barked out a laugh. "The better part of two days? We get to Velminth in less than a day, and that's traveling on a Shapers Path. I'm sure it's the same with getting to Ephra, especially as we all have made that journey before."

Two days on the Shapers Path. Tolan couldn't even imagine what that might have been like. And yet, a part of him wished he would've had the opportunity to go with Ferrah to Par, if only to see where she lived and what it was like. It was different than Ephra, but no less the edge of the empire than Ephra was.

A voice in the hallway outside the room caught his attention and Tolan sat up, glancing over at Jonas. "Did you go by yourself?"

"Did I go where?" Jonas asked.

"To the Selection, where else?"

Jonas pushed himself up and rubbed his eyes. "Why?"

"Did Draln go with you?"

"No. He was dragged along with a different Selector. I figured that was my reprieve from him."

"Do you know where he went?" Ferrah asked.

"Why would I have even asked about that?"

"Because all of us have been sent back to where we were Selected. Everyone but Draln."

"Maybe he didn't get to go along on a Selection," Jonas said.

Tolan hadn't seen Draln in the days since his return, so he didn't think that was likely, but what explanation was there?

Discovering involved asking around, though he wasn't sure he wanted to do that. At the same time, he wanted to know whether there was anything about the number of students Selected. The more he thought about it, the odder it seemed. Much like Ferrah had said, there really shouldn't be more than one or two people Selected from any city at any given time. It was rare enough to be Selected, and with so many having succeeded this time, it changed the dynamics of the Academy considerably.

Tolan got to his feet and headed to the door. By the time he reached it, he didn't hear the sound of voices out in the hallway anymore.

"Tolan?"

He glanced back at Ferrah and shook his head. "I'm just going to check on something," he said.

"Don't do anything foolish," she said.

"You know me. I wouldn't do anything too ridiculous."

"The problem is that I *do* know you."

He flashed a tight smile and headed out into the hall, searching for where Draln and his buddies had gone. The hallway outside the student rooms was quite a bit nicer than what they had in the first-level dormitories. Even before their promotion to this level, Tolan had been here, having come when he had been trying to help injured students after having just come to the Academy. Both had recovered, though he hadn't seen them since.

Twisted stone sculptures rested on the ground along the hall. Most were strangely decorative and he paused at one, wondering if it might represent a rune or whether this was something else. There was nothing about the pattern on the sculpture that left him thinking it was anything more than just a simple sculpture, but now he had spent as much time as he had in the Academy, he had to believe everything had some purpose. Even things that didn't quite look like they should.

He shook away those thoughts. That wasn't why he was here now. He was here to approach Draln.

He heard voices near the end of the hall and found

Draln and four other students sitting in the practice area. It was a part of the living area designed to prevent a dangerous shaping from escaping. It also was the place where he had found the injured students, and he wasn't surprised to see Draln here, though it had been weeks since he'd seen the man.

"Ethar," Draln said, sneering at him. "What are you doing here?"

"Probably the same thing as you," he said.

"I doubt that," Draln said, looking at the others. Tolan realized shaping built from each of them, a gentle, subtle sort of shaping that went from person to person. It was far more controlled than anything Tolan could have managed.

"Don't you need to be heading back up to one of the towers and working with your bondars?" Draln continued. "I hear there are plenty of first-level students you can work with. Maybe they'll help you feel more at home."

"At least I was allowed to go out on a Selection," Tolan said.

"And what makes you think I wasn't?"

"Jonas said you didn't go to Velminth."

"Velminth," Draln said, waving his hand. "What was there for me in Velminth? With my shaping ability, I would need to remain in Amitan to serve on the Council."

"I'm not sure the Council has any place for someone like you," Tolan said.

"The Council needs skilled shapers to guide us toward the future," Draln said. "If you would've been paying attention when we had members of the Council in the Academy over the last few months, you would have known that, but I suspect you were too busy trying to discover your connection to your element bonds."

"Where did you go if not to Velminth?"

"It doesn't matter where I went. The better question is *who* I went with."

"Who did you go with?"

Draln leaned forward, his sneer growing more intense. "The Grand Master."

He looked around at the others, and Tolan realized they were watching him with a bright-eyed intensity. All seemed to think Draln was somehow the key to their gaining power, and maybe he was. It was possible Draln and his connection to the Grand Master and to shaping would be a way to lead them toward a stronger position than they already had. If Draln was already politicking to serve on the Council, Tolan could imagine others were doing the same.

Maybe it was a mistake that he and Ferrah and Jonas weren't. At least Ferrah should. She was incredibly gifted, and he could see her serving on the Council someday, though from what he had seen so far, she wanted nothing more than to become a master librarian.

Jonas was a skilled shaper, but he could be impulsive, and that impulsivity led Tolan to believe Jonas had a different role. Maybe he would join the Inquisitors.

"How many were Selected?"

"What?"

"How many were Selected?"

"What does that matter?"

"I'm just curious."

"We found one. The same as we usually do. Great Mother, Ethar. You really are a strange one. I'm sure that comes from your time in Ephra and spending so much time near the waste, but you need to stop asking such odd questions." Draln turned away, looking at some of others behind him. "Maybe Ethar is the traitor they're looking for."

"What was that?" Tolan asked.

Draln glanced back at him, sneering. "A traitor, Ethar. I overheard the Grand Master while I traveled with him. There's a traitor at the Academy. They think the Draasin Lord is planning something and has to have someone on the inside responsible for it." He grinned at him. "Maybe it's you."

Tolan turned away and ignored the sound of their murmuring voices behind him.

Only one from the Grand Master. Only one with Ferrah in Par. And several from Velminth, where the Grand Inquisitor had been involved. And five in Ephra, where the Grand Inquisitor had been involved. And a traitor in the Academy who worked with the Draasin Lord.

While he wandered, not looking up, he nearly slammed into another of the second-level students. Haervn Voil was a dark-haired man from someplace far west in Terndahl. Tolan didn't know him well, other than that he was a shaper of moderate ability.

"Ethar. How long have you been back?"

"A few days," he said, blinking.

"Wasn't it amazing? The Selection is so much easier when you aren't the one worrying about whether you will pass."

Tolan flashed a smile. "It is a whole lot easier that way, isn't it?"

"And to think how nervous I was when I learned the Grand Inquisitor was going to be performing our Selection."

Tolan froze. So far, he would be the third person the Grand Inquisitor had been involved with. "How many were Selected?"

"That's the thing. We had more than usual. I can't remember how many are Selected each year, though I blame the Inquisitors on that. Most agree it's no more than one, and rarely two. We had four this year."

"That *is* impressive," Tolan said. "It's good to see you. We'll have to catch up later."

Hearvn nodded and wandered down the hall. He was friendly with Draln, but friendly in the way he wanted to ensure he didn't anger the man, and Tolan suspected he was heading toward Draln and the others to share how many had been Selected as a way of impressing him.

The Grand Inquisitor involved with the increased number of students Selected from these places left him feeling uncomfortable. He needed to find out more.

Maybe it was nothing more than a strange Selection and an increased number of students chosen. Combined with the last Selection and now this one?

Something was taking place, and while he might not know enough to be able to understand just what that was, he recognized there was something strange happening.

It might not be his role to uncover what it was, but he would pay attention, keep his eyes open, and be prepared. He had to anyway. Strange things seemed to happen both to him and around him. Unfortunately, he was afraid they were already happening and he had already been brought deeper into something than he had intended.

7

THERE WAS A SOMBER AIR TO THE INTERIOR OF THE LIBRARY, and as Tolan sat at a desk, staring at the books in front of him, he couldn't shake that sense. There was always a silence within the library. It was fostered by the master librarians to ensure anyone who came to the library had a peaceful place to study. Today was not that much different, but there was something more than just the somber atmosphere.

He looked around, trying to piece it together. Ever since returning to the Academy from the Selection, something had felt off. It came from the murmuring throughout the Academy, a murmuring that fit with his experience, the questions he'd asked, and it left him wondering if perhaps there was more going on than what the master shapers had shared.

He glanced at the dais, seeing Master Minden working with her back hunched over whatever volume she was reading through. There were times when he wished she would be more forthright with him, and yet she had provided him with much more than most of the master shapers had ever offered.

As usual when he looked over at her, the sense of a shaping built, though he was no longer certain it came from her. It was possible it came from the Convergence deep beneath the earth, and not so much from the master shaper.

"Tolan," Ferrah said, whispering. Even in, her voice carried far more than it should.

He jerked his head around to her, meeting her eyes.

"If you're this distracted, maybe we should not stay here."

"I can't help it," he said.

She nodded to the books in front of him. Nothing he'd managed to obtain provided him any real insight. So far, Tolan had found nothing more in the books on elementals, and he closed them, slipping them into his pouch. Eventually, he would have to return those books. He enjoyed having access to them, to continue to study them, and yet the longer he did, the more he realized he probably no longer needed them. How long ago had it been since he'd memorized everything within them? The time spent at the Keystone had given him a different knowledge and understanding of the elementals, and though he no longer knew whether that experience reflected reality or whether it was tied to that place alone, Tolan thought he did understand the nature of the elementals.

"Let's go then," Ferrah said.

"You're not finished with what you're working on."

She shook her head. "I'm not sure I'm going to find anything."

There was more to her frustration than what she revealed, and he figured he could wait until after they left the library.

She got to her feet, grabbing her stack of books and tucking them under her arm, and Tolan followed. He trailed after her out of the library, and when he reached the doors, feeling the strange tingling that was meant to be a seal around the library itself, a way of preventing anyone else from shaping, he glanced back at Master Minden.

He knew it wasn't imagined, and yet he couldn't help but feel as if she were something different.

The woman never looked up at him.

Ferrah grabbed his arm, dragging him through the halls.

"What was that about?" he asked.

She glanced at the books. "When I was back in Par, I spent some time in our archives. There's so much there I want to understand."

"And you think these books will help you understand."

"I don't know if they will or not, but they're a start. Master Jensen found some things for me, and I thought... I don't really know what I thought. I want to be able to understand the Par archives."

"Do you have people there you can ask?"

"That's just it. There isn't anyone at the archives who can help with this. They've translated parts of it, but not all of it."

Other voices caught his attention, the call of the new first-level students along with that of the older students. One of the voices stuck in his head, and Tolan glanced behind him to see Velthan walking with a group.

"Let's get moving," he said.

"Why?"

He shook his head and hurried through the halls, reaching the main door and then back outside. Once there, he started toward the nearby park, but every so often glanced behind him to see Velthan and the others were still following. He had no interest in dealing with him here. Even though he was a second-level student, and even though he had demonstrated the ability to shape and no longer had to worry about Velthan's insults, he couldn't shake that agitation.

What would happen if Velthan and Draln ever got together? Tolan prayed that didn't happen, and worried about the time it would. The two men would discuss his shaping ability, such as it was. There were enough rumors about him here that he didn't need Velthan to reveal his ties to the Draasin Lord, however false they might be.

"We could just go back to our rooms," Ferrah said, looking behind her every so often.

"I don't really want to."

"Where would you have us go?"

Tolan had reached the edge of the city without even

thinking about where he was going, and he started into the forest.

Ferrah grabbed his arm, pulling him back.

"Are you sure we should go there?"

He shrugged. "It's perfectly safe. They moved the Keystone."

"They might've moved it, but I'm not sure the Grand Master would want us to keep heading out to it. How would that look with what Draln told you?"

"I don't know that I care how it would look."

"Tolan!"

He paused, turning back to her. He needed to be more careful. He should be concerned about how things looked.

"We shouldn't be spending too much time beyond the borders of the city."

"You believe Draln?"

She looked around before settling her green-eyed gaze on him. "I think what he told you has some merit. When I was heading to Par, there was conversation about the movement of the disciples. You know they've been more active. It's at the point where we don't even have enough defenses within Amitan for their usual diligence. And then with the attacks on the Selections."

"Those were elementals. They weren't attacks."

She frowned at him. "You know as well as I do that the elementals are tied to the disciples. And if the Grand Master believes there's someone inside the Academy who is responsible…"

He held her gaze, debating how much to argue with

her. The problem was that he didn't know, and he wasn't convinced, either. More than ever, he wasn't sure there was anything to be concerned about with the elementals, and yet, everything he'd learned about the disciples of the Draasin Lord suggested they wanted to use the power of the elementals, combine it with the power of the element bonds, and rule.

He wanted nothing to do with that, either.

"I didn't get the sense there was anyone trying to instigate that attack," Tolan said.

"How can you even say that?"

"I can say it because it's true," he said. "Besides, I think Draln was just trying to impress the others. I have a hard time thinking there's a traitor here."

"I'm surprised to hear you say that," she said.

They had paused in the middle of the forest. The trees all around them rose high overhead, creating a canopy that shaded them. A soft breeze blew through, barely more than a whisper that brushed across his cheeks, a promise of power he thought he might be able to reach for. In the time since he'd been asked to leave the Keystone alone, his experience with wind and water had not been nearly what it had been before, and yet Tolan still believed he could reach them if given the proper motivation. Fire and earth remained potent for him, and yet of them, it was fire that was the most potent.

"Why are you surprised to hear me say that?"

"I might not have the same memories of everything"— Ferrah still held a hint of irritation in her voice as she spoke of the time they had gone down to the Convergence, and he wondered if there would ever be any way for her to regain those memories—"but I was there with you when you dealt with the Keystone and the attack. I understand what's been taking place and the fact none of this has been all that common. You know the last attack on Amitan had been nearly a decade previously?"

He frowned, shaking his head. "I didn't know that."

"And did you know the last time the Draasin Lord was this active was years ago?"

He remained silent. The last time he remembered the Draasin Lord being active was when his disciples had come to Ephra and claimed his parents. Now he understood the way his parents might have been responsible for making bondars, he thought he had a better understanding as to *why* they might have been claimed, only, where would they have been brought?

"And think about what we experienced on the edge of the waste. As far as I've been able to find, that hasn't ever happened."

"Ever?"

Ferrah shook her head. She held his gaze. "That attack is unusual. Even more unusual for the fact the master shapers were unable to figure out who was responsible or do anything about it."

Tolan let out a heavy sigh. Perhaps she was right. There had been quite a bit taking place, and the only thing he could think of was that the Draasin Lord was becoming more active, which meant another attack was imminent. He hadn't been alive during the last attack, but the stories of the Draasin Lord, the violence that had racked Terndahl, changing the landscape of everything, was something everyone knew.

"It's quite a leap to go from believing the attacks are signs of the Draasin Lord becoming more active to believing there's a traitor somewhere within the Academy."

"If what Draln said was true…"

Tolan sighed, leaning his head back on the trunk of one of the trees. The bark was rough, and standing where he was, he felt connected to earth the way he did any time he was within the forest. It was tempting to try shaping, but out here away from the city, with the rumors being what they were, he didn't know it was safe to do that.

"It's Draln, Ferrah. And you know how he can be."

"I know how he can be, but that isn't the kind of thing to start rumors about. Even he isn't stupid enough to do that." Tolan arched a brow. "Fine. Maybe he is."

"I'm less concerned with Draln's rumor than I am about why there were so many more Selected."

"It's probably nothing more than the fact they were ready," Ferrah said.

"It has to be more than that."

"I don't know that it is. I know you want to tie this to some grand mystery and want to believe the Grand Inquisitor is somehow involved, but I'm not sure we can make that connection."

"What if she's the traitor?"

"Tolan—"

He shook his head, looking all around him. The energy of the forest filled him, the sense of heat and earth and wind all around. He suspected he could reach for water if he tried, or at least had some connection to it that he didn't normally have.

"What better way to hide her actions?"

"I'm quite sure the Grand Inquisitor isn't involved. You do know she was one of the three who helped defeat the Draasin Lord?"

"I guess I didn't."

"She was part of the push to exile him from Terndahl."

"Nobody even knows who he is," he said.

"They know enough to know they defeated him. It wasn't just the Grand Inquisitor, but the Grand Master was there too."

Tolan knew that. It was part of the mystique of the Grand Master. He was one of the shapers responsible for exiling the Draasin Lord, ensuring power was removed from Terndahl, and yet as far as Tolan knew, there were none who actually knew anything about the Draasin Lord. No one knew where he went. No one knew if he lived or died. The only thing they knew was that the attacks stopped.

Or, they had seemed to stop.

There were places like Ephra where there was always the threat of attack. Rogue elementals would crop up infrequently, and because of that, there would be danger at the edge of the waste. Most believed it was because they were closer to where the Draasin Lord had disappeared, and yet as Tolan thought about what he had seen of the waste and the power that existed there, he couldn't help but feel as if no shaper would have been able to escape across it. How could they when there was an absence of shaping ability?

But then, the Draasin Lord was connected not only to his ability to shape, but to the elementals, tying them to him, forcing them to serve. After having seen the elementals at the Keystone, Tolan could easily imagine someone like that would be able to use that power and force the elementals to escort him across the waste and to safety.

"If there's a traitor, then we should help find them," he said. At least that would allow him to keep digging about why there were so many Selected.

"Now you're going to get us in trouble again."

"How is that going to get us in trouble?"

"Well, seeing as how you were after Jory—"

"Another traitor."

"Another traitor, but not the same. From what you said, he wanted the power for himself, and Draln says this traitor suggests they're in the service of the Draasin Lord, not trying to replace him."

"How do you know that?"

"Because I asked."

"You did what?'

She shrugged. "I wanted to know for myself. Whoever is working inside the Academy, working against us, is doing so in order to help expedite the return of the

Draasin Lord. But after what happened with Jory, and then with the Keystone, we've been far too involved. Maybe it's best if we sit this one out."

"I didn't say we would get actively involved and that we needed to try to interrogate people within the Academy, but I think we can stay aware. If we find something that's useful, then we can..." Tolan wasn't entirely sure what they could do with that information. Where would they bring it? It wasn't something he could easily bring to the Grand Master, and yet, he thought he would need to.

"If we find anything, then we can bring it to the Grand Inquisitor."

"Maybe you can do that," he said.

"You know her better than anyone in our level."

"That's not something I'm proud of."

"It's useful."

"I'm not entirely sure how that's useful, either."

"How many others can say they were Selected by the Grand Inquisitor?"

"This year? Quite a few. Previous years?"

Ferrah watched him, saying nothing.

"See? You recognize there's something strange going on."

"I recognize there's something off, but I still think you're reading too much into it."

"And I think you're not reading enough into it."

She sighed, throwing her hands up. "Are we going to involve Jonas in this?"

They hadn't involved Jonas when they went to the

Keystone, and yet Jonas was one of his closest friends at the Academy. How could he not include him?

"I can check and see how much he might be interested in participating, but I don't know if Jonas is all that excited about getting involved with the Grand Inquisitor. There's something about her that makes him uncomfortable."

"There's something about the Inquisitors that makes everyone uncomfortable, Tolan. You might not have seen the Inquisitors all that often around the periphery of Terndahl, but stories of Inquisitions are legendary."

"How so?"

"They pull shapers aside, take them for Inquisition, torment them until they get the answers they want. If they think someone is tied to the Draasin Lord, they will do anything to get that information from them."

Tolan shivered involuntarily. He was thankful that hadn't occurred in Ephra. At the edge of the waste, there had been very little exposure to the Inquisitors. The only experience he really had was when they had come through, but for the most part, the master shapers had been responsible for ensuring the city was safe.

"We should go back. We can study in the second-level rooms. Besides, we won't be able to find anything here."

"You go back. I just want to check on the park."

"Tolan…"

He flashed a smile. "I'm not going to do anything foolish. I'm just going to head out there, see how much is changed since the last time I was there, and I'll return. We can continue to try to figure out what's been going on afterward."

She watched him, and he worried she would want to come with him. As much as he enjoyed Ferrah's company —and he did—he also wanted to go to the park, to see whether that power would still be there, and whether there was anything he might be able to do.

"Don't be too long."

He nodded and hurried off into the woods, leaving Ferrah. They hadn't gone all that deep into the forest, which meant he had a bit of a walk before reaching the park. He was careful as he went, using his connection to earth to sense whether there was anything moving around him.

Ever since his time in the Keystone, his connection to sensing had increased, giving him a much easier time recognizing that energy, and he was able to feel the way it connected to him, the way his boots sank ever so softly into the ground with each step, the way he thudded, the reverberations of his footsteps echoing toward others who might be nearby, and the nature of how his presence within the forest influenced the creatures here.

The longer he was here, the more he knew his presence mattered. It was tied to everything. Within the forest, he was aware of the elements in ways he wasn't in other places. It was similar to the park near the Academy, and yet this was less controlled, and because of that, Tolan couldn't help but feel as if his connection were greater.

The clearing for the park opened in front of him, and

he paused at the edge of the forest. He looked around, using his connection to earth to see if there was anything to worry about, but the more he searched, the more certain he was there was nothing.

It was possible the disciples of the Draasin Lord were here, and yet with the Keystone missing, there would be no reason for them to come. This park was not otherwise special, at least according to the Grand Master.

Tolan studied the low stone wall surrounding the park. The symbols were still marked on it, symbols depicting the element bonds. Those runes meant that regardless of whether the Keystone was here, there would still be power present.

Could he use them?

He didn't know. He hadn't spent nearly enough time back here, and yet now he was here, he thought he needed to better understand the park.

He approached the stone wall slowly, feeling his way toward it, worried there would be some presence approaching, and yet found nothing.

If the disciples were out here, they had left this place alone.

Touching the wall, he felt nothing strange about it. When the disciples—and Master Daniels—had come before, there had been resistance, some sort of barrier preventing them from getting too close, and he couldn't help but think there was something about it he should better understand. Could it be tied to the runes? It was the only thing he knew was here, though it was possible it was tied to the Keystone itself. Then again, when Tolan had been here, using the Keystone, the power had seemed inactive until he had begun to use it.

He climbed up, taking a seat on top of the wall. When he did, he looked over the grassy square. It was large, set in the middle of the forest, surrounded by the stone wall, a field where shaping energy had been trapped. The elementals had been trapped. And as he sat here, he couldn't help but think some of that power remained, even though he wasn't able to access it.

There was something peaceful about coming here. That much hadn't changed. After his experience on the way to the Selection, Tolan thought he needed to better understand the elementals—and learn if there was some way of speaking to them.

If he could, he thought any rogue elemental would provide less of a challenge than it had. Could he summon anything from here?

He needed to try.

Scrambling off the wall, he took a seat on the other side, down in the grass, smoothing it around him. He pulled the furios from his pocket, resting it on his legs. He would start with fire, the way he always started with fire. If he could summon one of the elementals, then he could move on to earth. If he succeeded there, then he could try wind and water. He was a second-level student now. He had to continue to use the various elements. Eventually, there would be another test, and though he didn't know what would be involved, he suspected it would be as difficult as the last one had been.

He drew through the furios, and hyza suddenly surged into view. It happened the same way as it happened each time, the elementals springing into view, and he held on to that connection, watching as the foxlike creature prowled around him, before he released the hold on the elemental. The shaping disappeared slowly, and as it winked out, there was a sense of something more, almost as if he should recognize something about the elemental, but it faded too quickly for him to do so.

Tolan frowned, thinking about hyza again. He would continue to work with fire until he had it.

It was something he probably shouldn't be doing, and yet he wanted to better understand the elementals. How could he not when so much of what had happened at the Academy seemed to be tied up within them?

8

THE COURTYARD OUTSIDE THE ACADEMY WAS ONE OF THE nicest places within Amitan. Most of the students came to the courtyard after getting settled in, and Tolan was not surprised to find the first-level students no different. He and his second-level classmates had done the same thing when they had first come to the Academy, using that as an opportunity to get out of the Academy towers as often as they could. It wasn't that they minded the inside of the Academy, it was just there was something about being outside, surrounded by the elements, feeling the infusion of power.

That had to be the intent of the founders of the Academy. They would have known the students needed to return to a place like the courtyard, and that had to be the reason they had built it so close. There was water for water shapers, and a breeze continually gusted through. The rugged contours brought a proximity to earth, and the brightly shining sun that usually favored Amitan shone overhead, casting a certain warmth.

In the last few days, Tolan hadn't been able to uncover how many more people had gone on a Selection with the Grand Inquisitor but given the sheer size of the first-year class, he had to believe it was more than he had uncovered so far. It had to be more than him and Jonas and Haervn.

The first-level class was nearly twenty shapers larger than Tolan's class. That many students would put a burden on the instructors, and while Tolan hadn't seen any evidence of irritation out of them, he doubted he would. They would be far more skilled at controlling their emotions and their irritation. Most would probably be excited about the fact so many students had been Selected.

From what he had been able to gather, the fact only a few each year were able to be Selected was something of a disappointment to many of the master shapers. They wanted to increase their numbers, finding strength to overpower the disciples of the Draasin Lord, and he had heard murmurings that suggested many of the master shapers feared they wouldn't have enough numbers to really ever take on and defeat the disciples or the Draasin Lord if they didn't continue to bring in students.

Had they changed the Selection?

The fact the Grand Inquisitor had been there for his Selection, along with the Selection of several of these larger groups, had to mean something. Tolan wondered what it could be.

A large grouping of first-level students sat near the

small pond at the center of the park just outside the Academy. Tolan stayed off to the side, sitting on a bench, focusing on the book resting on his lap. Every so often, he fidgeted, slipping his hand into his pocket, and as he did, he came across the things he'd brought back from Ephra.

He hadn't paid much mind to them. They had been his parents' items, things he had wanted, if only for the memories they might hold. Now he knew his father—and possibly his mother—had some connection to the bondars, he wondered if perhaps these items weren't more important than he had realized before.

Tolan pulled a small ring out of his pocket. He had found it in his mother's wardrobe. Like so many of the items his parents kept, he wasn't surprised it was made of stone. It was an exquisite design. There was a spiraling pattern to it, twisting as the ring was formed, and he ran his fingers along it, tracing for some sign of runes, thinking maybe it was a type of bondar, but there were none found upon it.

Perhaps it was nothing more than jewelry.

Tolan had seen something similar before but couldn't remember where that had been. He traced his fingers around it, feeling the pattern and wondering how much time would have gone into its making. It had to be something his parents had made. There would be no reason for them to have a ring like this otherwise, but why this style?

Pulling the earth bondar from his pocket, he set it on his leg, rolling it over. It didn't take much to connect to that bondar anymore. It was almost as if it were designed for him to use, though that was more likely related to the fact he had spent so much time working with the Keystone, connecting to the element bonds in that way. Ever since doing so, his ability to at least reach the element bonds through bondars had improved.

The stone felt familiar.

What secret did his father know about the making of bondars? Tolan had tried—and failed—at making them, but if he could have an opportunity to figure it out, he could make one for wind and water, and then he wouldn't have to worry about attempting to shape the elements he wasn't able to reach easily. He suspected part of the testing for passage beyond the second level would involve demonstrating reaching a third shaping, but he didn't like the chances of doing so on his own. He would need help, especially when it came to wind and water.

He attempted shaping each of the elements through the ring, but nothing succeeded.

His parents being shapers made a different sort of sense to him. Some of the memories he had were of their attempts at helping him reach the various element bonds. He had told Master Marcella about their attempt to help him reach wind and earth, taking him to the mountains, and yet there had been other attempts. None had succeeded.

It was almost as if whatever abilities he had were muted.

Until he reached the Academy.

A familiar voice cut through his reverie and he looked

up. Velthan was standing with the group of first-year students at the edge of the pond. A shaping built from him, far more skillfully than Tolan remembered him capable of.

Water spiraled, turning in a tight funnel, and Tolan couldn't help but watch, marveling at the level of control Velthan demonstrated. It was impressive, as much as he hated to admit it.

He turned away and had started to get to his feet when Velthan's voice called to him.

"Ethar."

Tolan looked over. He shoved the bondar into his pocket and wrapped his hand around the ring, squeezing it.

"What is it, Velthan?"

Velthan glanced at the others, and Tolan noticed the slight twinkle in his eye. He had seen that look on the other man's face before.

Did he think he was going to use Tolan in some way to raise his stature here? Tolan wouldn't put it past Velthan to use the fact they knew each other to somehow make himself out to be more than he was, and Velthan already was a skilled shaper.

"We didn't get a chance to talk much when you were in Ephra," Velthan said.

Tolan stuffed the book into his pocket. He glanced over Velthan's shoulder, noticing the other students watching them talking. "The Selection doesn't allow for much of an opportunity to talk."

"I know, but… how is it you're here?"

"I was Selected, the same as you."

"But how are *you* here? I'm not disparaging the Selection process. The Great Mother knows I'm thankful I was Selected, but I just don't understand how it is *you* of all people managed to be chosen. You can't even shape!" He dropped his voice at the end, and Tolan thought for a moment that Velthan was being kind to him until he realized a soft wind shaping was carrying their words.

Irritation bubbled up within him. He squeezed the furios, letting fire begin to build, and sent it swirling around Velthan. He held it tightly controlled, pushing through a connection to hyza, summoning the faintest bit of a connection to the fire elemental. He didn't want to summon the entire elemental, not wanting to call upon fire quite so potently, but all he really wanted to do was create a funnel, to make Velthan aware he was something more than what the other man remembered.

Heat built and Velthan took a step back, his eyes going wide. "How are you able to do this?"

"I'm a second-level student at the Academy, Velthan. Do you think they would've promoted me if I didn't have any ability?"

"Why didn't you use it in Ephra?"

"Maybe I didn't want to learn from the shapers in Ephra."

Tolan gathered up the heat, suppressing it again. He didn't want to overdo it, and as he started to do so, he realized the heat continued to swell. He released the connection to the furios, letting go of it, the runes leaving a tingling on his palm.

Great Mother!

He closed his eyes for a moment, sending out a surge of connection to the elemental, begging for it to retreat. He didn't need Velthan to see him manipulating an elemental. There were already enough stories out of Ephra, and now Velthan was here, those stories would spread, more so if he were involved with summoning elementals.

The time in the park had made it so he summoned them far too easily. When there, they had disappeared quickly. Would it be the same now?

Please. Not now.

There came a sense of resistance. Tolan could feel it as if deep within him, and distinct from the stirring he felt when he attempted to shape. This was as if the elemental was trying to resist what he was asking of it.

Please.

"You've made your point, Ethar," Velthan said.

Sweat broke out on Tolan's face and he leaned toward Velthan. "I just wanted to show you what you can learn when you're at the Academy."

"You don't think I know what I'm going to learn at the Academy? I've spent years wanting to make it. And now I have. I'm going to be a master shaper. I'm going to be one who stops the elementals from escaping from the element bond. And I'm going to be a part of stopping the Draasin Lord."

There was an eagerness in his voice, and Tolan shook his head. "You might get your chance before you realize it."

"What does that mean?"

The heat continued to rise and Tolan tried again to beg the elemental, feeling as if that was the only way he would convince it to tamp down, but when that didn't work, he switched his grip, grabbing for the earth elemental, calling on jinnar.

He hadn't tried using them in this way before, but all he wanted was to suppress fire, and earth and fire were opposite enough that it should work.

The ground rumbled softly, faintly, and slowly the heat began to dissipate.

Tolan released his grip on the earth bondar, breathing out a sigh of relief. *Thank you.*

He wasn't sure if the elemental had been jinnar or not, but it seemed as if there came a soft echoing in reply.

"It just means the city isn't as safe as most believe. There have been several attacks in my time here. Be ready for whatever you might have to face," Tolan said.

"What kind of attacks?"

"The Draasin Lord."

Velthan grinned, and he glanced over his shoulder at the others. "I'll be ready. I'm not afraid to face the Draasin Lord, especially as I've already faced him in Ephra." His voice rose slightly at the end, and Tolan realized that last was not meant for his benefit—but rather that of the other students. "And if there's a traitor here like I've heard…"

He should have known better. How much of this conversation had been staged, Velthan's way of trying to prove himself more important than he was? Was it Velthan's way of trying to allude Tolan might be the traitor?

"You'd be surprised at how many think they are prepared for the Draasin Lord but find out when confronted by him that they are not," Tolan said.

"I grew up in Ephra. I'm ready for dealing with the Draasin Lord. If he were to come here, if he were to try to attack us, I'd be ready."

Tolan glanced behind Velthan before shaking his head. There was no purpose in staying and arguing with him. Velthan had always been arrogant, and perhaps he was one of the skilled shapers of his class. If so, there wasn't anything Tolan was going to be able to do to dissuade him from acting the way he was. In that, Velthan reminded Tolan more of Draln than anyone else. They were skilled shapers, and that skill gave them a bit of earned arrogance.

"I hope you are. And I hope when you're brought out to the waste with the rest of the first levels that you're brave and don't run away from it the way so many others do."

The words had the desired effect on Velthan. "They bring the first levels out to the waste?"

Tolan nodded. "They want you to know what it's like when you lose the connection to your shaping ability."

"I bet you ran. Didn't you, Ethar?"

Tolan flashed an angry smile. "Why would I run? I went deeper than anyone else."

Heading away and winding to the Keystone park, he found it empty. He reached the spot the bondar had occupied. The ground was smooth, almost perfectly so, and he suspected that came from a shaping designed to mask what had been here. The last time he'd come here, he hadn't gone to where the stone had stood.

He touched the dirt, shaping briefly and releasing it, ensuring that he could. When he straightened, he realized he wasn't alone.

"Shaper Ethar," the Grand Master said.

Tolan bowed his head respectfully, glancing around. How had the Grand Master found him so quickly? "Grand Master. I—"

The Grand Master only smiled. "You don't need to apologize. There is no harm in visiting this place. Most of the people who know of it understand what it is, and you are among them."

"How did you know I was here?"

"We have placed certain protections around it to identify whether someone would come here."

Then he would have known the last time Tolan had come. "You think the disciples might return?"

"It's quite likely they will. We wanted to be ready for that possibility."

"How did you get here so quickly?"

The Grand Master smiled at him. "We have ways that don't involve the Shapers Path."

Tolan imagined there were. He didn't know much about traveling by shaping, but the more powerful shapers had ways of transporting themselves from place to place. Some of the incredibly skilled wind shapers could travel on the wind. Others were skilled with water, and he knew they would use platforms of water for travel. Still others would travel on the earth, practically sliding over top of it. He wasn't sure how that one worked, though he had heard about it often enough to know it was possible. Fire was easier to understand, at least the way he used it but having control over it seemed difficult to Tolan. It was incredibly difficult to control the nature of fire.

And then there was the way some shapers could travel that involved combining the various elements, twisting the bonds together. They were able to simply move from one place to the next, far more rapidly than anyone could, even with the Shapers Path. That was a higher-level skill, and one he imagined they would learn as they continued to progress through their training. It involved reaching deeply into the bond in order to do it. What would happen when he was asked to do so? Would he struggle? Without having access to the bonds, it was possible he might not be able to do it.

"It feels different here."

"As it should," he said.

"Is it bad that I don't like it?"

"I wouldn't have expected you to have liked to the change. The change was for safety, though. It was needed. Had we left the Keystone where it was, there was a very real possibility the disciples of the Draasin Lord would have found it."

"Found it again?"

"Perhaps."

"I don't think they were able to use it," Tolan said.

"No. There is something about the Keystone that chooses those who have access to it."

Tolan wondered how much of that was true or not. He didn't have the sense he had been chosen by the stone, but there was a sense of power required to use this place. Maybe his connection to the element bonds and his understanding of the elementals was what allowed him to do it. It was possible there was another way, something that was simply different about him.

"You disagree," the Grand Master said.

"It's not so much that I disagree, it's just that I…"

The Grand Master smiled. When he did, his eyes softened, the weight he normally held behind them leaving, making it so he was almost welcoming and warm, something Tolan would never have normally described the Grand Master as being.

"It's just you had a different experience?"

Tolan nodded. "I did have a different experience. It was one that required a connection to the elements in a different way."

"And what can you tell me about it?"

How much should he reveal to the Grand Master? This was always the part of things where Tolan wasn't sure. He didn't know whether he should reveal anything about the elementals, particularly to the master shapers. What would they do if he told them he felt as if he were releasing elementals?

"Was it real?"

"Was what real?"

"The release of the elementals from the Keystone."

"Ah. That is an excellent question. You wonder if it's a shaping you were able to control or whether it was the elementals?"

Tolan shrugged.

"To be honest, we have spent considerable time studying, trying to understand whether it is the elementals themselves or whether it was simply our shaping. The Keystone was a connection to an ancient power, and that ancient power could have many different forms. Some suspect it simply allows us to connect to the element bonds more effectively, while others wonder if perhaps the truth is something different."

"Such as reaching the elementals."

"Possibly, though even that seems unlikely."

"Why is that?"

"There is a difference between what you might find here and the rogue elementals we have encountered that have escaped. The rogue elementals are more violent and agitated. What we found here seemed almost subdued. Controlled. And, I suspect you noticed, they weren't allowed to leave the park. There is something that confines whatever we do here. Considering what we know of the elementals, such a confinement should not be possible."

Tolan hadn't considered that, but it made sense. The elementals *were* trapped here. He had been thankful of that when he had felt as if he were freeing the draasin. If it wasn't the draasin, then he had some hope that whatever it was he had done, whatever shaping he had created, had not really freed anything.

"What do you think the purpose of this place was?"

"It's hard to know what the ancient shapers intended. We have many examples of their shaping, but oftentimes they are difficult to understand. This one, so close to the Academy, is intriguing in its power. Much like the sense of the Convergence is different in its power."

They fell into silence. Tolan watched the Grand Master for a long moment. "Are the rumors true?"

"Rumors have a way of often coming from the seeds of truth."

"About a traitor within the Academy."

The Grand Master looked around before turning his attention back to Tolan. "Unfortunately, we believe it must be. Not only have these attacks on Amitan suggested the Draasin Lord has increased his activity, but the attacks on the Selections made it clear they knew when we were starting our search."

"What does that mean?"

"For you? Nothing more than you continuing your studies. I think you should not attempt to return here, though. It will be dangerous for you."

"Why?"

"There will be changes, Shaper Ethar."

"What kind of changes?"

"When the Draasin Lord attempts to infiltrate the Academy, we must take action. That means Inquisitors." He took a deep breath, and Tolan had a sense the Grand Master didn't care for that. "You need to remain close to Amitan or you will draw the attention of the Inquisitors. That means not visiting this place, and not pursuing your search for the Keystone."

"I don't have any intention of searching for the Keystone," he said.

"Good. You already have found two places of considerable power that help protect Terndahl and the Academy. It's unusual for someone so young and so early in their training to discover these sources of power. I would caution you not to continue looking for others. And avoid the Inquisitors if you can. Focus on your studies."

The Grand Master flashed a smile and focused on a shaping, and with that, he disappeared into the sky faster than anyone Tolan had seen before.

He remained in place, looking around the park, worried it would be a while until he could see it again, before heading back toward the Academy.

9

As they headed to their fire shaping session, Tolan saw the first of the Inquisitors.

They were dressed in black cloaks. All wore serious expressions. Some carried swords. He counted five on the way to class but suspected there were more.

Ferrah pushed him. "Don't stare."

"When he said they were going to come to the Academy, I knew we'd see them, but I didn't…"

She shoved again. "Keep moving."

Tolan let his gaze linger as he looked at them but forced it away. Staring would only draw their notice, and he definitely didn't want that.

A faint haze hung over the fire-shaping classroom as Tolan entered, taking a seat near the back. It took him a moment to realize the haze came from a shaping, leaving smoke swirling around the classroom, filling it. Master Sartan stood near the front of the room, his hands pressed on his desk, and a shaping radiated from him. Probably this shaping, Tolan decided.

Ferrah took a seat near the front of the class, pulling her notebook open in front of her, her pen ready. Others continued to file in, and Tolan was thankful he wasn't the last to have arrived. On the first day of their second-level shaping lessons, he didn't want to be the last one to arrive.

Jonas joined him, flopping down in the chair and looking over at him. "Where have you been?"

"All over the place," Tolan said.

He had stayed mostly in the library since meeting the Grand Master, deciding the best use of his time was to try to understand the Selection. He might not be able to find the traitor—and now the Inquisitors were here, he doubted he needed to—but he could understand that. He still hadn't uncovered anything about the Selection that would help him understand it any better than he already did. And maybe he wouldn't be able to understand any better. The books Master Jensen had dug out for him had not been very helpful. Tolan had been reading through them, trying to understand everything he could about the nature of shaping, but all he was left with was a sense that shapers from that time, at least those who had made notes and left them behind, had a very different understanding of shaping than what the master shapers of today did.

From what Master Minden said, that present knowledge of shaping was better, though Tolan wasn't completely convinced. Maybe it was better, but it was just as possible their understanding of shaping was just evolved. That didn't make the shapers of before any less talented. They had to be talented, especially as they had been the ones who had started the Academy.

"Don't tell me you've been digging into your concern about the Grand Inquisitor."

Tolan shook his head. "I'm not even sure where I would start, but there *is* a traitor at the Academy. The Grand Master admitted as much."

"Because you shouldn't. I don't know what you think you might have uncovered with her, but I doubt it's anything nearly as exciting as what you have imagined. Besides, did you see them?"

He nodded, not needing to ask what he meant. "I think we're going to see a lot of them."

Tolan turned his attention to the front of the class, where Master Sartan was beginning to take a seat. That indicated the start of his lessons, and Tolan was not interested in upsetting him. Most of the time, Master Sartan was accommodating to him.

"Today we are going to talk about smoke," Master Sartan said.

Someone groaned off to the side of the class

Master Sartan smiled slightly. The smoke began to thicken. "You don't believe working on smoke is beneficial?"

With the rising haze in the classroom, Tolan couldn't tell who he was directing the question to. He could barely see the end of his table now and he coughed, hurriedly covering his face with his jacket so he didn't breathe in the smoke.

"Many people feel fire alone is a weapon, and it is, but there are aspects to fire few people think to utilize. We've gone through steam, and how that can work with water, the two of them surprisingly much stronger than what they would be otherwise. Today we are going to go through smoke, and we will spend the next few weeks mastering it."

"The next few *weeks*?" Jonas asked near him. "I'm not sure I have the patience for spending a few weeks on something so simple."

"Is that right?" Master Sartan's voice came from much closer than he had been before. How had he snuck up on them so easily? "Most feel summoning smoke is easy, but they would be mistaken. There is nothing simple about summoning smoke in this manner. In fact, when you learn to master smoke, you will find the shaping is far more complicated—and subtle—than many of the other shapings you might attempt. Now, if that is about all from you?"

The smoke around Jonas cleared enough for Tolan to see his friend nod. They had to be careful. Master Sartan was an incredibly gifted fire shaper, and with the smoke being his creation, it wouldn't be surprising if Master Sartan was completely in control of clearing it up. He might even be able to see through it, unlike the rest of them.

Master Sartan's voice came from a different section of

the room. Tolan wished he were able to see him more easily, but the haze made seeing anything far too difficult. "You will find controlling smoke is difficult, but partly because you expend far more of yourself when you do this than you do with fire. Fire is focused, direct, whereas smoke is everywhere. But it is that reason that smoke is far more powerful. You can use it to obfuscate, concealing, but you can also use it to incapacitate."

The smoke thickened once again, and several people around the classroom began coughing. As Tolan had his arm covering his mouth, he wasn't breathing in nearly as much as he would have otherwise, but still he took in a mouthful of smoke, much more than he wished he did. He could see the value in a shaping like this. It would be incredibly powerful, and it would provide the ability to hide.

"Today I would like you to focus on creating smoke around you. Nothing more than that. The shaping is a matter of focusing on flame but twisting it in such a way that you are constantly tamping it down, forcing the heat to dissipate. Not only are you asked to form a flame, but you're also asked to quiet the flame." The air suddenly cleared. Master Sartan stood in the center of the class-room. "Which is why smoke is one of the most difficult shapings for students to master."

He made his way to the front of the class, and once there, Master Sartan took a seat and reached into one of his drawers, pulling a tray loaded with bondars out and setting it on his desk.

More people than usual got up from their seats and went to grab a bondar. Jonas was among them. When he returned, he glanced over at Tolan and shrugged. "If he said this was one of the more difficult shapings, I figured I might as well have some assistance with it."

Tolan reached into his pocket, thinking of what elemental might be beneficial. He had some ability with forming smoke already, though that was tied to both shiron and esalash. Both were smoke elementals he had some experience with, though not enough experience to be able to control them. He glanced over at the bondar Jonas had borrowed, and he saw a marking upon it that he recognized.

"Can I borrow that?" Tolan asked.

"Don't you have your own?"

"I do, but I'm not necessarily able to pull it out while in class," Tolan whispered. He worried Jonas's voice had carried too far. He didn't want—or need—others to know about his possession of bondars. The first had been hidden since he initially came to the Academy, but the earth bondar was something else entirely.

Jonas handed him the bondar and Tolan took it, rolling it in his hands for a moment. He held it out, focusing on shiron. That was the marking he'd seen on the bondar, and he had enough experience with the elementals and recognizing the patterns that he identified the one that would be beneficial.

Focusing on the marking—Tolan didn't know whether

it was a rune or not, though had long ago realized it didn't matter—he imagined what he could of shiron.

With this elemental, he didn't want to have complete obfuscation of everything and let smoke fill the room. That would be the role of esalash. He wanted to create a small band of smoke. That was something shiron was more suited to.

He continued to focus, holding the image of the elemental in his mind, and slowly—far more slowly than what he was accustomed to—smoke began to appear. A sense of stirring started, and with that, he latched onto it, connecting to what he could imagine of the elemental, using that knowledge to help him focus on shiron. As he did, he tried to call to the elemental, to guide it. He didn't want the elemental to burst into view. All he wanted was enough of an appearance that he would be able to demonstrate smoke for the day.

Streamers of smoke began to swirl. Tolan held onto those streamers, trying to thicken them. As he did, he sent them swirling around himself.

Shiron listened and cooperated.

It wasn't that the elemental obeyed. Tolan never had the sense he was commanding the elementals, not when he attempted to use his shaping in that way. Rather, he had the sense he was guiding them, asking them to join him, and when they cooperated, they were able to work together.

Perhaps it was all in his mind, and if it was, he didn't

care. Whatever it took to help him be able to shape was all that mattered.

"Okay. Now you've proven you can do it, can you let me borrow it?" Jonas said.

Tolan released his connection, and the smoke continued to swirl around him. He handed the bondar over to Jonas and focused on the elemental. This was the part he still needed practice with. He didn't know if he was actually calling an elemental or not, but dismissing the shaping—or the elemental, whichever it was—was the hardest part for him.

Thank you.

There seem to be a slight stirring within the smoke, but then it started to dissipate.

"Who taught you to shape like that?" Master Sartan asked as he approached Tolan.

The smoke had faded, leaving nothing around him.

"I was just doing what you instructed," Tolan said.

"That is not what I instructed." He motioned around them, and Tolan looked around the room before seeing what Master Sartan meant. Most of the other students were attempting faint wisps of smoke, nothing quite like what Tolan had done. He had convinced shiron to swirl around him, creating a haze covering him. Would the same thing have happened had he focused on esalash? It was possible it would, though he hadn't wanted to strain for that much elemental power quite yet. It was better to connect to them cautiously, rather than rushing in.

"I don't know. I must've seen a shaping like that before."

"That is an interesting level of control," Master Sartan said. "Many students never master that degree of control."

"What degree?"

"Where they cover themselves. You were using smoke to hide within." He cocked his head to the side, staring at Tolan for a moment. "Or were you not aware of that?"

"I didn't quite know what I was doing. That's the problem."

"Perhaps." He frowned a moment longer before making his way through the classroom.

Jonas elbowed him. "Now you're getting on Master Sartan's good side? Pretty soon you're going to be his favorite."

"I have a hard time believing I could ever be his favorite."

"I don't know. He seemed awfully impressed by your shaping. Although, I have to admit, seeing as how you were able to shape the way you were compared to everyone else, it *was* impressive. Look at everyone else's shaping. No one is doing anything quite like what you managed."

Tolan looked up at Ferrah. If anyone would be able to do anything similar, it would be her. She was a skilled shaper and already had some talent with fire, so it wouldn't surprise him to see her able to control fire and shape exactly the way Master Sartan had wanted.

Except Ferrah was struggling, or at least seemed to be.

148 | D.K. HOLMBERG

She had smoke, but not as much as Draln had managed. He could practically see the tension within Ferrah. It was the rigid way she sat, her stiff neck, and the occasional glance around her that told him just how agitated she was.

"So, what's the secret?"

"You just have to do as he says," Tolan said.

"I've been trying to do that, but all I managed to do is create sparks in my hand. And I'm pretty sure he doesn't want us to light ourselves on fire today."

"Not today, but maybe on another day," Tolan said, forcing a smile.

"Is there anything you can suggest that will help me shape the way you did?"

"I don't know. I just focused on smoke."

"Focus on smoke," Jonas muttered, squeezing the bondar as he pointed at his hand. A flicker of flame appeared there and immediately began to dissipate, smoke streaming off of it. Jonas was doing what Master Sartan had instructed, but the instructions didn't fit with what Tolan knew to be necessary to create smoke.

The connection between his shapings and the elementals was almost enough for him to go to the Grand Master. The moment he did, Tolan suspected he would be treated differently. Already he was treated differently enough because of everything he had been through. He didn't want more reason for people like the Grand Master to treat him any differently than anyone else. More than that, he wanted to stay at the Academy and his studies.

"We can practice more after class," Tolan whispered to Jonas.

"I'm going to have to. If he said this is a shaping all must master before they leave the Academy, you know what that means."

"I don't know what that means."

"It means it's part of some testing."

"Do you think it could be?"

"You heard what he said the same as I did," Jonas hissed. "Honestly, Tolan, sometimes I don't feel as if you pay attention."

He sighed and turned his focus back to the front of the class. Eventually, they would end the lesson and Master Sartan would begin talking about elementals. At least, that was the way lessons had gone before.

This time was different. As everyone either finished or gave up, Master Sartan got to his feet. "Everyone join me on the peak."

Tolan and Jonas shared a look. "The peak?" Jonas whispered.

Tolan shrugged. They filed out of the classroom, Draln and his buddies the first to make their way up the stairs, following after Master Sartan. Tolan slowed and Ferrah joined them, her jaw still clenched with her frustration.

"How did it go?" Jonas asked. "I nearly burned my hand, but Tolan here was able to create some sort of smokescreen all around him. He became Master Sartan's favorite in the process, though I'm not surprised. Some of the things he's done with fire have been—"

Tolan elbowed him, silencing him. Ferrah glanced at both of them before hurrying up the stairs after the rest of the class.

Jonas shot him a look. "What?"

"Can't you see she doesn't want to talk about it?" Tolan asked.

"Is it because she's not the best at something?"

"I don't think that's it," Tolan whispered.

Jonas made his way up the stairs, leaving Tolan as the last to follow. He didn't understand Ferrah's frustration when it came to fire. It wasn't that she wasn't talented. He had seen frustration escape from her before, though today was more than he had noticed before.

Maybe it was the fact Tolan had managed the smoke so quickly, though he had never seen her upset with his ability to shape fire, mostly because she knew he was using the bondar to do so. She didn't need the bondar. If she had, and if she had used it, she probably would have been able to do much more of a shaping.

At the top of the stairs, he emerged on an open platform. The city spread out below them. Though they weren't nearly as high up as they would be when taking the Shapers Path, it was still high enough that he felt a sense of distance from everything else.

He took a deep breath, letting it out, and looked around. Master Sartan was near one of the low walls surrounding the peak, little more than a short drop before he would fall, though as most were shapers, a fall shouldn't be deadly. At this point, most should have enough control over at least one of their element bonds to be able to save themselves were they to fall.

"Up here is a protected space much like the spaces within your student sections. Up here, you can practice with fire the way you would anywhere else, only in this space, our intention is to begin planning to battle elementals."

A steady murmur built around the peak, everyone's voices rising.

"Many of you think you will need to have more training in order to face elementals, but I'm here to tell you that you might not get any more training than what you already have. Some of you, as you have seen, will not pass on beyond this level."

Tolan looked around the room, realizing they still didn't know how many had passed beyond the first to the second level. There hadn't been many who hadn't, otherwise he would've recognized it the moment they returned, and yet, as he looked around, he realized there weren't nearly as many people as he remembered. How many could be missing? Maybe two or three, possibly more than that. Ferrah would know. She was great at keeping track of such things.

"Regardless of how long you remain at the Academy, you will have to know how to be prepared for the possibility you will be asked to stop an elemental attack. Many of you will spread throughout Terndahl, providing defense, providing services through your shaping ability. Some of you will return to teach at your local shaping school, while others of you will move onward, preferring to take a different approach. Regardless of where you go, the Academy graduates are expected to serve Terndahl and prepare for an elemental attack."

Master Sartan pulled a bondar from his pocket and focused. Slowly, a streamer of fire began to emerge, twisting in place.

Tolan recognized the elemental Master Sartan was intending to create, though there were some differences. He was trying to generate isaw, though from what he knew of the elemental, it was more ropey, a spiraling sort of elemental that created heat and flame. What Master Sartan had generated was thicker and didn't put off nearly as much heat as Tolan suspected it should.

Most backed away, putting space between themselves and the elemental, though Tolan remained fixed in place. There was nothing dangerous about this. While it might be the image of an elemental, it was shaped rather than real, which he could feel. How come others could not? It was no different than when they had played Imaginarium.

Maybe they could but didn't know it. Tolan recognized the power of shaping building from Master Sartan, flowing through the bondar. It surprised him he would hold onto a bondar in this way, though the bondar would allow him to shape with much more strength than he otherwise would be able to do.

Tolan was tempted to use the furios to summon the elemental himself, though were to do so, he would raise questions, and he had no interest in having others question him about how and what sort of connection he had to the elementals.

"Can anyone identify this elemental?"

"That is isaw," Tolan said, though he immediately realized he should have waited a moment.

Master Sartan turned his attention to him. Tolan was the closest to him now, barely a step away from the elemental. There was heat from it, but with as much fire as Master Sartan was putting into the shaping, having heat flow into the elemental wasn't shocking, but there wasn't the same nature of heat Tolan would have expected. Isaw was a combination of heat and fire, but there was another aspect to it that Master Sartan hadn't managed to add within it. From what Tolan knew of his readings about the elementals, isaw was not only of fire, but also of wind, though not nearly as strongly as some. There should be more of a wispy quality to it, and it should flow, spinning in the air.

It was an interesting elemental for Master Sartan to have chosen for that reason. If he wanted them to know what it would be like to stop a fire elemental, Tolan would have expected him to have chosen an elemental that would have been fire exclusively rather than one that had aspects of wind within it. But then, seeing the way he summoned the elemental, maybe Master Sartan didn't know.

"Very good. This is isaw. This elemental was once incredibly powerful and found within deserts and occasionally in higher elevations. Now the elemental is nothing but a part of the bond." The shaping waned and the form of the elemental dissipated suddenly. It happened far more rapidly than any time Tolan attempted to remove the presence of the fire elemental, which left him wondering whether Master Sartan was doing things the same as he was or whether his control was simply that much better.

"How would you have handled an elemental like this?" Master Sartan asked Tolan.

"I would probably have focused on earth," he said, thinking about what he knew of suppressing elementals. That wasn't really what he would have done, though he didn't want Master Sartan to know his first attempt would likely have involved him trying to speak to the elemental. Any time he had tried to dismiss an elemental on his own by using another element, he had failed.

"And what sort of shaping would you have used?"

When Tolan had no answer, Draln strode forward, glancing over at Tolan. "I would use a layering shaping. I would use it to trap this elemental, confining it, and then I would smother it."

"That could possibly work," Master Sartan said, glancing from Tolan to Draln. "And now you have confined the elemental, how would you return it to the bond?"

"I would..." Draln frowned, biting his lip as he considered how to answer. "I would use a suppression shaping." When he answered, he looked at Master Sartan, and Tolan bit back a laugh. A suppression shaping? What sort of thing was that?

"A suppression shaping would allow you to tamp down the strength of the elemental, but you would need to force the elemental back into the bond. That is what we are going to work on today."

Tolan couldn't believe Draln had gotten away with an answer like that, but more than that, he wondered whether he would even be able to do what was asked of them next. He had no idea how to perform a suppression shaping, and it was possible such a shaping wouldn't even work for him.

Once again, Master Sartan built a powerful shaping using the bondar. As before, the shape of isaw flowed from the end of the bondar, taking on the snakelike appearance, though still too thick. What would it look like if he added a hint of wind to it?

"I thought it wasn't safe for us to him to demonstrate shapings like this," one of the students said.

"Safety is in the nature of whoever is holding on to the shaping. We aren't demonstrating an actual elemental, other than my shaping forth the appearance of isaw. And I have enough control over this shaping that I'm not afraid of losing my connection. If you had someone without as much control, there would be danger in shaping, but as it is, there is no reason to fear."

"It's like Imaginarium," Tolan said, glancing over at Ferrah.

She wore a troubled expression but didn't say anything.

"Who will try first?" Master Sartan asked. His gaze darted around the line of students before falling on Draln. "As you seem to think a suppression style would be most effective, why don't we have you attempt this?"

Draln nodded and stepped forward, already starting to shape. Power built from him and the ground rumbled, flowing upward toward the shaped appearance of isaw. As it did, sections of earth surrounded the shaping, confining it.

"Now you have confined it, what would you do next?"

"I would try my suppression."

"Go ahead."

Draln glanced up at Master Sartan, tearing his gaze off the trapped elemental. "Do I need to hold the shaping confining it?"

"You see the challenge now, don't you?"

"I don't know if I would have enough shaping strength to be able to keep it confined and still force the elemental back into the bond."

"It is possible, but it's also difficult. There's a reason many of these shapings require multiple shapers. One will attempt to confine and control the elemental while the other will try to force the elemental into the bond. What you will experience is elementals confined by one shaper of a particular ability while the shaper with the strength in the element similar to the elemental would be responsible for forcing it into the bond. In this case, someone who was particularly powerful with earth shaping would confine the elemental while the fire shaper would force the creature back into the bond."

"You still haven't explained how," Ferrah said.

Master Sartan turned toward her. "I have not. And your classmate has made a reasonable observation, or at least as reasonable as one could expect. Pushing the elemental into the bond is not an easy task. Suppression is perhaps the best way of describing it, but in reality, it is more the matter of pushing on the elemental and forcing it deeper into the bond, tying it more deeply to that connection once again. If you can do that, you can overcome the natural inclination of the elemental."

"What's the shaping like?" Tolan asked.

"In order to demonstrate it, I would need someone to be able to hold onto a shaping similar to this."

"Ethar can do it."

Tolan shot a glare toward Draln, hating he had volunteered Tolan for something like this but more concerned about the possibility of what would happen if he attempted to shape isaw. He didn't know how to create a shaping the same way Master Sartan had. If he were to attempt it, more likely than not, he would actually shape isaw into existence.

"Typically, when we demonstrate the first shaping, we have a master shaper doing both," Master Sartan said. "The suppression shaping is complicated, but it is similar for each element bond, so if you managed to master one, it appears likely you will be able to handle the others."

Tolan breathed out a sigh of relief. It sounded as if Master Sartan wasn't going to have him try to do a shaping like that.

"Do you think you can shape this?" Master Sartan asked.

All eyes turned to Tolan, and his entire body tensed. Warmth crept from his stomach, working up from deep within him before settling in his neck and face. Sweat beaded on his forehead.

"I don't know I have the necessary control," he said.

"Look. It sounds as if Ethar is afraid," Draln said, his voice carrying. Other students chuckled, and Master Sartan did nothing to settle the other students down.

"You need to do it," Jonas whispered.

"I don't need to do anything," Tolan said. And he didn't want to do anything, either.

"I know Draln," Jonas whispered. "He's going to keep on you. If you don't do this, he won't let it drop."

Tolan sighed. He knew Draln well enough too. And Jonas was right. It was likely—and probable—he would keep harassing Tolan. If he didn't do anything, he would never live it down.

What was the harm in attempting to shape the elemental, anyway? He could suppress it if it were necessary, and even if he couldn't, Master Sartan was going to be demonstrating the necessary shaping so he would be the one forcing the elemental back into the bond.

Only... There was a part of Tolan that wondered if that harmed the elemental.

He had to stop thinking like that. He had to stop believing the elementals were something to protect. There was a reason the shapers of old had suppressed them. Those shapers had known something about the elementals, and they had made a decision to confine them to the bond. If they hadn't, something worse might've happened, and Tolan couldn't allow himself to believe he knew better than shapers who had preceded him, shapers who most certainly knew far more about shaping and the elements and the element bonds than he had begun to learn.

He took the bondar from Master Sartan and glanced down at it. He rolled it in his hand, looking for signs of isaw on it. If there was no symbol for isaw, it would be an easy thing to prove he couldn't shape. He didn't have to worry about failing, as he would be unable to do anything but fail.

As he looked at the bondar, he noticed there was a symbol for isaw.

The symbol for isaw looked much like the actual elemental, a tight spiral, though it had lines coming off the end. Those lines reminded Tolan of the wind and the markings for that. He would have to be careful, but could he give a warning to the elemental? Maybe he could send some sort of signal to disappear the moment the shaping began to build.

Master Sartan studied him a moment. "There is no shame if you struggle with this shaping."

"I will do my best to hold onto it."

"We need you to hold it long enough for the others to have a chance to observe the necessary counter. The suppression is not necessarily an easy thing to accomplish, and I need for you to hang on as long as you can."

Which meant if he did summon an elemental, he needed to hold on to that connection for a long time.

He started to focus, thinking of the shape of isaw, but also about aspects of it. Isaw was of wind and fire, though mostly of fire. It was heat and flame and spirals. Isaw was the power of the fire funnel.

"Look. Ethar can't do it. Not surprising, especially as—"

The elemental began to appear. As it did, Tolan focused on it.

This is for demonstration only. We're not trying to harm you.

He wasn't sure if the warning would make a difference or not, but he began to feel a slight reverberation, an echoing, and he continued to push that warning through the summons.

As he held onto the shape of the elemental, Tolan continued to send a warning. He needed the elemental to know it should disappear the moment it needed to, but he also needed for the elemental to hold on for as long as it could. It was a difficult contrast, and it was one Tolan wasn't sure he was able to maintain very effectively.

"It looks different. Will that matter?"

Master Sartan positioned himself in front of the elemental and focused on it. Unlike the shaping he had used, the one Tolan created had more of a wispiness to it, with hints of wind causing the shape of isaw to spiral slowly.

"I doubt it matters, though I am uncertain why Shaper Ethar decided he needed to modify the shaping."

"I'm sorry. It's just this is what I was able to make."

"This has wind as a part of it," Master Sartan said.

He wasn't surprised Master Sartan recognized the wind in a part of his shaping, but he did wish he wasn't revealing so much about the elemental.

He continued to send a plea across the connection, hoping the elemental would know what he needed of it.

Master Sartan's shaping built.

As it did, isaw began to writhe beneath the power of the shaping. It twisted, forced back, and Tolan continued to hold on to the summons, trying to fight off what Master Sartan did. The elemental struggled, and it seemed to Tolan there was some agitation within it.

You can return. I will summon you again.

The elemental surged, almost creating a sense of connection within his mind, and then it began to fade. Tolan didn't fight, letting the connection to the elemental disappear, and finally, it was gone.

He sagged, taking a step back, and nearly dropped the bondar.

Master Sartan stared at the space where the elemental had been. "That was interesting."

"I didn't recognize everything about the shaping," Draln said.

"No. You will need to see the suppression shaping more often in order to fully master it. I think Shaper Ethar is a good candidate for helping us learn." He cocked his head, turning to Tolan and studying him. "If he can maintain a shaping like that a little longer, perhaps we will be able to all learn together."

Tolan licked his lips, staring at the space where the elemental had been. Now it was gone, he felt a strange sort of emptiness, but it was more than that. There was a sense of pain from what had happened to the elemental.

More than ever, he was convinced the shaping used to force the elementals back into the bond harmed them. Worse, he realized he wanted nothing to do with forcing the elementals back into the bond. He didn't want to be the one who harmed them.

As he stepped back into the line of his classmates, not only did Master Sartan watch him, but other classmates did as well. Among them was Ferrah, and she looked at him with an expression mixed with concern and fear.

10

THE LIBRARY WAS QUIET, THOUGH TOLAN HAD WAITED until late in the day to return, passing a pair of Inquisitors along the way. He thought he'd detected a shaping from them but wasn't certain. He had wandered throughout the Academy grounds, trying to stay by himself, avoiding anyone. He even avoided going to his room, not wanting to face any sort of questions. Not that he had any answers.

After leaving the fire-shaping class, several of his classmates had come up to him, asking him to demonstrate how to make an isaw shaping. That was the last thing he wanted. Even if he could demonstrate what he'd done, Tolan also doubted anyone else would have the same ability. What he did seemed to be unique to him.

What he needed was to understand what was happening with him. If he could understand why he was able to shape in the way he did, and why that shaping seemed to depend upon the elementals, maybe he could come to terms with what he was.

He didn't want to talk to anyone about what sort of shaping he had managed to do, and had no interest in sharing any secrets, but he doubted he would be able to avoid questions for long. Too many people had seen the shaping, and all were interested in what he had done and wanted to see if they could do something similar.

When he took a seat at the table in the library, he rested his head on his hands, staring down. He had the books on the elementals and he pulled them out, flipping through the pages of the book describing the fire elementals until he came across the section on isaw. He reread it, though he didn't really need to. He had looked through the book many times over the months since Master Minden had lent it to him and had done so often enough that he had practically memorized everything within it. There was nothing here that would be a surprise to him.

"Back to the elementals, I see."

Tolan glanced up at Master Minden. She had moved quietly enough that he hadn't even been aware she was there. "We had our first lesson on suppressing the elementals."

"And what class was that in?"

Tolan nodded to the book. "Fire."

Master Minden glanced over his shoulder, staring down for a moment. "Isaw? An interesting choice. Few realize there is an aspect of wind within isaw, though for the type of lesson they would teach, it's unlikely to be necessary to know."

"I don't think Master Sartan recognized wind was supposed to be a part of it."

"Is that right?"

Tolan glanced down. "His was a little thicker than what isaw should be. There wasn't the same rotation, either."

What was he doing sharing that with Master Minden? He didn't need her to question him, and he certainly didn't need her to know how interacted with the elementals—if that was indeed what he did. Of all of the master shapers at the Academy, for some reason, Master Minden made him the most uncomfortable. It was a combination of her knowledge and that she had a strange power others didn't seem to have, including the Grand Master and the Grand Inquisitor.

"Even among the master shapers, few take the time to try and understand the elementals well enough to know the necessary way to shape them."

"Why not?"

"Most feel as if they understand the elementals well enough. Perhaps even more is that once they learn the way of suppressing the elementals, they have no need. The shaping is the same, regardless of which elemental. The only thing that changes is which element bond you are forcing the elemental into."

"He had me hold the shaping, so I didn't get to see the shaping he used."

"A master shaper had a second-year student holding the elemental shaping?"

"I was using a bondar," he said.

She nodded. "Of course."

"Even Master Sartan was using the bondar."

"That is not surprising. To summon an elemental is incredibly difficult. Even if the elemental is not real, it is difficult for most to create anything resembling an actual one. The power involved is enormous, but even more so is the level of control required to maintain it."

What she left unsaid was that allowing a student to demonstrate it was equally surprising, for exactly that same reason. If it was an enormous expenditure of energy, it would require a significant exertion on his part, and yet... Tolan had managed without really struggling.

"I have the sense he intends for us to continue working on learning to suppress elementals."

"It is one of the more critical tasks expected of Academy shapers," she said.

"Why?"

"You in particular should understand why it would be necessary for Academy shapers to be a part of the suppression," she said.

"Me in particular?"

"You have experienced an elemental attack both in the Academy and in your homeland. Very few people have the same experience. That gives you a unique perspective. I would expect you would have wanted nothing more than to suppress the elementals."

Tolan turned his attention back down to the book, staring at the page. "Do you think it harms them?" He didn't look up as he asked the question, not wanting Master Minden to give him a disapproving look. With everything taking place at the Academy these days, it was a dangerous question to even ask.

Master Minden chuckled softly. "That's interesting. I don't know that anyone who has researched the elementals has ever questioned whether they suffer during the process of replacing them within the bond."

Tolan looked up. "If they are living creatures, don't they deserve the same respect we would give to any living creature?"

"Well, Shaper Ethar, they are living creatures, but they aren't the same sort of creature as what you know. They are of a deep and powerful energy, a part of the world, but not in a way horses or wolves or the squirrels or birds would be. Many of the elementals are rumored to have indefinite life, and a creature like that would need to have some controls set upon it."

"It doesn't mean they don't—and can't—suffer."

"You make a good point, but I doubt you will find many of the master shapers agreeing with any decision to treat the elementals with compassion. All master shapers want is to return an elemental to the bond if they manage to escape. None want to spend much time trying to understand how to do so compassionately."

"And from what I've seen, no one wants to understand why the elemental tries to escape the bond."

"Do you think we should?"

"I don't know."

"I suppose that's as good an answer as any. That means you are willing to keep searching for your own understanding. That's all we can ask of any of our shapers." She glanced down at his book before looking up at him. "I take it you would like to hold onto these for a little while longer?"

"If you don't mind," he said.

"I suppose that I can make do without them for now. Are you interested in getting the other volumes today?"

Tolan glanced toward the dais and nodded. "I think I should. There's more I can learn from them."

"With works like those, some would say you could continue learning throughout your entire life."

She hobbled away, leaving Tolan watching her depart. He turned his attention back down to the book, flipping through pages as he stared and tried to understand elementals. There had to be something in these pages that would help him. He'd gone through these often enough over the months since he'd acquired them and still came up with nothing more than a basic understanding.

Master Minden returned, handing the books over to him. "As you know, you must return these before leaving."

"I know."

When she was gone, Tolan slid the new books out of the way and returned to looking through the book on the elementals. He was flipping pages, reading one after another, when Ferrah took a seat across from him.

"I've been looking for you," she said.

"Why?"

"Maybe because you've been hiding from everyone since classroom today."

"I thought it was for the best."

"Because you helped with the lesson, or because you were afraid during your shaping?"

Tolan sighed. Ferrah knew him far too well, and he couldn't hide from her the fact he'd been uncomfortable. "You know how I shape," he whispered.

"I understand how you *think* you shape, but all that tells me is that you're more talented than what you let on. Look at what you were able to do today with Master Sartan."

"What I was able to do today was nearly releasing an elemental."

"I doubt that's what you were doing."

"You might, but I don't. The shaping I did was basically a release. I don't know how else to explain it, and certainly don't know whether anything would've happened had I lost control, especially as Master Sartan was there and holding onto his shaping, but that's why my shaping, my connection to the elemental, was different than his demonstration."

Ferrah studied him for a moment before leaning back and pulling the stack of three books over to her. "I was wondering about that, but I figured it was only because you have a little different understanding of the elementals than most. Who else but you spent so much time reading through books like these to try and understand them?"

"You?"

She waved her hand. "I don't spend any time doing that. I might spend some of my time in the library researching, but I haven't devoted nearly as much time to the elementals as you."

He smiled to himself. "No. You research other things."

"So?"

"I'm not saying it's bad, I'm just saying you have other things you research."

"There are plenty of people who come through here who have other research interests," Ferrah said.

"I know that. I also know the things you spend your time researching have more to do with your homeland." He thought about what she had told him of Par and remembered her describing depictions on some of the ruins of draasin flying. "Is that why you have been so disappointed with your ability with fire shaping?"

She clenched her jaw and sighed. "I should be able to shape fire better than I can. It irritates me that others have continued to improve with their shaping, but I have been stagnant."

"It's because you refuse to use a bondar."

"I shouldn't need a bondar. I have enough of a fire shaping ability, I shouldn't have to use anything like that. If I can master my shaping without using a crutch, I'll be even more talented."

"It's not a crutch to use something that allows you to reach for shaping you wouldn't have otherwise."

"You're starting to sound like some of the master instructors."

"Which master instructors?"

"Master Sartan has been trying to convince me I need to use a bondar so I can understand a shaping. Once I understand the shaping, he's convinced I won't need the bondar any longer."

"And you think you know better than Master Sartan?" he asked, smiling.

"It's not that."

She leaned back, pulling on the books Tolan had set aside and leaning back. She held on to them and started to flip through the three restricted volumes, looking through the pages, and after a moment, she started flipping more slowly, taking her time to read through them. She glanced up at Tolan before turning her attention back to the book. A frown crossed her face and her mouth pressed into a tight line.

"These are restricted."

"How do you know?"

"Just the type of information that's in them. How do you have restricted text?"

"I asked for information about the Selection, and they gave me these. It's better than asking about the traitor who may or may not be at the Academy."

"The Inquisitors will find out if there is someone here,"

she said, continuing to flip through the pages of one book before going on to the next.

He didn't know how much of it she was reading and how much was more a matter of her just flipping pages and trying to get a sense of what was within the book. When she moved on to the third one, she was shaking her head. "Why these? What's in here they thought would be valuable?"

"Well, this one is apparently from the first Grand Master of the Academy," he said, tapping at one book. "And this one is from the first Grand Inquisitor."

"What of the third one?"

"That one apparently is from another founder of the Academy, and also happens to be related to Master Minden."

"Really?" She started flipping through that book, suddenly more intrigued than she had been before. "Why did Master Minden suggest you read this one?"

"Master Minden didn't. Master Jensen was the one who gave me these books."

"Master Jensen got books for you from the restricted section?" She looked up at him, her mouth twisted in a frown. "I would've expected that from Master Minden. She seems to have taken an interest in helping you that's different than many of the other master shapers, but not from Master Jensen. He hasn't even given me some of the books I wanted."

"I think it has more to do with the fact they brought

students out on the Selection, so Master Jensen figured we were allowed to have access to some of those books."

She grunted. "That's an interesting approach. I guess I wouldn't have thought to even ask."

"It's not as if I asked for restricted books. I just asked for anything that might help me understand the Selection process. These are what he gave me."

"Why am I not surprised he gave you books like this?"

"What is that supposed to mean?"

"It's just you tend to have a way with the master librarians."

"Not all of them," Tolan said.

"Enough. I think it stems from Master Minden, but the others react differently to you. You'd better be careful or they might pull you in to become a master librarian."

"I thought that was what *you* wanted."

"It is."

Tolan closed the elemental book and stuffed it back into his pouch. He was thankful Master Minden hadn't asked for it back. There would come a time when he would learn everything he could from the books, but he didn't feel as if he had reached that point yet.

"Have you ever asked for the book on spirit?" Ferrah asked, jolting him from his solitude.

"The book on spirit?"

"You have one on each of the other elementals. I just figure there has to be some book on spirit."

"They told us spirit is different."

"That's what they told us, but they've also told us they know more about the elementals than they do. You've proven many of the master shapers don't know quite as much about the elementals as they would like us to believe. I just wondered if perhaps you'd found anything on spirit."

He shook his head. "I could always ask, but I have a sneaking suspicion spirit is something they keep restricted."

"Restricted like these?" Ferrah asked.

"I guess so."

"Then you should ask."

He frowned at her. "You only want me to ask because you're curious."

"I'm not going to deny that. If there's a book on spirit elementals, think about how much we might learn."

"I doubt it will help us reach spirit any faster, if we're ever able to do so."

"I think we both know you'll eventually reach spirit, Tolan. Whether or not I do is a very different matter. It might involve me combining a shaping of each of the element bonds, but since you've been immune to spirit shaping, I suspect you'll reach spirit on your own. Wouldn't you rather know all you can? It's not like you want to learn everything from Master Aela."

He shrugged. "I don't know."

"You might not, but I trust you will. Do you mind if I read these?" she asked.

He shook his head. "They've made a point of telling me

every time I've been here that they aren't allowed to leave the library."

"Because they're restricted."

"Because they're restricted," he said, smiling. He got up and made his way toward the dais.

Master Minden was sitting there, and she looked up when he approached. "Is there something else I can help you with, Shaper Ethar?"

"I've been thinking about the elementals."

"Haven't you spent quite a bit of time thinking about them already?"

A warm flush worked into his cheeks. What did she think of his interest in the elementals? Would she accuse him of asking the wrong sort of questions? His curiosity was certainly enough that it could get him into trouble, but he *had* helped the Academy in his time here.

"Well, I guess I've been thinking more about them, but I was wondering if there are similar books on spirit elementals."

"We've had this conversation before," she said.

"There has to be something." Tolan looked around the inside of the library, marveling at the sheer number of books spread throughout. "With as much knowledge as is here, and as many years as people have studied these things, it seems as if there would have to be something." A thought occurred to him, and he wondered why he hadn't considered it before. "All of the elementals have escaped the bond before, but I've never heard of a spirit elemental escaping from the bond."

"Are you so certain?"

"Are you saying spirit elementals have escaped but they've shaped it so we don't remember?"

"I'm not saying anything of the sort. It seems as if you are."

Tolan studied her, trying to decide if she was making a joke or not, and ultimately decided he couldn't tell. "Are there spirit elementals who can escape from the bond?"

Master Minden set her hands on the dais and straightened her back. "The element bonds aren't meant to confine indefinitely. They are meant for shapers to reach the power stored within, but nothing more than that. It is not possible for the elementals to remain trapped within the bonds forever."

That wasn't an answer, but maybe it was all she would give him. "Do you have anything that would help me understand the spirit elementals?"

"I have something that might help you understand spirit, but typically we reserve that for those who first understand their connection to spirit. Are you making the claim you have a connection to spirit?"

Tolan debated how to answer. On the one hand, if he told her he thought he had a connection to spirit, it sounded as if she might allow him to take the book and continue to learn, but on the other hand, he wasn't sure how many people he wanted to know he might have that connection. At least, until he understood whether or not he did, and if he did, what that meant for him.

"I might, but I don't know for sure," he said.

"Indecisive. I suppose that is as much as one could be when it comes to spirit. Not everyone is aware of their connection, and it's possible you do. Most of the time, people come to us looking for understanding about a connection they've discovered."

"Do most people uncover their spirit connection in the spirit classroom?" Master Aela was fine, but he didn't really think he'd learn what he needed from her. She was too vague about her approach.

"Surprisingly, no. Most who come to understand they have a connection to spirit find spirit classes aren't designed to take them to reach it. The spirit classes are more designed to help you understand the use and nature of spirit, but for most people, that is the end of it. Most aren't able to use spirit any other way."

She climbed down from the dais, making her way over to the stack of shelves. Tolan thought she was going to head toward the same stack where she had initially grabbed the books on the elementals, but she surprised him by taking the stairs, winding her way up to the second story.

Once again, the restricted stacks.

He waited, looking around the library, noting that other than he and Ferrah, no one else had come into the library. The only other librarian here was Master Shore. He was an older shaper and had a serious expression practically burned on his face. He made his way around the library, constantly re-shelving books, never taking a place upon the dais and sitting next to Master Minden.

When Master Shore had been in the library before, Tolan had seen him doing the same thing. Maybe he viewed his responsibility to ensure the books were appropriately shelved, or maybe it was his assignment.

Eventually, Master Minden made her way down the stairs, and she did so carrying a small book. It was about the size of his hand, and not very thick. It was more a pamphlet than a true book, and quite a bit less significant than any of the books on the elementals he had borrowed. She made her way toward him, and she and Master Shore shared a strange glance. When she reached Tolan, she held the book in both hands, squeezing it, almost as if afraid to hand it over to him.

"This is another incredibly rare book, Shaper Ethar. Much like the other three, this one is not allowed to leave the library."

"Because it's restricted?"

"Because the shapings upon the library keep it intact. If you were to remove this, the book itself would disintegrate. It is much older than the other three, and among the oldest we have. I would ask that you sit up here when you look at it so I can ensure its safety."

Tolan tensed, feeling as if he were being granted some great gift, but not sure he was truly worthy. He had told her he might be a spirit shaper. Would reading through this book somehow change him in any way? Would it have information he was not meant to have unless he really was a spirit shaper?

He held onto the book and followed Master Minden

up to the dais. Once there, she motioned for him to pull out a stool he hadn't seen before, and he took a seat next to her. The view from up here was different—unique. Situated only five steps above the rest of the library, he felt as if he were still quite a bit higher than he really was.

Ferrah glanced over in his direction, her eyes widening slightly, and then turned her attention back to the three books.

Tolan flipped open the book and started reading, looking for anything that might remind him of the elemental books he'd already borrowed. While this one referred to spirit, it also referenced the heart and the mind, and seemed quite a bit different than the other books on the elementals.

Unfortunately, Tolan didn't feel as if this would give him any real insight about spirit, but he persisted, flipping through the pages slowly.

As he did, he made note of the writing. At first, he hadn't realized there was something unusual about it, but the more he looked at the pages, the more he realized it wasn't written in the common tongue.

Despite that, Tolan was somehow able to understand what he was reading.

How was that even possible?

He glanced over at Master Minden, but she remained preoccupied with the book she worked on, ignoring his questioning glance.

Was anything to the writing that would help him understand what he was seeing?

It wasn't in the lettering, and it wasn't even in any depiction of spirit elementals as there was for the other elementals. The pages, too, were considerably thicker than what he'd found in some of the other books.

He flipped it closed, looking at the depictions on the surface, but found nothing there that would help him. The cover was silvery and smooth. He ran his fingers along it. It felt metallic, but not the same way some of the other covers had felt. The cover for the earth elemental had seemed to be both metallic and made of stone, a strange combination.

This one was quite a bit different than those. Opening the book again, he started through it once more. As he had before, he was able to read the book while at the same time recognizing he should not be able to.

"I don't understand," he said.

Master Minden was watching him, and there was a strange light in her eyes.

"What is it you don't understand, Shaper Ethar?"

"What is it about this book? Why did you give me this to read?"

"I gave you this because you wanted to know something about spirit."

Tolan looked down at the book, staring at the page. "What if I can't read it?"

"Can you?"

There was something more in the question, and Tolan knew his answer would determine what more she would do for him. Was he willing to admit he could read the words written on this page?

He stared at the first page, the language filling his head, almost as if he had seen it before. "I don't understand."

"This is written in one of the most ancient of languages, Shaper Ethar. Very few without appropriate training are able to understand what's written on the pages."

"Do you?"

"I have studied for my entire life to be able to read this language. And even then, I wouldn't be able to understand it were it not for a special gift that had been given to me."

"What gift was that?"

"The gift of a shaping."

"A shaping?"

She nodded. "In order to understand the writing within this book, one must have knowledge of it shaped into them. And I wonder, now I see you staring at the pages, how is it you seem to understand this language?"

TOLAN LAY IN BED, UNABLE TO SLEEP, STARING UP AT THE ceiling. The others in the room with him were all sleeping soundly, having drifted off long ago. He knew he should fall asleep, but he just couldn't. As much as he wanted to, he just couldn't shut down his mind enough to get enough rest. It was as if everything was changing.

Tolan was left with questions, but there were no answers. Every time he went looking for answers, he came across new questions.

Master Minden hadn't known why he was able to read through the ancient book on spirit shaping. Tolan hadn't had any answers, either. At first, he'd thought she was playing a game with him, but the way she'd stared at him, the intensity in her milky gaze, left him fully aware it was serious. That he had no idea why he would be able to read the words in the book mattered to her, though he didn't have any explanation either.

It was why he lay restless, struggling for sleep, straining to understand whether there were any answers. Who had shaped that knowledge into his mind?

As far as he knew, he couldn't be spirit-shaped. The Grand Inquisitor had tried, and she had failed—at least, he had *thought* she had failed.

What if she hadn't? What if rather than trying to wipe his mind, she had given him knowledge? But what purpose would there be in giving knowledge like that?

If Master Minden knew the answer, she hadn't said anything to him.

And he didn't have any answers, either. So he stared at the ceiling, trying to come to terms with what he had learned, but he struggled with the attempt.

He got out of bed. If he wasn't able to sleep, there was no point in lying there. He could remain all night, restless, his mind churning through what he had experienced, and still be no closer to any answers. And perhaps that was the way it was going to be.

What he needed was to return to the library and see if there were any other similar books he could read. Master Minden would have to allow him an opportunity to try to read them. If she did, maybe he could uncover more about himself. At the same time, he had no interest in returning to the library this late, not without knowing which of the master librarians he'd find there. If it wasn't Master Minden, there would just be more questions, and likely the kind of questions he had no interest in—and perhaps no ability to—answer at this time.

Instead, he headed down to the kitchen.

The smells of the kitchen—of breads and meats and pastries—all lingered, though it was late enough that none of the cooks was still here. Students weren't forbidden from heading to the kitchen at any time, so he wandered through and reached the cabinet near the back where leftover pastries would be found. It would fill his stomach, probably not much more than that, but it would be enough to satiate him, and maybe it would be enough to finally be able to sleep.

Fumbling for a way to see through the darkness, Tolan grabbed for the furios and shaped a hint of flame through it, adding a connection to saa without thinking much of it. The flame burst into view, floating in front of him, giving enough light for him to see everything within the closet. Shelves were filled with jars, and row upon row of sacks filled with grain and flour and sugar lined the floor. It was incredibly neat and tightly organized, and the sense of a shaping to preserve all of this lingered overtop everything.

He found a loaf of bread and pulled off the end of it, grabbing a hunk of cured meat to go with it. Unfortunately, there were no pastries, but he would make do with this. When he went back out into the main part of the kitchen, he took a seat at the counter, holding on to the shaping of flame. He'd long since released his hold on the furios but maintaining a connection to saa wasn't all that difficult regardless.

As he was eating, the door to the kitchen opened and Tolan tried to release his connection to the shaping, but the elemental hovered for a moment before flashing out, practically waiting for him to beg to it to disappear.

"Shaper Ethar," a voice called out.

Tolan sat up stiffly, looking over toward Master Irina. "Master Irina. I was just getting something to eat. I was having a difficult time sleeping."

"And why would that be?"

"Just my studies."

She approached him slowly, and in the darkness, it was difficult to tell how she studied him. As she neared, it seemed she looked at him with an unreadable expression. "What is it that troubled you about your studies?"

"The same as troubles most students, I suppose," Tolan said.

"Most students struggle with mastering complex shapings, though from what I hear from Master Sartan, you have demonstrated an incredibly complex fire shaping. He was interested in how you knew how to do it, but I think also impressed, though he would never share that with a student."

"I was just recalling a shaping I knew," he said.

"Intriguing. And what shaping is it that you knew allowed you to perform such a complex shaping?"

"I'd seen it before," he said, his mind racing as he hurriedly tried to come up with anything that would explain why he would know about that shaping. "I think it was from one of the upper-level students when I was first here, and—"

"I see. Would this be the same upper-level students who thought it appropriate to create elementals with their shapings?"

Tolan froze. That would be as good an answer as any, and at least offered an explanation as to why he would have known how to do that, but would Master Irina believe it?"

"I can see you don't want to betray them, though I suspect many of those students have already moved on."

"Many have," he said.

"But not all. I see." She studied him for a moment. "You will find the masters are most impressed by complicated shapings out of students they don't expect it from."

"Such as me?" he said.

"You would be such a case. As you know, you did come to the Academy without much natural shaping ability. The fact you have progressed as far as you have is quite impressive. Many are surprised you graduated to the second level."

"What about you?"

"Ah, but I'm not necessarily the right person to ask. I saw you knew something unique. Though I recognized you had no idea what you were doing, I didn't have any problem with you presenting yourself for Selection."

What did she mean, she saw he knew something unique? That was an odd comment, and yet, it was surprisingly fitting. He *did* have something unique about him, though Tolan wasn't entirely certain what it was. Perhaps Master Irina wasn't entirely certain, either.

"Do you often come here late at night?"

"Not usually," Tolan said. "Most of the time, I'm able to sleep."

"And yet you don't think it's unusual that tonight of all nights you're unable to sleep?"

"I've come here before in the middle the night," Tolan said. Having the Grand Inquisitor with him gave him an opportunity to ask questions. Maybe he could find something. "All the talk of the traitor at the Academy and the Inquisitors…"

She regarded him. "It can be difficult to believe, but the Inquisitors are here for your protection."

"I understand."

"I'm not sure you do. Thre has been enough activity from the Draasin Lord lately. We recognize the danger of what he intends, though we might not know his plan. Finding this traitor will allow us to uncover those plans."

"Will the Inquisitors question the students?"

"Do you think they should?"

Tolan tensed, his food forgotten. "I want to keep the Academy safe from the Draasin Lord too. This is my home now. I guess that's why I wasn't able to sleep and came down here."

She smiled tightly. "Not all students take advantage of the kitchens. It's rare for anyone to come this late at night, though I find it also soothing."

"Were you unable to sleep, as well?"

She shook her head. "I never struggle sleeping. It's a simple matter to place a shaping upon yourself to allow yourself to sleep, but in this case, I find it helpful to process what I've been thinking about. Movement often allows me to think more clearly. With what we are dealing with, I must have a clear mind."

"Movement?"

"Getting out of my rooms. With the activity in the Academy, the daytime isn't often the most productive for me. It's not until evening that I'm able to finally slow down and be able to get my bearings."

"I thought the Academy was quieter now the Council has moved back out."

"Quieter, but still not quiet. And I have become accustomed to staying up. With the new students taking up residence within the Academy, there has been a need for some attention to them."

There was an odd statement for her to make, and Tolan couldn't help but wonder what sort of attention she thought the new students needed. What could the Grand Inquisitor offer that master shapers did not?

"Don't mind me, then," Tolan said.

"Oh, Shaper Ethar, it would be my pleasure to sit and have a quiet bite with you."

She wandered to the same closet he had gone to and was gone for a few moments before returning. In the time she was gone, Tolan debated running off and returning to his room, but doing that would only raise questions, and he wanted to avoid her focus as much as he could. Maybe it was best to just remain and deal with whatever conversation she intended to have with him.

When she returned, she was carrying a plate laden with cheese. She set it down between them. She nodded to the hunk of meat, and he handed it over. Master Irina pulled a knife from a pocket and began slicing off chunks of meat. Tolan realized he had just been sitting there, not eating, and not doing anything other than waiting for her return.

"Are you going to eat?" she asked.

"I'm sorry, I was just lost in thought. Maybe I'm more tired than I realize."

"Maybe you are. I'm sure you have a busy day ahead of you tomorrow, but I would appreciate the opportunity to converse with you for a little while."

Tolan could only nod. What choice did he have? "What do you want to converse about?"

"How was your experience in Ephra?"

That wasn't the question he had expected of her, and he shrugged. "I suppose about as well as I expected."

"I understand you weren't eager to return to your homeland. Most of the students who were offered an opportunity to return did so willingly, and one might say almost excitedly. You, on the other hand, were one who was not necessarily eager to return."

"I don't have much family there."

"Not family, but you did have a friend. Are you disappointed he was not Selected?"

Tolan had spent some time thinking about it, and realized he wasn't upset Tanner hadn't been Selected. He should have been more disappointed, losing out on the opportunity to have his friend at the Academy with him, but surprisingly had not been. The part that troubled him the most was the idea Tanner wouldn't have remembered he had visited. With the spirit shaping, Tanner wouldn't remember anything about Tolan's visit and only would know a disappointment in having Velthan suddenly disappear.

He pushed away those thoughts. They did him no good. As he had Master Irina here in front of him, it was an opportune time to see what he might be able to find out about her and the connection to an increased number of students being Selected.

"There are rumors going around the Academy," Tolan said, taking a careful bite of food.

"There are always rumors going around the Academy."

"These are different."

She arched her brow at him. "How is that?"

"These involve you."

He waited, worried she might react poorly, but she didn't. She only watched him, her gaze lingering on his face for a moment before taking a bite of cheese. "There are always rumors going around the Academy about me, too."

"Why were so many students Selected during this time?"

"Would you rather have fewer students at the Academy, or more?"

"I guess I want there to be the right number of students at the Academy. Ideally, everyone who is Selected has the right ability."

"And who determines who has the right ability?"

Tolan shrugged. "Presumably spirit shapers, but—"

Master Irina shook her head. "That is something many people get wrong. Most believe the Inquisitors responsible for making the Selection, but it is not on us to make it. We confirm it, but we aren't the ones choosing who joins the Academy."

Tolan frowned. "If not the Inquisitors and the Selectors, who is it?"

"What was your experience when you came for your Selection?"

"Mine was different."

"How so?"

"Because I went to support a friend. I probably shouldn't have, but I guess that was the price for my going."

"You still believe you don't belong?"

"I guess I know I should be here now."

"You guess. And yet, everything you have done and seen since coming here has proven how you belong at the Academy."

Tolan nodded, taking another hunk of bread and chewing it slowly. "What does that have to do with the Selection?"

"Because who chose you?"

Tolan frowned. "You did."

"I did nothing. I performed the shaping necessary for the Selection, but I didn't choose you. In some respects, you wouldn't have been one I would have chosen." She smiled and shook her head. "That's no slight, Shaper Ethar. It is simply a matter of tradition. We have typically Selected those who have demonstrated shaping ability. It makes the time spent at the Academy more fruitful, but as you have shown, that is not necessary. You have given us as Selectors something to think on, and because of that, the process has changed somewhat."

"It changed because of me?"

"It changed because we realized we were flawed in assuming only those with shaping ability could be Selected."

Tolan chewed thoughtfully, thinking of everyone who had been Selected in Ephra. As far as he knew, everyone there had the ability to shape, unlike him. "Were any Selected who weren't able to shape?"

"Not this time."

"This time. Which means you think it's possible in the future someone might be Selected who isn't able to shape."

"That remains the possibility, Shaper Ethar. And it gets back to my original point."

"And what point is that?"

"The point of who is responsible for your Selection."

"You're saying you weren't, which means you believe I am responsible."

"You are the one who presented yourself for Selection. Because of that, who else can you credit with it?"

"But that doesn't change anything."

"Doesn't it? I think it changes everything."

"Why?"

"If you're looking for someone to either blame or give credit for your Selection, you need to look inward. And you need to continue to take ownership of your place here." She got up, gathering the plate of cheese, and started away.

Tolan leapt to his feet. "Master Irina?"

She paused, turning back to him.

"Is there anything with Master Daniels I should have been aware about?"

"Master Daniels was not a faithful servant of the Academy," she said.

"I know he wasn't, it's just…" What did he want to admit to her? "I feel betrayed."

"Many of us feel betrayed."

"He seemed to have some ability with spirit."

"We've spoken of this already. He was not a spirit shaper."

"Could he have used a bondar?"

She frowned, turning toward him. "The bondars allow an easier connection to the element bonds. There are bondars that allow access to each of them. Spirit is no different."

That was the first he'd heard of that. "Are there spirit bondars at the Academy?"

She studied him for a moment before her mouth

pressed into a tight line. "Get some rest, Shaper Ethar. If you don't, the next day will be difficult for you."

Tolan almost shivered as she walked away, worried she knew something.

12

THE INSIDE OF THE SPIRIT-SHAPING CLASSROOM WAS ALMOST uncomfortable. After having spent the night having difficulty sleeping, then sitting alongside the Grand Inquisitor, Tolan wasn't sure he wanted to have a day in his spirit class, but seeing as how they had these infrequently, he needed to attend as many as he could.

There were fewer students here than he expected. Could some have decided they weren't going to reach spirit and simply abandoned class?

The classroom setting was oftentimes difficult to sit through. When it came to spirit, Master Aela was particular about how she used it, ensuring the students sat organized across the floor in a specific pattern. A thick rug spread across the floor, which she claimed was designed to help them feel as if they could reach something more.

"Today I would like all of you to focus your minds. We are going to work on opening yourself up to each of the elements. As all of you have reached the second level, all of you have potential for spirit within you."

"We can all be Inquisitors?"

The question came from the front of the room, and there was a nervous sort of chuckling after it.

"Not all will become Inquisitors. The Inquisitors are those who have a natural spirit shaping ability, not the way we are going to practice today. I know their presence around the Academy can be somewhat intimidating, but the Inquisitors are here for all of our protection."

Tolan glanced at Ferrah. She sat in front of him and over a few rows, and seemed to recognize he was looking in her direction. When she glanced back at him, she shook her head slightly.

She didn't want him to do or say anything, though he didn't know if there was anything to do or say.

"What we're going to work on today is your way of opening yourself up to each of the elements. Now, I don't have a bondar for each of the elements the way some of you might need"—her gaze paused on Tolan for a moment before drifting around the rest of the room—"but as each of you has the potential to shape each of the elements, you are all capable of at least reaching for their power. It doesn't have to be shaped in order for you to open yourself up to spirit."

"It's not going to work," Jonas grumbled next to him.

"How do you know? If we can reach spirit, think of how useful that might be for us."

Jonas looked over, shaking his head. Tolan and Ferrah

hadn't gotten him involved in much of anything, not wanting to dig into the rumors of the possible traitor at the Academy. The presence of the Inquisitors all around had limited their desire to do so. For the most part, Tolan —and everyone else at the Academy—went about their studies but did so in a way that would hopefully keep them from drawing too much attention.

He had a pair of bondars with him, both the earth and fire, and with them, he wondered if he might be able to reach for aspects of the spirit shaping Master Aela was trying to teach more effectively. He couldn't help but feel as if there was some way he needed to reach spirit, and if only he could, he might be able to know more about the Selection, and he might be able to better prepare himself if he were ever spirit-shaped again.

Considering everything that had occurred throughout the Academy, and all of the times he'd been challenged, Tolan thought having some way of protecting his mind from spirit would be beneficial. Wasn't that what each of the master shapers were teaching these days? They all wanted to demonstrate there was something more, and in doing so, they were trying to help everyone else reach for a way of protecting themselves.

He didn't know that spirit would help protect them from the elementals, but when it came to the elementals, Tolan no longer knew if he even needed to be protected from them.

He tried to push that thought out of mind. It was dangerous.

"What I would have you do is focus your thoughts internally. When you do, think about what you know of each of the bonds. As each of you have been here for nearly a year, your knowledge of the bonds is far greater than it had been before you arrived. What I would ask you to do is think about your connection to each of the element bonds. Use that, connect to it, and let that knowledge flow through you. As you do, you need to press that power together."

"That's it?" somebody near the front of the class asked. Tolan shifted, trying to see who it was, but he wasn't able to make them out. It wasn't Draln. He sat rigidly, focusing on Master Aela, likely determined to reach for spirit. If any was going to be an Inquisitor, Tolan suspected it would be Draln.

And after having seen the Inquisitors throughout the Academy, he couldn't help but feel as if Draln was the last person who should become one. Draln was the kind of man who would abuse that power.

"When you can shape independently, reaching for each of the elements, something a few of you are capable of doing without a bondar, then you can learn to bind those element bonds together. As you do, then you can reach for more power than you would otherwise, and perhaps you can reach a semblance of spirit. Those who are able to reach spirit on their own feel it is a pale reflection of true spirit, and yet it does manage to accomplish many of the same tasks."

Tolan frowned to himself. That might explain Master

Daniels. As much as he had thought the other man had been using some other technique, it was possible Master Daniels had simply been binding each of the elements together, using that type of shaping in order to reach for power he should not have had.

And knowing what Tolan did now, that his parents likely were responsible for creating bondars, he couldn't help but think Master Daniels had power added.

"Begin."

"I can't believe that's all the instruction she gives us," Jonas muttered.

"I'm not sure it would help, anyway," Tolan said. "Seeing as how I can only shape two of the element bonds, I don't know it would matter."

"You can shape two, but you can sense four," Master Aela said, approaching.

A heat washed through him. He hadn't known she was so close, and he looked down.

"You are showing incredible growth, Shaper Ethar. I would suggest you continue to work on reaching for each of the element bonds. It's possible in time, you will be able to reach for water and wind as effectively as you can earth and fire."

Tolan looked up. He hadn't realized Master Aela had been following him closely enough to know he was able to reach for those two elements the way he did.

But then, he had to believe the master shapers all spoke about the students, likely planning what was necessary for them to survive the next testing, if that was what they wanted.

He leaned back, closing his eyes. He focused on fire and earth, using those first, and the connection to both of the elements came quickly. It was much more quickly than it had been before, but then, he was touching the bondars, using them to help him reach for power.

The real challenge would be reaching wind and water. Though he could do so in the classrooms now with bondars, doing so outside of the class, finding some way to shape without needing the bondars, was still beyond him. Eventually, Tolan would need to better understand what it would take, and there was a part of him that suspected the potential was there, if only he could find it.

Fire and earth overwhelmed his ability to reach for wind and water.

He released his hold on the bondars, focusing on wind. As he did, he breathed in and out steadily, using his connection to his own breath, to that of the breathing around him, thinking if he could find some way to connect to it, he might be able to reach for power.

There came no sense of the stirring, the telltale sign suggesting he could reach for the element bond. He had grown accustomed to knowing that sense, and the more he focused on it, the more certain he was there had to be something there, if only he could find it.

What about water?

Licking his lips, testing the moisture in his mouth, he started there, thinking from that to the way his heart beat, focusing on the blood within him. Those were the lessons he wanted to take. As he did, he didn't find anything that would make a difference.

He wasn't able to reach them.

But he could reach his ability to sense both wind and water. At least that much had changed. Always before, he had struggled, knowing the elements were there, but also that he had no way of truly reaching them.

A sense of shaping built all around him. All of the second-level students were trying to mingle their shapings together, trying to combine that power, and Tolan wished he were able to do the same thing. The more he thought about it, the more he realized he could not.

"Are you able to do anything?" Jonas whispered.

"No."

"Me neither. I wonder if perhaps I would've been able to do it when I was in my testing for the second level. At least then I had one of the bondars for each of the elements."

"I don't think they cared if we reached spirit at that time," Tolan said.

"You think that'll be the next test we have to face?"

"You're already thinking about that?"

"We need to be thinking about our next test all the time, Tolan."

Jonas was right. Instead of focusing on the identity of the traitor within the Academy, and instead of worrying about what it meant that the Inquisitors were here, wandering the halls, he instead needed to be more focused on his own abilities. He had to be prepared for what he could do and what would be asked of him in the coming months and years.

If he were to stay at the Academy, he was going to need to continue to progress. That was one constant he had experienced in his time here. The more he learned, the more it felt as if there were other aspects he needed to know. It wasn't just reaching each of the elements through the bondar. Eventually, there would be another test, and the potential for another promotion.

Why wouldn't it be connecting each of the element bonds together to forge spirit?

Then again, Tolan didn't know if that made the most sense. The master shapers had the ability to reach each of the element bonds without a bondar. In his mind, that would be the next test.

At that point, they would shed even more students, leaving the upper-level ranks more barren. Those who didn't pass would be allowed to continue to work, but in time, Tolan understood those who didn't pass would eventually be released from their Academy responsibilities, allowed to head back home or wherever their assignments took them.

That wasn't the fate he wanted. The longer he was here, the more he had an opportunity to shape each of the element bonds, the more he felt he wanted to understand shaping. He wanted to master it. He had come a long way from where he'd begun, and now it was all about knowing the elements.

And, when he was honest with himself, the elementals.

It was dangerous, and if the Inquisitors were to uncover him out in the park, working with the elementals, he would likely end up within the Inquisition, which was part of the reason he had refrained from heading out to the park.

"How long do you think we need to stay and continue to practice?" Jonas asked.

"I haven't had the sense Master Aela was too eager to allow us to leave before the end of her training time."

In many of the other classes, if the shaping assignment was complete, they were allowed to leave. Spirit was different. When he was here working with spirit, and working with Master Aela, he often felt as if he needed to linger, waiting to ensure there wasn't any part of the assignment he'd missed.

But then, part of that came from Tolan's interest. He wanted to know the elements, wanted to know spirit in particular, and he thought there might be something he could learn from Master Aela that he couldn't work on anywhere else.

"I haven't, either. I just don't know if I'm opening myself up the way she wants."

"With the two of you be quiet?" Ferrah whispered.

Tolan nodded quickly and Jonas grunted.

"Of course, she probably can reach each of the elements. She's probably shaping spirit right now."

Knowing Ferrah as he did, Tolan didn't think she was.

He closed his eyes again, thinking about what Master

Aela asked. If part of the assignment was mixing the various elements together, then he needed to do so in a way that would allow him to use them.

He focused. Wind and water first. As he did, he let the knowledge of them flow to him, letting that sense roll through him, and tried to find a connection to shaping those elements, but it didn't come. That didn't mean it couldn't, only he wasn't able to do so now. Rather than trying to force a shaping that wasn't going to work for him, he focused instead on sensing each of the elements, letting awareness of them flow to him.

Would there be any way of mixing element sensing together?

It was different than what Master Aela suggested, and yet the more he thought about it, the more he wondered if that were perhaps possible.

He had recognized spirit shaping before. He had been exposed to it more than most within the classroom, and if he could at least summon some sort of spirit sensing, he had to think the next step would be understanding what would be necessary to mix together in order to shape it.

The sense of shaping continued to build all around, and as he focused on each of the elements, he became aware of something else.

At first, Tolan wasn't sure what it was or whether he was detecting anything accurately, but the more he focused, the more certain he was that it truly was spirit.

And it wasn't just the sense of spirit—it was a shaping of it.

Was there someone here who had managed to reach spirit shaping?

It would be an advanced shaping, and it would signal someone within this classroom would have the potential to be an Inquisitor. He looked around, searching to find whether anyone here had shown any sign of it. He had to think that Master Aela would have acknowledged it if that were the case, and yet as he looked around, it didn't seem as if anyone was having success.

Perhaps in time they'd be able to. Or perhaps Master Aela would allow them to use one of the Tracker bondars like the one Ferrah had borrowed. Using something like that would open them to the possibility of spirit in a very different way.

As he looked, he realized the shaping came from Master Aela herself.

It washed over the students.

Why would she be shaping them?

It was a spirit shaping. Tolan understood what would happen with a spirit shaping, though only if that were her intent.

She did it subtly, a soft touch, and he frowned to himself as he paid attention. She started in the front row of the classroom, letting spirit sweep over each of the students.

Could she be trying to unlock something within them? It wouldn't be unheard of for one of the master shapers to use a connection like that in order to free them, but spirit was its own troublesome element. There was danger in using it like that, danger that came from how others could be influenced, and there was danger in how they could destroy someone's mind, taking away their ability to think for themselves.

He didn't want to be spirit-shaped. He didn't want *anyone* to be spirit-shaped, but in particular, he didn't want *Ferrah* to be spirit-shaped. She was angry enough about the shaping she'd experienced before, and he could easily imagine what she would do if she learned Master Aela was trying the same thing.

When she finished the end of one row, he noticed the way she neared Ferrah.

"Master Aela?"

The shaping shifted, drawn off Ferrah. It swept toward him, and he steeled himself against it. Instinctively, he shaped fire, adding earth, drawing it through the bondar. He could feel the spirit strike his shaping, rolling past it, and he held her gaze, terrified she was somehow using it on him, but nothing seemed to change.

Master Aela watched him, frowning. "What is it, Shaper Ethar?"

"I think I've managed to mix each of the elements."

Somewhere nearby, someone chuckled. Tolan didn't have to look over to realize it was Draln.

"That would be an advanced shaping, Shaper Ethar."

"Can you let me know if I'm doing it right?"

Next to him, Jonas frowned, watching him, and Tolan ignored him. He ignored the way Ferrah watched. If nothing else, he wasn't about to let her get spirit-shaped until he better understood what was taking place.

"I seem to recall you do not have the ability to shape wind and water without the bondar."

His heart hammered. "Not yet, but I think maybe I managed to make this work."

She frowned at him. "It's unlikely, Shaper Ethar. I am attuned to spirit shapings, and if any of you were capable of merging the elements, I would have detected it."

"That's what you were doing?" he asked.

She stared at him. "I was searching for spirit. There is a telltale signature, and there is a particular spirit shaping that allows me to uncover it."

He nodded, taking a seat. "I'm sorry. I just thought I might have succeeded. With as hard a time as I have reaching any of the elements..."

She nodded to him. "Don't despair, Shaper Ethar. Seeing how much you've been progressing, I suspect you will one day show potential even with spirit."

She turned away, and her shaping stopped.

Tolan breathed out heavily, staring straight ahead, not wanting to do or say anything.

"I think that is enough for today," Master Aela said. "We will resume this in another week. You will continue to work on opening yourselves to each of the elements, and when you do, then you can see if you can uncover any way of reaching for spirit. I hope this has been enlightening for all of you."

Everybody began to get to their feet and started to

shuffle out. Shapings burst from the edge of the spirit-shaping classroom as shapers used their preferred shapings in order to lower themselves back down out of the spirit tower. Tolan paused at the edge, and Jonas looked over at him. "What was that about?" he whispered.

Tolan shook his head. "Not now."

"You weren't able to do anything. Why would you claim it?"

Ferrah shaped, dropping to the main level. Tolan used fire and earth, dropping alongside her, and Jonas joined them on wind.

They headed out of the tower, passing a pair of dark-cloaked Inquisitors who watched them. Tolan couldn't help but think they were attempting to shape them, though he didn't feel anything from them. Perhaps they weren't trying to test anyone. Then again, they were Inquisitors. With the nature of their shaping, it was likely they were so skilled with it that no one would be able to detect what they were doing.

"When do you want to talk about this?" Jonas asked.

Tolan hurried, racing up toward Ferrah. She was heading toward the second-level quarters, and when he caught up to her, she shot him a look.

"What?" he said.

"You don't need to draw attention to yourself. With everything you've done, I think drawing attention is dangerous."

"You don't understand," he said.

"I'm sure I don't. Why don't you tell me?"

They had reached the main part of the second-level quarters, and he motioned for them to follow him back to their rooms. When they were there, he waited, giving Jonas a look until the other man shaped wind around the room, attempting to seal it off. Thankfully, Wallace wasn't in the room, so they didn't have to worry about him. Then again, Wallace wasn't there very often.

"The only reason I did that was because Master Aela was performing a spirit shaping on everybody in the room."

Ferrah watched him, her brow clouding.

"You heard what she said," Jonas said. "She was using her shaping to see if any of us had the potential."

Tolan nodded. "I know that now, but at the time, I didn't. I didn't like the fact she was sweeping her spirit shaping around the room."

"You were trying to protect yourself by drawing attention to yourself?" Jonas looked over at Ferrah, as if trying to get her to agree with him. She remained silent, though Tolan recognized the irritation on her face. Hopefully it wouldn't be directed at him this time.

Tolan shook his head. "No. She shaped me when I called attention to myself."

"Then why would you do it? Honestly, Tolan, I think Ferrah is right. You really have to be more careful. Everything that's happened these days has you involved, and with the Inquisitors here, and with the rumors spreading, we need to be careful."

Jonas released his shaping, heading out of the room and toward the commons area.

It left Ferrah and Tolan alone.

"You did that for me, didn't you?"

He inhaled deeply, letting it out slowly. "She was getting closer to you with the spirit shaping. I didn't know the purpose of it, but knowing you'd already been exposed to spirit shapings before, and knowing that those shapings have influenced you, I…"

Tolan shook his head, glancing toward the door. He had been foolish. Here he'd begun to think Master Aela was doing something to them, but she was only attempting to find spirit. And when her shaping had washed over him, he hadn't felt anything strange. There had been no sense of her trying to harm him. The only thing he'd detected was the way the shaping washed over him, sweeping beyond him, and it left him knowing there was nothing else within it to fear.

More than that, he had drawn attention to himself, the way Jonas and Ferrah had suggested. He had enough of that, and he should know better than to do so, and should know better than to draw that attention to himself, especially as it served no purpose other than to make him the target of the Inquisitors. With their presence in the Academy, he *should* do whatever he could to avoid their notice.

Ferrah sat next to him, taking his hand. "Thank you. It *was* stupid of you. If her shaping was only determining whether or not we were reaching for spirit, then what you did wasn't necessary, but I know why you did it. And thank you."

He sat there for a moment with her, quietly, and yet, he couldn't help but wonder whether the spirit shaping had done something else to him, or perhaps that was nothing more than his imagination.

What he did know was that he had some time before the next spirit class session, and he was determined to go in prepared. If that meant he would need to continue to work with each of his element bonds, then he would do so. The time with the bondars had to matter. He had to be able to reach each of the elements on his own. He was determined to figure out what was necessary in order to reach spirit.

And Jonas was right. He needed to focus on the future, on what it might take to pass the next test. There was always another test.

13

ATTEMPTING TO SHAPE IN THE EARTH-SHAPING CLASSROOM as a second-level student went much better for Tolan than it did when he was a first-year student. Partly that was because he had spent so much time with the Keystone and the bondars, but partly it was because he'd been able to practice with earth on his own.

Master Shorav seemed less and less surprised by Tolan's ability to shape within the classroom. That had begun during the ending of his first level and at the time of his testing, and it had continued, allowing him the opportunity to feel almost as if he could be an earth shaper.

He still felt dependent upon the bondar. As in all shapings, he defaulted to using it, not considering it a crutch the same way Ferrah did. For Tolan, it was a necessity.

"It is time for you to attempt your shaping," Master Shorav said from the front of the class. He pulled a tray of bondars out, and everyone filed toward the front of the room.

Tolan hesitated, remaining seated, and Jonas glanced over at him.

"You don't need a bondar for earth anymore?"

Tolan considered getting up but decided to use the bondar he'd found at his parents' home. Why shouldn't he? If nothing else, the bondar his father had made might be more effective than any of the others. He also needed to practice with it, using what he could to shape through the bondar so he could become better aware of its limitations—along with *his* limitations. There would have to be some, though when it came to understanding how to use this bondar, Tolan wasn't entirely certain what limitations there might be.

"I'm going to try without it today."

"Weren't you the one who was commenting on Ferrah and her inability to shape fire without a bondar? I seem to remember you talking about a stubbornness."

Tolan started to flush, his gaze drifting toward Ferrah, who sat at the front of the class. Unlike with fire, she was strong with earth, and she had no need to use a bondar for her shaping. He wasn't surprised she hadn't taken one.

"If I can't do it, I'll go and get a bondar."

Jonas frowned at him. "If you say so." He went to the front of the class and took his bondar before returning and taking a seat. As he did, he set it on the table, glancing over at Tolan. "Are you going to shape?"

The shaping Master Shorav wanted from them

shouldn't be that difficult. He had wanted them to create a specific shape, and they cleared the table out of the way, taking a seat on the ground so they could use that natural connection to perform their shaping. There was something about the earth tower that seemed more open than in other places. Because of that, he was better able to use the earth shaping here than elsewhere within the Academy towers. Any shaping here didn't really disrupt the contours of the structure. Tolan still hadn't discovered if it was some extra layer of shaping upon the Academy or if it was something else.

He focused on an elemental. In this case, there was one elemental he thought might be helpful, an earth elemental called grosn. The only connection he'd had to this elemental had been at the Keystone. Without using a bondar, Tolan didn't know if he would be able to reach it now, but he focused on what he needed of the elemental.

It came to him slowly. There came a soft rumbling, and Tolan opened his eyes to see if it was from him but realized it came from Jonas working next to him. He had a powerful shaping building from the bondar, forming an enormous frame encompassing much of the floor. Jonas held onto it before releasing it again.

"You really should try using a bondar," Jonas said.

"What would you be able to do without the bondar?"

"With earth? Probably a much smaller version of this. I'd fought using it, but there's no point. Why shouldn't I get a better sense of the shaping? It's better for me to do it this way than to fight it and think I know better."

Tolan chuckled. "I'm not saying I know better."

Jonas held out the bondar, but Tolan didn't take it.

"See? Stubbornness."

Tolan shrugged. "Again, I'm not so sure I'd call it stubbornness. More a determination."

"You and Ferrah both."

Tolan continued to focus on the elemental. If he could manage that, then he wouldn't feel as dependent upon having a bondar available anytime he needed to perform a shaping.

Holding the image of the elemental in his mind, he continued to attempt a shaping. All he really needed was that sense of stirring within himself, the connection that would allow him to grab hold of the elementals. It didn't come.

Jonas was watching him, and he seemed waiting for Tolan to fail.

The way Jonas looked at him reminded him far too much of the way others had looked at him in Ephra. It was similar to the way Tanner had always looked at him. Tolan hated that look. It was one that dismissed him.

Irritation bubbled up within him, and Tolan reached his hand into his pocket, gripping the bondar. Once he did, he focused on the elemental again. This time, there came a faint stirring from deep within him, and he latched onto that. Connected to the stirring in that way, Tolan focused on the elemental, forming it. It emerged slowly, a steady rumbling, and it built larger and larger.

As it did, Tolan realized he'd made a mistake. He

hadn't focused on a size. Rather, he'd used everything he could to simply generate the elemental.

Tolan tried to push away the elemental, trying to dismiss it, but now he'd summoned it, there was no way he was going to be able to dismiss it so easily.

Please, he begged.

The earth elemental ignored his plea, continuing to rumble.

Tolan continued to focus on it, trying to suppress it, but it wouldn't dissipate.

Was there anything else he could do?

Fire.

He grabbed for the furios, squeezing it and attempting a subtle shaping, but in his panic, he drew too much and saa burst from him, striking the elemental, and the two of them wound together before both collapsed.

Tolan sank back, sweating.

Jonas was watching him, but that wasn't all. Others in the room were also watching him. Including Master Shorav.

"What was that?" Jonas whispered.

"That was a shaping."

Jonas shook his head. "That's not the kind of shaping we were asked to do."

"You did one quite a bit larger than that," Tolan said.

"With the bondar. You were doing it without, and then... Did you lose control of it? It looked like there was fire, but it was there and gone so quickly, I wasn't sure."

Tolan waved his arm across his forehead, wanting

nothing more than to be invisible so others wouldn't turn their attention to him. Unfortunately, everyone looked in his direction, waiting for him to respond.

"I'm not feeling so well," he said. He got to his feet, heading out of the earth classroom, and staggered down the steps.

He actually wasn't feeling well, but it was different than some sort of sickness. It was fear.

He was losing control of his shapings. With Master Sartan, he would have lost control of his fire shaping had the master shaper not been there. In Master Shorav's classroom, Tolan would have released earth somehow had he not managed to combat it with fire. Would the same thing happen if he attempted wind and water?

This wasn't the kind of thing he should be doing these days, not with the Inquisitors at the Academy.

At the branch point of the stairs where he could head down, he turned toward the student section. All he wanted to do was rest. And maybe that was his problem. Maybe he was tired from lack of sleep the night before. Master Irina had warned him he needed to get his rest, almost as if she had anticipated something like this happening, though Tolan doubted she would have been able to predict he would release an elemental—or nearly so.

When he reached his room, he dropped onto the bed. He laid back, his eyes wide as he stared up at the ceiling. Maybe he should get some rest but after what he'd done— or nearly done—he thought he needed to disappear.

Everyone had been looking at him.

And now he would be attracting attention. Others would see him, and would they accuse him of dangerous shapings?

They *were* dangerous. The more he performed them, the more convinced Tolan became that they were tied to the actual elementals. They had to be, especially as uncontrollable as they were. With that being the case, and with him not having a connection to them, he should stop—only shaping in this way was the only way he knew how to shape.

A soft sound of the doorway caught his attention and he looked up to see Ferrah standing there. Concern wrinkled the corners of her eyes and she shook her head softly. "What was that?"

"It was nothing."

"It was more than nothing." She took a few steps and a shaping built from her, sealing off the room. "You need to talk to me, Tolan. You need to talk to someone. Even if it's not me."

He sat up, looking around. "It was a shaping."

"I'm quite aware it was a shaping. I'm just asking how. The shaping you performed was more powerful than what any of the rest of us performed. Even those with bondars."

Tolan pulled the bondar from his pocket and held it up. "I used a bondar."

Her eyes widened. "You stole one from Master Shorav?"

Tolan shook his head, handing it over to her. "Not from Master Shorav. This one came from my home."

"Your home? I don't really understand what you're getting at."

"When I went back to Ephra for the Selection, I visited my home. It had been a while since I was there, and I came across this. It was in a back corner, hidden, and I wasn't sure at first what it was, but the more I studied it, the more certain I became it was a bondar."

"Why would your parents have a bondar? I thought you said they weren't shapers."

"I didn't think they were shapers." He stared at the bondar for a moment, thinking back to the memories he had of his parents. "And I think they had a bondar because they made it."

She started to smile before seeming to realize he was being serious. "Your parents made bondars?"

"It seems that way. When I was young, they were taken by the Draasin Lord. I never really understood why my parents. If they were able to make bondars, then I could understand why the Draasin Lord would take them."

Ferrah examined the bondar, rolling it over in her hands. A shaping built from her, and there was a tentativeness to it, the shaping building slowly, rolling off her, and when it struck the bondar, he felt the way it surged.

Her eyes widened slightly and Tolan smiled to himself.

"It *is* a bondar."

"I told you it was."

"I guess... I guess I wasn't convinced it would be."

"Why not?"

"Because I haven't heard of anyone succeeding in making bondars." She looked up at him, her shaping easing off. "I know we tried but making a bondar is a difficult skill. I looked into it a little bit since we last tried, and everything I've been able to come up with tells me you have to be a powerful shaper, but you also have to understand the workings of the element bond in a way that is greater than even many of the master shapers understand."

"You're saying my parents were master shapers."

"I'm saying they would have to be if they were making bondars. Which is why I have a hard time believing they made this. Maybe they'd acquired it, not made it. You have to admit that would make a lot more sense."

Tolan took the bondar back from her, holding it in his hand, looking at the surface and at its design. It would make more sense to have that explanation than the one that involved his parents making bondars. They were craftsman, but it was possible they had acquired a bondar and were attempting to copy it.

If only he had clearer memories of that time, he might be able to better know and understand what might've happened, but his memories from that time were faint, faded. The only memory he really had was one that came from the Selection. All the other memories of his parents and the time before their disappearance had faded, disappearing into the back of his mind, leaving him with a sense of nothingness. "I suppose that makes more sense," Tolan said.

She took a seat on the bed next to him, meeting his gaze. "No one's going to accuse you of serving the Draasin Lord."

He looked up, meeting her eyes. "With what's taking place these days, that's not true, and you know it."

"Why do you say that?"

"Think about everything you know of what I've been able to do since coming to the Academy. Everything has been tied to the elementals. And who else is tied to the elementals?"

"No one's going to accuse you of being responsible for that."

"Are you sure?"

"Tolan—"

He shrugged. "That's what I fear. If the Inquisitors decide to blame me for what happened, I don't know how I'll be able to justify my role in everything. And maybe I'm not supposed to."

"You're not supposed to justify your role? You're not making any sense."

"Everything I've done has been tied to the elementals. And the longer I'm here, the more I begin to wonder if I'm posing more of a danger being here or whether there's something else for me."

"What something else?" Ferrah asked, watching him carefully.

"Nothing like that," he said.

"Like what?"

"I see the way you're looking at me. I'm not going to run off and serve the Draasin Lord."

"That wasn't what I was thinking."

"Your eyes were telling me you're thinking."

"You need to talk to someone about this. Whether it's the Grand Master or one of the master shapers or even the Grand Inquisitor, you need to share with someone."

"What happens if they feel as if I'm somehow tied to the Draasin Lord?"

"At least you've raised the question. There has to be someone you feel comfortable going to."

He thought of Master Sartan but didn't know if going to the fire shaper would be the right choice. Going to Master Shorav wouldn't be helpful, either. Master Marcella wouldn't offer him any real advice. He suspected she would react strangely, more likely than not making comments about his shaping. He'd already heard some from her and didn't like the idea he'd hear more. The only person who made any sort of sense to go to would be the Grand Master, and they needed to do it now before anything else happened.

"I can go with you, if you want."

Tolan nodded and got to his feet. "Okay."

"Okay?"

"Let's go."

"I didn't realize you'd want to go so soon."

"If I'm going to do this, I want to do it before I change

my mind. Besides, you're right. I do need to go to someone."

They started out of the room, and voices down the hall caught his attention. The rest of their class was returning from the earth shaping, and he glanced over at Ferrah.

She shrugged. "I left early."

"*You* left early?"

"It seemed like you needed help."

"Thanks."

They had made their way through the common area and reached the stairs heading down when they ran into Jonas. He glanced from Ferrah to Tolan, a question burning in his eyes.

Ferrah smiled widely. "We're going to get some food."

"Just the two of you?"

Ferrah shrugged.

Jonas watched them as they continued down the stairs. Tolan couldn't help but feel as if he were betraying his friend. Jonas deserved honesty, but there were things he didn't feel comfortable sharing, and he worried if he attempted to share, Jonas wouldn't understand.

When they reached the main part of the hallway, they passed a pair of Inquistors. The sense of shaping built from them and Tolan did his best to ignore it.

Ferrah walked with him as they headed toward the Grand Master's rooms. They reached the door, and she urged him forward until he knocked.

There was no response.

Tolan knocked again, stepping back to wait, looking

around the hallway. A few of the older students were making their way through the halls, and one of them—an older man named Charles—grinned.

Tolan turned away, focusing on the door and practically willing it to open.

"He's not going to be here," he said.

"Then we will have to return."

"I don't know if I can."

"Tolan—"

They were turning away when the Grand Inquisitor came down the hallway.

"She's the last person I want to talk to about this," Tolan whispered.

"You don't have to."

As she made her way down the hallway, Tolan realized she wasn't alone. The Grand Inquisitor came with two others, both dressed in the same deep black cloaks of the Inquisitors.

"Where do you think they're going?" Tolan asked.

He looked over at Ferrah, but her face had drained of color.

She stood rigid, fixed, and he wondered what bothered her.

"Shaper Tolan Ethar," the Grand Inquisitor said, approaching.

Tolan turned his attention to her, feeling a shaping building from the Grand Inquisitor. "What is it?"

"You are to come with us."

"I am? Why? I'm not the traitor."

The Grand Inquisitor didn't answer, staring at him.

Tolan started to turn toward Ferrah but caught himself. If they were after him, he wasn't about to drag her into anything.

Where was the Grand Master? He had to believe if he could find the Grand Master, anything that might have upset the Grand Inquisitor could be resolved.

The two Inquisitors behind the Grand Inquisitor came around her, and they grabbed Tolan and dragged him away.

The shock of it all kept him from even thinking about resisting.

THE ROOM WAS DARK, AND HE SAT THERE ALONE. THERE was the presence of stone all around him, and as he had grown bored with sitting, he had attempted a shaping, but had found shaping on the stone had failed. It was almost as if he were cut off from shaping, though not entirely. Had he been cut off from shaping, he wouldn't have been able to attempt one. It was more that any attempt to shape was wiped away when it struck the stone. Strangely, it reminded him of his time in the waste.

He sat on a hard chair, all of his belongings out of reach. His pouch rested in the corner, and his cloak was stacked on top of it.

He stared at it. If the Grand Inquisitor decided to search through his belongings, she would find the bondars. Why had they brought him here?

Tolan had lost track of time. He'd been sitting here for over an hour, and possibly longer. The Inquisitors had said nothing as they had dragged him through the halls, and he had seen a few older students and knew gossip would already have spread about him.

After everything else, this would happen to him?

He got up and started pacing, but it did nothing to calm his mind. Thoughts raced through his head and he struggled to try and understand, to make sense of what had happened, but no answers came to him.

He was tempted to go to the cloak and search through it to ensure his bondars were there but decided against it. If they came upon him clutching a bondar, what might they do to him?

He tried to think about why he would have been brought by the Inquisitors, and the only thing he could think of was that someone had recognized he had released an elemental. If that were the case, he wasn't sure how he would answer to the Inquisitors.

He paced, his mind working through what he might say and what he might do, but no answer really came to him.

Eventually, he took a seat once again.

When the door finally opened, Tolan had long since lost track of time. He looked up and the Grand Inquisitor entered, dragging a chair with her. She placed it in front of his chair and took a seat upon it, sitting with her back straight as she studied him. He had a sense of a shaping radiating from her, but nothing more than that.

Was this a spirit shaping? Was she trying to force him to answer? Could she be sealing off the room, trying to make it so no one else could hear what they were about to discuss?

"Shaper Ethar. Do you know why you're here?"

Tolan didn't trust himself to answer so he shook his head, meeting her gaze.

"We know the Draasin Lord has sent someone to infiltrate the Academy. You have been observed performing shapings of great strength."

There it was. She was after him because of the shapings. They had known about the elementals, and he wasn't even going to have an opportunity to approach the Grand Master with his concern and explain to him what he'd been doing. Had he only gone to him sooner, maybe none of this would be an issue, but he had been afraid. And now it would be too late.

"I was going to talk to the Grand Master about it, but—"

"The Grand Master is indisposed at the moment, which leaves you with me."

A chill worked along his arms and he resisted the urge to rub them and warm himself. It seemed to Tolan that was exactly what she wanted out of him.

"What do you want from me?"

"Generally, in these, I'm the one who asks the questions."

"And what is this?"

She cocked her head. "Another question. This is your Inquisition."

Tolan's heart seemed to stop. Sweat beaded on his forehead and his mouth was suddenly dry.

An Inquisition?

He'd heard stories of an Inquisition—everybody probably had. They were designed to question people considered dangerous to Terndahl, and they had been used ever since the founding of Terndahl, the primary role for the Inquisitors and a way to ensure safety for all of Terndahl. Why would they need to perform an Inquisition on him?

They worried he served the Draasin Lord.

They worried *he* was the traitor.

It all came back to the elementals.

He had been far too free with his attempts at shaping them, far too relaxed with using his connection, drawing out that power, and now it would come back to haunt him. He should have known better, especially with the rumors around the Academy.

"I will ask you again. Why do you think we have brought you here?"

Tolan swallowed, and her shaping built. He had the sense she was trying to convince him to answer, to admit something, and maybe if he said nothing, he would avoid incriminating himself.

"I don't know."

"Interesting. I never took you for the cautious type. You always seemed so willing to step outside of what was considered right and proper."

Tolan licked his lips. How could his mouth be so dry

when sweat was dripping from his forehead? "I don't intend to step outside of anything."

"And yet you do. Ever since you came to the Academy, you have stepped outside of yourself, taking risks most would never have considered."

"I didn't do anything."

"That is what we are here to determine. Why do you think you were summoned here?"

"I don't know."

"Still with that as your answer? I would think you should come up with something better."

"What would you propose I come up with?"

"An answer," she said.

"I've given you an answer, and I've told you I don't know why you have me here."

"And I have told you that you were observed performing a shaping you should not have been able to do."

Tolan breathed out heavily. What would he have to say to get out of here? He didn't have any idea what Master Irina would ask of him. "I don't know what you need from me."

"Better, but you still haven't gotten quite what we need."

She sat back on the chair, the shaping that she was holding building. As it did, the air seemed to take on a tension, and Tolan resisted the urge to fight through it. Even if he wanted to oppose Master Irina, he didn't have any ability to do so. She was far stronger than he, and the only thing he was able to resist—so far, at least—was her placing a spirit shaping upon him. If she succeeded in that, what would happen to him? Would she be able to reach into his mind and uncover secrets he might be holding?

She watched him, a steady grin rising on her face. It was almost as if she knew what he was thinking, but she couldn't know he was trying to come up with some way of stopping her.

"Very few students face an Inquisition. Are you aware of that, Shaper Ethar?"

"I was not."

She watched him a moment longer, seemingly waiting for him to say something more, but he refused. "You are interesting. You have been so ever since I came across you in Ephra, and as I told you then, your presenting yourself for Selection may have been a mistake."

"I thought you told me the other night that it was my choice."

"I told you the Selector doesn't make the choice. They put each candidate through the shaping, and from there, only those who have the potential to serve the Academy are Selected. As I think I told you, there has not been one who doesn't have the ability to shape Selected for the Academy before. In that, you are unique."

Tolan didn't like being unique. Ever since his parents disappeared, he had felt that way. At first it had been unique in his family, and the fact his parents had disappeared, seemingly going with the Draasin Lord, and since coming to the Academy, it had been a uniqueness in his shaping, something that had set him apart, making it so he felt different. And then *he* had made himself unique. It had been his fault he had gotten involved with things like the pursuit of the Convergence and then the Keystone.

And here he had intended to take his second level at the Academy to avoid notice. If nothing else, he had wanted to be in the background, and yet he had been unable to do so.

"What do you think I did?"

"That's what we are attempting to discover." She glanced at his belongings. "Before we go any farther, I thought I would give you one last chance to share anything you might have that would explain things. We find it's often easier on those we bring to the Inquisition if they admit what they did."

She waited, and Tolan considered saying something about the bondars, but perhaps she wouldn't find them.

She went over to his pouch and pulled the bag out, dragging it toward him. When she reached him, she opened the flap and set it on the floor in front of him. "What will we find in here?"

"Books."

"Indeed. I can see there are books in here. What sort of books have you decided to bring with you? What is it you value so much you would carry it around?"

Tolan glanced at the bag. As he did, his heart seemed to stop again. Not only had he shaped elementals, but the books he had were about the elementals. He licked his lips again, finding no moisture.

"You would continue to say nothing?"

She watched him for a long moment, and he decided there wasn't anything he could say. As he watched her, he could tell she'd already come up with her own conclusion and anything he might say wouldn't matter. How could it, when she believed he was responsible for freeing the elementals? And there wasn't anything he could do or say that would counter that. He *had* freed the elementals.

It was all too easy to believe he was the traitor. Everything that had happened with him fit with that story.

She reached into the bag again and removed the stack of books. There should be no harm in studying that, and yet, with everything he'd been responsible for, he worried perhaps he'd made a greater mistake than he'd realized.

Master Irina stacked the books on her lap and began to sort through them, going from one book to next, her eyes narrowing. "An interesting selection for you to have, especially considering everything you've experienced."

"I wanted to know more about the elementals."

"And you decided you would prefer to learn this way rather than from what the master shapers would teach you?"

Tolan almost said something he would regret, nearly admitting he didn't feel as if the master shapers were all that current with their knowledge on the elementals but decided against it. If he would've said that, he would have essentially admitted he was responsible for freeing the elementals.

"Where is the Grand Master?"

"You are here for an Inquisition. As I said, you will not be questioning me."

Tolan looked around. Irritation flashed within him. "Is it typical for a student of the Academy to be questioned like this without anyone else present?"

"I would advise you to be careful."

"And why should I? You've already judged me. You can't even know what happened."

She leaned toward him, her smile widening, a predatory gleam in her eyes. "And now you admit something happened?"

"I don't admit anything. All I admit is that you have decided your judgment already. You haven't even taken the time to understand anything."

"Because there's nothing I need to understand. You were observed shaping without a bondar and performing a shaping of incredible strength. It was not the first time you were observed having such shaping prowess, and such ability raises questions, though the nature of the books you have with you raises additional questions." She continued to sort through his pouch before setting it down and turning to his cloak. When she reached it, she went through his pocket, and Tolan's heart sank as she pulled out first the furios and then the earth bondar.

"How is it that a student has not one but two bondars?"

What was the best course of action here? Tolan wasn't entirely sure how he should respond. Honesty might get him free from this, but it also might not.

He swallowed again. "I was given the furios by Jory."

"Jory?"

"The Selector who attacked the Academy, trying to free a draasin."

Her eyes narrowed. "How is it you know this?"

"Because I was there. You might have tried to spirit shape me, but it didn't work." He wasn't sure how much to say about this point, worried that if he shared too much, she might become angry, but *he* was starting to get angry. Why was it that she felt as if she could treat him like this?

"My spirit shaping failed?"

"Much like the spirit shaping I imagine you're attempting now," he said.

She leaned back, crossing her arms over her chest. The two bondars rested on her lap, and Tolan wanted nothing more than to grab them and shape himself free, but doing so would reveal his connection to the elementals.

"What makes you think I'm attempting a shaping now?"

"Just a guess," he said.

"A guess? This from someone who continues to use bondars kept by the master shapers."

"The other one isn't from the Academy."

"And how would you have acquired a bondar if not from the Academy?"

"In Ephra," he said.

"Is that right?"

There were plenty of ways he could take it, but only one that made sense to him. "Master Daniels had it in his shop."

Her eyes narrowed and she said nothing, watching him for long moments. "Where would Master Daniels have obtained a bondar?"

"I don't know. He was a craftsman, so I wouldn't be entirely surprising to me if he managed to create it himself. It's an earth bondar, and he was a powerful earth shaper."

She turned her attention to the bondar and her shaping built, directed toward the bondar.

"He wouldn't have been able to create a bondar. It takes a knowledge of runes and the elementals he doesn't possess," she said absently.

"It would if he served the Draasin Lord, as we know he does."

Her eyes narrowed again and she looked up from the bondar. "And perhaps you did along with your mentor. When did you acquire this?"

"During the Selection. It's not the same as the bondars we have here. I didn't take those." He allowed himself a moment of hope, thinking if nothing else, she might only be concerned about his possession of the bondars. If that was her primary concern, then maybe—just maybe—he could get away with little more than a warning. He could get out of this Inquisition, and he could... What? He doubted she would return the bondars to him, and without them, he would have no way of shaping. He needed the bondars, and he needed to be able to access them in order to shape in the way he was familiar with.

"I can see it is different." She continued to study the bondar, a trickle of shaping power coming off her.

It was clear to him the way it pressed into the bondar, the shaping energy flowing out from her and into the room. If he were to do it, he would create an elemental, and when she did it, all he noticed was power flowing away from her. How could he do something similar?

Mostly, it seemed to have to do with control. Others had it, whereas he did not. His connection to shaping wasn't one of control. It was one of almost desperation. When he reached for power with shaping, he did so without an expectation he would succeed in reaching it. Even with the bondar, he often failed to reach the elemental, though these days, it was less and less often that he failed.

What he would like would be an ability to do as Master Irina did and have some way of shaping a controlled shaping into the bondar rather than depending upon dumping out power from the elemental.

"Where did you find this in Master Daniels' shop?"

"It was in the back of one of his cabinets. He had tools below it, and I was surprised the tools were still there. Since the shop had essentially been abandoned, I expected the tools would've been stolen."

"The shop should not have been abandoned. When you were Selected, and when he was recalled, another was to handle his responsibilities."

"Did those responsibilities involve working in his shop?"

"The shop gave him something to do while watching for movement from elementals. It is that way for all who serve the Academy."

He kept his gaze locked on the bondar. He longed to have it back. Watching her, noticing the way she held on to both the earth bondar as well as the fire bondar, he doubted he would see them again.

And here he had feared this was all about his reaching for elementals. That wasn't it at all. Instead, she was far more concerned about his use of the bondars and shaping power he shouldn't have.

"Why are you concerned about my shaping?"

She looked up. Something had shifted in her when she had discovered the bondars, and either she realized he wasn't lying to her or she had her answer. Tolan wasn't entirely sure which it was.

"You have been one we haven't known quite what to do with," she said.

"I'm aware of that."

"What better way to infiltrate the Academy than to send someone who can learn from us and who can facilitate a shaper in finding something that should be hidden from him and then to reveal an attack on the city."

He began to understand what she implied, and his heart raced. Did she think he was somehow a part of what had transpired?

"I don't serve the Draasin Lord."

"It has been difficult to detect what you do serve. With most, I have some ability to test them, and I can understand what they might be doing, but with you... I have found it difficult. It's almost as if you had some ability to spirit shape before you ever came to us. And that is incredibly rare."

Tolan sat stiffly, staring at her. "I don't know how to spirit shape."

"It's possible you don't. Unfortunately, the questions continue. Were it only one situation, we would have questions, but we wouldn't have brought you in like this. The fact you continue to be involved in various situations raises the concern that you serve the Draasin Lord."

"I don't. I wouldn't."

"And yet everything you have done, including these," she said, patting the books and then holding up the bondars, "suggests you are involved far more than you have admitted. I will get you to answer, Shaper Ethar. You will reveal your connection to the Draasin Lord, and when you do, we will have our answers."

Tolan's heart hammered. What sort of answers did she think he had? If she believed he served the Draasin Lord, then would she think he would have information about where he'd been?

Tolan met her eyes, wishing for some way of getting her to understand he wasn't a part of what she thought. Master Irina looked back at him, no compassion in her eyes, and he knew she wouldn't believe anything he would have to say.

"There will be more questioning. You will find we will get the answers we seek. Eventually, you will share with us what we need to know. The city—and Terndahl—will be protected."

She got up and left, setting his pouch along with the books and the bondars in the corner of the room. A shaping built from her, and he suspected it was one that created a barrier around the bondars and his pouch, and it wasn't until she was gone that he went to try to reach for them and found he couldn't.

It was almost a taunt. As much as he wanted them, and as much as he might want to shape, he was still so far from being able to get to them.

He stared at the door, unable to say anything. He was trapped, and he had no doubt other Inquisitors would come to him, questioning him, and when they did, what would he say? Would he continue to be able to withstand their shaping?

Eventually, he suspected he would fall. This was an Inquisition. Eventually, everyone succumbed.

15

Sounds outside the door stirred him awake and Tolan sat up, rubbing the sleep from his eyes. It had been only a few hours since the last questioning, and he didn't even know the name of the Inquisitor who had been here demanding answers. There had been a steady stream of Inquisitors, one after another, and with each one, he felt as if his ability to resist was crushed more and more.

The door opened and the Grand Master entered, joined by the Grand Inquisitor.

"I will be fine with this one," the Grand Master said.

The Grand Inquisitor looked at him. A shaping built, directed at the Grand Master, before she nodded and turned to the door. "We will have answers from him," she said.

"I have no doubt you will."

The Grand Master stared at the door for a moment

until it closed, then he turned to Tolan. "How are you holding up?"

"I didn't do these things," he said. "I'm not the traitor. I don't serve the Draasin Lord."

"I know," the Grand Master said. "You forget, Shaper Ethar, I was there along with you. I know you didn't have a hand in this."

"Then why are they still holding me?"

"Because the role of the Inquisitors is to obtain information about those who have betrayed Terndahl. They take that role quite seriously, even if they haven't needed to use it recently. In the days when the Draasin Lord was gaining power, many were accused of serving him. The Inquisitors were there, helping to ensure the safety of Terndahl, as he was quite persuasive. It was his ability to shape spirit, as I suspect you know. With that ability, he managed to convince many others to side with him. Doing so allowed him to gain strength, and with strength and numbers, he gained credibility. Were it not for the Inquisitors, it's possible the Draasin Lord would have succeeded in his goal of overthrowing Terndahl and releasing the elementals for him to subjugate."

Tolan glanced at the door. "Why won't they release me?"

"Eventually, they will. They have no reason to hold you, and there will come a time when they have no choice but to release you. As long as you don't keep anything from them, and as long as you aren't in fact serving the

Draasin Lord, there would be no reason for them to hold you."

Tolan shook his head. "I've been trying to tell them what they want to know."

"I'm sure you have. And I'm sure this is terrifying for you. It's unusual for the Inquisitors to hold a student like this. And I have been trying to convince them to release you, but when it comes to this, I'm afraid the Grand Inquisitor is the one who must make that decision."

If Tolan were to understand what the Grand Master was saying, all he needed to do was find a way of holding out, and when he did, he could be released. There wasn't anything to share, as he didn't have anything he was keeping from the Grand Inquisitor.

Other than the fact he was using the bondars to shape the elementals.

So far, they hadn't asked that. The accusation of his connection to the Draasin Lord had been enough, and she hadn't begun to question him about the nature of his shaping. And perhaps she wouldn't. If she continued to attempt spirit shapings, would there come a time when he wouldn't be able to withstand it?

"Do you think you can hold out?" the Grand Master asked.

Tolan met his gaze, wishing the Grand Master was the one who was doing the Inquisition, but he nodded while knowing that eventually, he would fall to the spirit shaping.

"Do you?" he asked again.

Tolan nodded.

The Grand Master smiled. "Good. I will keep my pressure on the Grand Inquisitor to get her to release you, and eventually, this will be over." The Grand Master clapped him on the shoulder before nodding and making his way to the door. When he was there, he tapped on it, and a shaping Tolan hadn't felt was released. The door opened and the Grand Master departed, leaving Tolan alone again.

He took a seat, not knowing what else to do, and stared at the walls. His belongings still rested there, out of reach as a taunt, the kind of thing that told him the Grand Inquisitor knew exactly what she was doing when it came to him and his shaping—or inability thereof. She had left them as a way to remind him that without his bondars, he was unable to get to his belongings, but had he some normal way of shaping, it wouldn't be an issue.

He dragged himself over to it, reaching for the bondar, but his hand hit the invisible barrier. He had reached fire without a bondar—and earth—but each time he had, there was no real control. What he needed was a way to slide through the barrier and grab his belongings. He didn't care quite as much about the books on the elementals. Those belonged to the library, and he had little doubt they would be returned. Besides, he had long since memorized the contents. If he were pressed, he would be able to recite everything about the elementals written within the pages.

Which connection would give him the best chance of reaching through the barrier?

Probably earth, but only if he were able to burrow beneath the barrier. That required a level of finesse and control with shaping thast Tolan wasn't sure he could manage.

Seeing as how he had time, he took a seat in front of the barrier. As he sat there, feeling the pressure from the barrier, he ran his hands along the surface. Power radiated from it, though he wasn't able to push through. He rested his hands along the surface of the barrier, waiting, and focused on earth.

What he needed was some way of finding a link to that deep connection within him. If he could somehow tap into that stirring sensation, even without the bondar, maybe he could reach beneath the barrier and grab the bondar.

And if he could do that, did he really even need the bondar?

His thoughts turned back to the Grand Inquisitor. This was what she wanted. She wanted to prove he didn't have any shaping ability—and he didn't. She wanted to force him to reveal his lack of shaping ability. And with that, what did she hope to accomplish? Did she think to get some sort of confession out of him?

He didn't serve the Draasin Lord, regardless of what she said, and he would do everything in his power to withstand her attempting to accuse him of that.

Irritation bubbled within him, and Tolan struggled to tamp it down. Getting irritated and angry would do nothing. He needed calm. He needed to have quiet. He needed to be able to find peace. It was there, somehow, within him.

If only he could find that stirring sensation, that deep part of him that connected to the elemental.

What had he done when he had reached earth before? There had been fear. During the attack on the city when the disciples of the Draasin Lord had come, he had somehow found a way to resist. He had used earth, and he had created elementals, drawing them out of the bond, and had shaped without a bondar.

There came no sense of earth.

What of fire?

Tolan had more experience with fire, and had even managed to nearly release a draasin, though he didn't know whether that was real or not. If he could use that knowledge, could he unleash the same shaping?

If he did it, he would need to find a way of pushing through the barrier. Fire would be destructive, nothing like earth that he thought he could burrow beneath, and if he managed to destroy the barrier, Master Irina would know.

That was something he didn't want to reveal—not yet.

He wanted to get the bondars and hide them.

Focusing on fire, he tried to slip it beneath the barrier. There came a faint burning, and Tolan tamped that down, connecting to that fluttering as he converted it, shifting it toward smoke. For some reason, he was able to do this without needing to connect to a bondar. It wasn't nearly as strong as what he'd done in the classroom, and as the smoke continued to build, he tried to force it beneath the barrier, but there was nothing he could achieve. The barrier went into the stone.

Of course, it did. Master Irina would have expected him to try. Even if he were able to shape stone, it was possible he wouldn't be able to get beneath the barrier.

He sat back, reaching for his connection to fire, and let smoke twirl around him. He imagined the various smoke elementals, first esalash and then shiron, and allowed the smoke to dance, twisting in front of him. He was able to control it, having the smoke spiral around. Tolan tried to urge it, sending it toward the barrier, but it always bounced off.

Tolan shifted his focus, thinking of saa. The elemental was that of flame, and it burned, a flickering that hovered in the air before him. He smiled at it. There was beauty in the fire. Flames had always appealed to him, drawing to him, and stories of the draasin had always seemed both terrifying and amazing. Having seen a draasin—at least, what he imagined to be a draasin—he still found the creatures to be amazing and terrifying.

The flame swirled, flickering, creating a gentle sort of heat pulsing into the air. Though he knew he would be able to draw upon it more strongly with the bondar, the fact he was doing this shaping on his own left him feeling proud. Maybe he didn't need the bondars as he had always believed.

What of a more complicated elemental?

He shifted to hyza, thinking of that elemental, and let

that power flow. As it did, it grew, the small foxlike shape forming and prowling around him. Tolan sat and stared as the elemental circled him. Heat radiated from it, crackling in the air. The effort of shaping hyza was much more than it took with the other elementals, and he couldn't hold onto it for long. As he released it, the elemental sent a strange pulsing back.

He shouldn't be strong enough to be able to draw an elemental on his own, but there had been something real. Surprisingly, he felt lonely with the elementals gone.

Could he call upon something smaller?

There wasn't much that was smaller. He tried reaching for fire again, but he was tired from everything he had already attempted.

Even if he could reach a shaping that would allow him beneath the barrier, he still didn't know whether he wanted to. What he wanted more than anything was to be able to reach the earth.

He took a deep breath, focusing on the ground in front of him. He thought of jinnar, the earth elemental he had the easiest connection to, though not the only earth elemental he was able to summon. He had some experience with other earth elementals, and it was possible he would be able to reach for more than jinnar. Jinnar was a useful elemental, powerful enough that it would cause the ground to rumble, but not so powerful that he worried about losing control.

Without the bondar, he didn't have any reason to worry about losing control.

He steadied his breathing, focusing, thinking how easy it had been to reach for fire by summoning the elementals.

The stirring began to build within him.

It was a strange sensation, a feeling that his stomach was unsettled. As it came to him, he reached for it.

All he needed was the ability to tap into that power. Once he did, then the elemental could do the rest.

It faded, leaving him empty.

Another failing.

And yet, he *had* begun to feel the stirring. That was the first step. If he could manage to do that more effectively, he could reach for the elemental.

He took another deep breath and had started to focus on the ground when words written in the books Master Minden had lent him began to flash through his mind.

He lost his focus, but he didn't care. There wasn't any reason to maintain his focus if he was able to do something else.

What was in those books that he could use?

The first Grand Master of the Academy had written one. Tolan had looked through it enough to know there was information he could use. He searched his memories, but he came up with nothing.

What of the book from the first Grand Inquisitor?

It was a different style, a philosophical approach to shaping, and in that one, he thought there should be something he could remember, but it too eluded him.

He sighed deeply and sat back. Strangely, it was the memory from the book of Master Minden's ancestor that came to him most of all. He thought about what was in there, the comment about how to access each shaping, reaching for some deep part of the shaper. As he thought about it, it seemed to him it was describing his technique of shaping, not that which the master shapers at the Academy tried to teach him.

He thought about what had been written in that book about earth.

Earth was a difficult element only because it was so massive and extensive, and reaching it meant you had to connect yourself to earth. Each shaper was a part of something greater—the earth bond—but each shaper had that power within themselves, and once they reached it, they could draw upon the power of earth and command it.

That was what the master shapers would teach.

The book Master Minden's ancestor had written described something different with earth. There was power to it, but that power came from the shaper. It was innate, rather than a part of the earth bond.

Tolan wondered if that was why his ability with shaping was so different. Was it because he didn't reach for it in the same way?

He focused again and, rather than thinking of the elemental, he focused on that stirring within him. He thought about the connection he had to the stone, and he thought about the way he felt when jinnar or whatever earth elemental he was trying to shape came into exis-tence. There was a sense of satisfaction, a sense of rightness, and a sense it was meant to be. All he needed was to reach that sensation and he could shape earth.

Not to control it. To be a part of it. To use it. The same way the elementals used that power. All in service of the bond, but not using the bond.

Power built from deep within him, and he felt the connection to earth.

It was different than any shaping he had felt before. This was earth. This was that natural power. And this was enough that he thought he could reach through it.

Rather than focusing on an elemental, he focused on what he wanted of earth.

It was a request rather than a command. It was an idea. He imagined having the ground roll up around him, creating a seat for him to sit upon. He focused on his connection to the ground, to the earth he felt beneath him.

Everything rumbled. The earth lifted him into the air, holding him upright.

He had shaped. And he had done so without an elemental.

Or had he?

He didn't know if jinnar was a part of that shaping, but even if it was, did it matter? Tolan wasn't opposed to connecting to jinnar. He had wanted that elemental connection, and it didn't mind it. Connecting to the elemental like that was worthwhile, only he didn't think he'd used the elemental for this shaping. If he was right, it had come from within him.

Which made the shaping even more valuable than before.

Unlike other shaping, this one didn't retreat when he released it. It maintained its position, holding steady, and the chair remained in place.

Could he remove it? Now he had brought it forth, the next step was to eliminate any evidence of what he had done. He focused on pushing back down, returning the earth to the way it had been. Once more, he was able to use that power from deep within him.

Slowly, the ground began to rumble, the shaping retreating and easing back into the earth, disappearing from view.

Tolan sat up triumphantly. Exhaustion swept over him.

He rolled over, looking at the place where the shaping had been, pleased to see there was no evidence of what he'd done. There would be nothing anyone would be able to see to reveal he'd been here.

Would they have detected his use of shaping?

From what he'd been able to tell, there weren't all that many people who could detect shaping. He was one, but there had to be others like him. Even if there weren't all that many, there had to be some way of shaping that would allow master shapers to detect that power being used around them. Tolan took a seat on the chair, sitting and watching the door, and waited, counting the moments as he expected the door to open and someone—likely an Inquisitor—to enter.

No one did.

He looked in the corner, studying the barrier, but without any way of shaping beneath it, he didn't think he would be able to rescue his belongings.

He had a victory, but it might be a hollow one, and without the bondars, what else would he be able to do?

Tolan lost track of how long he stared at the door, waiting for one of the Inquisitors to enter, constantly on edge. After a while, he gave up waiting and took another seat on the floor, focusing on shaping, and wondering if he might be able to find some way to reach the power of the other element bonds.

If he could, maybe there would be some benefit to his Inquisition.

16

THE DAYS PASSED AND TOLAN LOST TRACK OF TIME. HE considered scratching the count on the floor, shaping a record, but decided against it. What point would there be in reminding himself how long he'd been here? He was at the mercy of the Inquisitors, and while the Grand Master had visited him once, he had not returned.

The time spent alone here gave him an opportunity to continue to search to see if he had some way of connecting to the element bonds. The longer he did, the more he continued to feel the building power and presence of shaping from within him. It became easier to connect to fire and earth. He still hadn't managed wind or water, though there was a faint stirring with each, enough that he wondered if it would be possible to eventually reach them.

Each day he was here, he continued to try different shapings. He practiced those he had learned about from

Master Sartan and Master Shorav. None required a bondar, and while all had aspects of the elementals associated with him, in none of them did he feel as if he were using the elemental powers in order to reach for the shaping he attempted. What he was doing now was different than what he had done before—drawing now from within himself—and he began to wonder if he were finally reaching the element bonds the way he was meant to.

Strangely, he was still able to access the connection to the elementals. When he thought about them and only focused on each of the various fire and earth elementals, going through them in his mind as he shaped them into existence, he found it was increasingly easy to do so. He was able to keep them from emerging fully formed, drawing them forth just a little—enough so he could feel the connection to the elemental.

As he worked alone, he attempted several times to reach for the bondars, but had never managed to break through the barrier.

Having this time with nothing more than an opportunity to shape was helpful. It allowed him to focus. To run through shapings. To practice. It was something he had never done before.

Each day that passed, the Inquisitors came to him. With each passing day, Tolan managed to resist any sort of shaping. He was convinced they were trying to spirit shape him, but at the same time, he was also convinced that he was refusing to allow them to spirit shape him. He wasn't sure why he felt so sure other than that he still had memories of everything that had taken place here. He didn't think they were placing any thoughts or memories in his mind but began to wonder if perhaps he was wrong. Maybe their steady appearances were breaking down his ability to withstand their shaping.

After a week or more alone, Tolan began to wonder a different fear. What if the spirit shapings were allowing him to reach for shaping in this way? If so, then he should open himself up to them, to let them work their abilities upon him, to help him find more ways to shape. If he could reach for water and wind, then he would continue to progress through the Academy and might be useful.

After another week, the questions, allegations of working with the Draasin Lord, were unchanged and Tolan decided they hadn't unleashed any shaping potential within him. His days were a blur. They blended together from sleep to alertness. Food trays were delivered to him, never anything exciting, and he ate and drank everything he was given, wanting to maintain his strength. He needed it for what he did when he was awake.

When he was awake, he attempted to shape. When he was sleeping, he was dreaming of shaping—and elementals. They danced in the forefront of his mind, like the pages of the books he couldn't quite reach. Rather than only fire and earth, the two elements he'd practiced with when awake, all of the elementals danced across his mind. The only one that didn't was spirit.

When the door opened again, after a time that Tolan suspected was several weeks into his capture and Inquisition, he looked up to see the Grand Inquisitor.

She took a seat across from him, settling down and motioning for him to rise. "You have been here longer than I expected."

"How long did you expect me to be here?" His voice came out hoarse, and his throat hurt. How long had it been since he'd had any water?

"I thought perhaps you might last a few days, but never this long."

"How long has it been?"

"The better part of a month."

A month. What must his friends be thinking? Rumors had to be going through the Academy about him. It would be just like being back in Ephra. He would be different. Separated. When he had come to the Academy, it was a chance for a fresh start, an opportunity to find himself, and regardless of his inability to shape, he had relished that opportunity. Discovering the use of the bondars had given him a chance to fit in, even if that chance was different than he wished it would be.

Now he would be back to people talking behind his back. There would be whispers, and some people would avoid him. Others would be like Velthan, throwing it in his face. Tolan expected Draln to be one of them and hated that he feared the kind of comment Draln would make to him.

"Why have you kept me here a month?"

"Because you haven't told the truth."

"You accuse me of serving the Draasin Lord. There is no truth in that."

"I think there is far more truth in that than you realize. I've begun to suspect you were spirit-shaped, only you were done in such a subtle way as to hide the fact you serve him."

"How could I ever have served the Draasin Lord? I grew up in Ephra."

"A place on the border of the waste."

"I've been to the waste."

"I'm sure you have."

"All students go to the waste. I walked upon it the same as everyone else. I was cut off from my shaping ability the same as everyone else."

"The reports I've heard are that you ventured farther than anyone else."

Tolan shook his head. "That doesn't mean I serve the Draasin Lord. It only means my shaping is so weak, I don't have the same connection as others do. I have less to fear."

"Yes. I imagine you were taught to say such things. I have ways of unlocking hidden shaping."

"If you have ways, then why haven't you used them?"

She glanced behind her at the door. Who was she looking for?

"Why are you keeping the Grand Master from visiting me?"

"What makes you think I've prevented him from visiting?"

"He came once, and he hasn't come since. He said he was trying to free me."

"The Grand Master knows better than to interfere with an Inquisition. Such a thing would not look good to those who observe them."

"I don't care about how things look. You've kept me here for a month. I've done nothing."

"During the time you've been here, we've had no further strange events."

Tolan frowned at her. "What kind of strange events?"

"The kind that have been occurring ever since your arrival at the Academy. I find it interesting that your confinement has coincided with this silence." She leaned toward him, pressing the tips of her fingers together, her eyes locked on him in an icy stare. Power built from her, a shaping, and it started toward him.

Instinctively, Tolan pushed out, wrapping himself in a barrier of fire. He had practiced this in the days he'd been trapped here, and he used a faint shaping, little more than a trickle, making it so it would be invisible. He'd practiced working on shaping so the heat would be pressing upon him rather than outward so anyone else wouldn't detect the nature of his shaping. That last part had been the trickiest, and the more he'd worked on it, the more he'd taken aspects from what he'd read of the elementals to help him.

The shaping struck his fire barrier.

Tolan *felt* it when it did. It was a strange sensation as it washed over him, parting around him.

Strands of her shaping mixed with him, and while holding onto his fire shaping, Tolan could detect what those strands were. Within them, he thought he could reach for more.

Master Irina sat up. "What was that?"

"What was what?"

"That shaping. Where did you learn it?"

"From Master Sartan."

She frowned, shaking her head. "Master Sartan would not have taught you such a technique. I felt nothing other than my shaping splitting. I should not have been aware of even that other than I was trying to see whether you were doing anything to actively work against me."

"Why wouldn't I actively work against you?"

"Because I am the Grand Inquisitor."

"Who has kept a student at the Academy captive for a month." He knew he should be careful with her, but he was growing tired of simply sitting by and letting the other Inquisitors question him, the same series of questions coming over and over, no different than before, never satisfied by his answers. Tolan was tired of fearing the arrival of the Inquisitors, terrified he might say something that would lead them toward another line of questioning. He was tired of sitting on this chair and in this cell.

He wanted out.

"Where did you learn that shaping?"

"What else have I had to do?" Tolan asked.

"Contemplate telling the truth."

"I've contemplated telling the truth, which is the reason I have told the truth."

Had he gotten so far along into this that he was convincing himself of that? He hadn't been completely honest with her, and with his tie to the elementals, he no longer knew what the truth was. Now he was able to more easily reach earth and fire, he didn't have the same desire to attempt to free the elementals, though there remained a question within him. Why *should* he suppress them?

That line of questioning was dangerous, especially here within the Inquisition. If he began to ask that, he ran the risk of prolonging it, or worse.

"Perhaps it was good I came today. I got to see first-hand some of the knowledge you've been keeping from us."

"Have you ever had others separated so long?" Tolan asked.

"More questions from you. You really do need to understand the nature of the Inquisition."

"I understand the nature of the Inquisition. Isolation. You think the longer I'm here, you'll force me to admit something. Either that or you think to shape something into my mind, either a way to force me to say something I wouldn't otherwise, or perhaps something else. I won't do it. And the longer I won't do it, the more I think it makes you angry."

"The only thing that makes me angry is having a traitor within the Academy."

"All I've done is serve the Academy. Even these times when you think I've been a part of whatever has taken place, I still served the Academy. I didn't always know what I was doing, but you can ask the Grand Master about my role. I'm sure he would tell you the truth."

"Why question the Grand Master when I can question your friends?"

The comment hit him like a bucket of cold water. It felt almost as if he were shaped with ice, and his breath caught, leaving him to stare at Master Irina. In all the days he'd been here, Tolan hadn't given any thought to what was happening with his friends other than fearing gossip and stories about him would spread. He had expected that and had given up thinking about whether there was anything he could do to stop it.

He'd never thought his friends might be questioned.

"Who have you interrogated?"

"Do the questions never end with you?"

"Who have you questioned?" He started to stand when a shaping wrapped around him, forcing him back into the chair.

She smiled at him tightly. "You may be able to prevent a spirit shaping, but you have much to learn about shaping in general. We are having a conversation. There is no need for anything more combative."

"What have you done to my friends?"

"You would think your time here would have endeared

you more to them. Your friend from Velminth, Shaper Golud, has been most enlightening."

What would Jonas have said? He wouldn't have known anything, especially as Tolan hadn't shared anything about the connection he had with the elementals, but Jonas might have said something about bondars. And with the distance between them recently, he worried Jonas might have said anything to end the Inquisition.

"And then there is the other young man who shares your room. A Shaper Wirthlin. He revealed your interest in bondars," she said, her gaze drifting toward the corner. "And here you were the one who told me you discovered this at Master Daniels'. Perhaps you were the one to create the bondar."

Tolan breathed out, resisting the urge to look over into the corner and stare at the bondar. He wouldn't do that. "You've already learned I came to the Academy without any ability to shape. Why wouldn't I attempt to create a bondar to make it easier for me to shape when everyone else has such an easy time doing so?"

"Creation of a bondar is restricted."

"I didn't know it was restricted."

"You thought you would simply begin making a bondar? Such a thing is dangerous. It's the reason we confine the bondars to the various classrooms. And yet, you, Shaper Ethar, thought you didn't need to be confined to shaping with the bondar. You thought you could be excluded from that. Why am I not surprised?"

"I wasn't trying to be excluded from anything. I was trying to learn how to master my abilities."

"Yes. Your abilities. I must say I am a little surprised you were able to master creation of a bondar as a first-level student."

"I haven't managed to make a bondar," Tolan said.

Resignation began to set in again, making him fully aware of how trapped he was. If she had interrogated Jonas and Wallace, he had little doubt she would have done the same with Ferrah. Of all the people he didn't want interrogated, Ferrah was the one. She knew more about him, had been a part of more with him.

His desire to protect her was more than that, though. Not only did he want to keep her from any sort of interrogation, he wanted to protect her from the possibility of another spirit shaping.

"Lastly, I went and interrogated your friend, Shaper Changen."

There it was.

Tolan stared, feeling helpless. How much would Ferrah have revealed? He knew she wouldn't have done so willingly. Ferrah was a true friend, and he doubted she would have revealed anything that would've placed him in a difficult situation. She'd been the one who had wanted him to go to the Grand Master to discuss what was happening with him and the way he was shaping, but he had been unwilling.

He should have done so sooner. Maybe if he would have, none of this would've happened. He should've gone to the Grand Master when he first uncovered the way he shaped and his connection to the elementals.

Then he might have been exiled from the Academy, though it was difficult to believe his strange connection to shaping was different enough that it would raise questions even with the Grand Master, a man who seemed so open and willing to entertain different ideas.

"What did Ferrah say?"

"She was most enlightening."

Tolan studied her face. In the times he'd been working with her, he'd begun to notice something. Her eyes twitched a little when she was lying. He doubted Master Irina would see it as lying. She'd probably view it as an interrogation technique, but when she accused him of something she didn't have strong evidence for, the corners of her eyes narrowed slightly. It was the slightest movement, barely enough to notice if he wasn't paying attention to it, but after what she'd said about Ferrah, he'd been watching.

There it was.

When they twitched, he allowed himself a moment to relax.

Ferrah either hadn't said anything or all of this was a ruse, trying to get him to speak.

"How was she enlightening?"

"How do you think she'd be enlightening? As I've said before, it's easier for you if you are open and honest about these things. The Inquisitors will take this under a greater consideration. We will consider it cooperation.

Given what you've gone through, don't you want to cooperate?"

"Given what I've gone through, I think I have cooperated just about enough."

She smiled sadly. "Unfortunately, Shaper Changen thought the same."

Her eyes twitched again.

What had happened with Ferrah?

Had she managed to avoid having the Grand Inquisitor spirit shape her?

It was something that had angered Ferrah—the one thing that had bothered her the most. The idea that her mind might be changed, thoughts and memories could be wiped, angered her. And Ferrah *had* been pursuing ways of reaching spirit. Maybe she'd found one.

Or maybe she'd borrowed the spirit bondar again.

The idea of her using the bondar to hide her actions from Master Irina was almost enough to make him smile. And he wouldn't be surprised if Ferrah *had* found some way of twisting the various element bonds together in order to protect herself.

"She didn't tell you anything," Tolan said. "Because there's nothing for her to have said. She would've told you that we found the Convergence when we chased Jory into the depths below the Academy. Jory was not me. *He* was the one responsible for what happened. *He* was the one responsible for the attack on the Academy. *He* was the one who intended to free the elementals. Not *me*."

He emphasized the last, trying to draw attention away

from him and place it on Jory, though he wasn't certain whether he was successful.

"She would've told you how I revealed the Keystone to her. She would also have told you how I worked with her to stop Master Daniels and the disciples from attacking—after we had already managed to stop the disciples attacking on the Shapers Path."

"Are you done?"

"Do I need to be?"

"You make these bold claims, Shaper Ethar, but in all, you neglect one thing."

"And what is that?"

"If you have served the Draasin Lord as I believe, all of this would've been possible."

"How?"

"The Draasin Lord would have coordinated it with you. Why would he not when doing so would ingratiate you to those within the Academy?"

Tolan stared at her, and as he did, he began to laugh.

There was nothing else to do or say. Regardless of what he did, Master Irina was going to believe the worst of him. And he wasn't even sure she truly believed what she was accusing him of. That was the hardest part in all of this to wrap his mind around. Part of this was her way of attempting to break him—he was certain of it—and he was so close to letting her. Of admitting whatever she wanted from him. Simply needing to get out of this room.

But if he did, he would be banished from the Academy. He didn't have any idea what punishment there would be, but service of the Draasin Lord would involve death most likely.

"I'm afraid I don't understand what you find quite funny."

"You. This. The Inquisition. All of it." Tolan sighed, throwing his hands up in the air. "I could say anything, and you would twist it however you want. You've already made up your mind, deciding I'm guilty, regardless of whether or not I am. It matters not that I have served the Academy. It matters not that I came here with barely any ability to shape. And it matters not that I had nothing to do with anything that's happened at the Academy. In your mind, you will continue to blame me, calling me a traitor. If there's a traitor, you're looking in the wrong place."

She met his eyes, studying him. "Are you sure?"

"I've told you everything."

"No, Shaper Ethar. You have *not* told me everything."

Tolan groaned, leaning back. "What more do you want me to say?"

She got to her feet and stood with her hands clasped in front of her for a moment, watching him.

Tolan wanted her to disappear, to leave him, if only so he could continue to practice shaping. It was the only relief he had these days, the only reprieve he had from the torment that was his boredom.

Instead, she remained staring at him.

A shaping was building.

It took him a moment—too long—to realize she was

holding onto a shaping. What purpose did she have to be building a shaping as she did now?

He started to build the fire barrier once more, and as before, he inverted it, rotating the heat so that pressed upon him. He ignored the dry heat, ignoring the way his mouth lost all of its moisture, and ignored the slight burning along his skin. There was probably some way of buffering even that, and when he had more time, he would practice. Eventually, he would master all of these things.

Master Irina cocked her head to the side, and, faster than he could react, she reached forward and grabbed each of his wrists.

The shaping flowed out from her. It rolled through him, bypassing the barrier, and Tolan rocked back, collapsing to the ground.

WHEN HIS EYES OPENED, HE LOOKED AROUND. HE WAS NO longer in the room where the Inquisition was taking place. Wherever he was, faint sunlight streamed through a crack in the door. There was a certain warmth hanging over everything, a comforting sense he thought he should recognize, though he didn't. He looked down and realized his head rested upon a pillow. It was softer than any pillow he could remember, and it was covered with a bright yellow silk pillowcase. Embroidery was worked around the end and he ran his fingers along it, feeling a slight bumpiness.

It was pleasant. He couldn't identify the room. He sat up, looking around, and realized wooden walls surrounded him. He was on a bed as plush as the pillow, and silky sheets as soft as the pillowcase covered him.

Had they taken him out of the Inquisition?

He looked toward the source of the light. It wasn't a

door, as he had thought, but a window. A curtain covered it, and he got to his feet, pulling it back. He looked outside and almost stopped breathing.

His parents worked outside the window.

"Mother?" he whispered.

The voice that came out was not his own. It was softer, more childlike, and when he looked down, he realized he was dressed differently than he should be. He was shorter, for one, and he wore a long, flowing gown.

None of this made any sense.

Tolan headed toward the door and pulled it open. As he did, he found himself in a narrow hallway. Walking along it caused everything to shift, to blur past him, and when he reached the end of the hallway, he was in a large room lit by softly glowing orbs. It seemed as if he'd been here before. A smell lingered in the air, a mixture of sawdust and spice. Hanging over everything was a faint char, that of smoke. He took a deep breath, inhaling it all.

It was familiar.

Why should it be? Tolan didn't know this odor and didn't think he'd ever been to this place.

A table along one dimly lit wall caught his attention. A variety of tools rested atop the table. Some, like a rasp or saw, he had seen when working with Master Daniels. Others were different. They were long, slender rods, and still others were even stranger. Pointed ends, of varying thickness and sharpness, were arranged neatly. A large metal file was set at one end of the bench.

It came to Tolan slowly why he felt as if he'd seen this before.

These were the kind of tools his father had kept. They were tools he'd used in his craftsmanship to create items of incredible beauty, items he would turn around and sell, keeping the family housed and fed.

Tolan ran his hand along the bench. It was smooth and cool to the touch. He worked his way along it, feeling for something else, wondering if there might be other tools he would find that would remind him of his father.

He turned, and everything spun again. Now the glowing orbs had taken on a brighter light, illuminating a space at the center of the room. Set upon a table was a half-built length of stone. Striations had been carved into it and Tolan reached for it, running his fingers along it. Resting next to the length of stone was a piece of metal, and he lifted it, twisting it between his fingers, feeling as if he had seen it before, but how—and where?

Setting the metal back down, he walked around the table, staring at the stone. There was power within it, though Tolan didn't know quite why that should be. It seemed to hang within the air, a kind of power that filled the room, a sensation of warmth.

He turned, and once again everything spun, blurring past him.

Now he stood in front of an enormous lacquered table. Chunks had been broken free, and parts of the tabletop seemed as if they had been burned, while others were still smooth, slicked over, flattened. A gentle breeze blew through the room, catching his cloak. He was seated at a bench, and he looked down at hands more callused than he remembered. He was running a file over a piece of stone. Within the stone was power.

Of course, there would be. He had placed that power there. It had taken a shaping, storing it within the stone, but adding to it the memory of other powers, combining them together so others would be able to reach for that same power.

He worked slowly, using the rasp to run his hands along the stone, but it wasn't the metal that did the work. It was a shaping that drew out from his hands, drawing along the length of the stone, and within that shaping came the power needed to change it.

With each steady movement, the stone continued to change, growing, evolving.

As he worked, he became aware of how the stone was changing. It wasn't so much how it was changing outside, though that was a part of it. Placing the runes upon the surface gave it power, locking it in, but it was how it was changed inside that really mattered. There was a connection required, and within that connection, he was able to add patterns, twisting very subtle strands of metal he'd woven within, forming a series of connections that shaped the overall bondar.

Tolan spun, and everything swam around him again.

A bondar. He had memories of a bondar being formed?

How was that even possible?

He knew how it was possible. The Grand Inquisitor had placed those memories in his mind, forcing him to recall it so she could accuse him of more. He had little doubt she would use that against him. Regardless of whatever he might do or say to deny it, she was determined to make him out as the traitor.

When the movement stopped, he was in a different place. Light streamed in through a window. A long counter rested in front of him. A roll of dough sat untouched near the window. It was rising, giving a smell of bread and yeast. The oven radiated heat, giving off a soft warmth, and now he stood there, rolling his hands along the surface of the counter, twisting the strand of dough as he worked.

As he did, he recognized it wasn't dough at all but something else.

Twisting had purpose. Power flowed into it. The same way as before, there were shapings placed, runes added, a series of them, so many he could barely keep track. Dozens upon dozens, all tiny, smaller than any eye could see, and woven in such a way they were all interconnected.

The band was sealed, and hands were cupped around it. The shaping that built was unfamiliar to him, but the power that came from it was incredible. As it built, it flowed into the band, power rising more and more until it crackled within the air.

When the hands were removed, the smooth, silvery surface was revealed.

Tolan had seen this before. He wore one on a necklace taken from his home, but if that were the case, could there really be that many runes worked into such a tiny shape?

He turned and came face to face with his parents.

"You shouldn't be here already," they said.

"Where am I?"

"It's not time for you to be here."

"Why? What did you do?"

His mother took his hand and he felt the warmth of her touch, a soothing caress, and a familiar sense of comfort that came from her. She smiled at him, all the pain and fear fading away, leaving him with a sense of hope—and purpose.

"You need to go now, Tolan."

"I don't know what's happened."

"You do know what's happened. Just as I know you shouldn't have managed to unlock it so soon. As I said, it wasn't your time."

"What did I unlock?"

"Secrets."

"What kind of secrets?"

"The kind of secrets the Academy has wanted."

"I don't understand?"

"You will, but now is not your time."

Tolan glanced from his mother to his father. Was any of this real?

Somehow, he didn't think it was. He might be having this vision, but none of it was happening in the real world, which meant it was all happening within his mind. He remembered the Grand Inquisitor grabbing his wrists, holding onto them the same way as it felt as if his mother did, and her shaping flowed into him.

"Yes."

"Yes what?" Tolan asked.

"That is what happened. It is up to you to prevent that knowledge from escaping."

"Where would it escape to?"

"The Academy."

"Why can't it escape to the Academy? I serve the Academy. I was Selected."

"Of course, you were."

"Of course, I was? I'm not a shaper!"

Was he actually having an argument with his parents within his mind? The idea seemed impossible, and yet—that was what he was doing.

If this was real—if he was having memories of his parents unlocked by the spirit-shaping he suspected coursed through him, was there anything more he could glean from it?

"Were you taken by the Draasin Lord, or do you serve him?"

"Yes," his parents said at the same time.

"That's no answer."

"You must find your own answers, Tolan."

"I'm trying."

"You must continue to try. We've done everything we can to protect you. Unfortunately, it might not have been enough."

"Protect me from who? From what?"

"You must continue to learn. Grow stronger. You will be needed soon."

"I will be needed for what?"

"Find your ancestor."

The image of his parents began to fade and Tolan reached for it, trying to grab it, but it dissipated.

He strained, grabbing again, trying to understand what it was they had done. They were responsible for this, though he had no idea how.

He turned again, expecting everything to spin, but nothing did.

He was standing in his old home. Could that have been where he'd been all along? If so, then what had they wanted him to see?

He turned, walking through the kitchen. There was no strange sense of movement as there had been before. The light he'd seen pouring through the window had faded, leaving it dark. Shadows danced around the edge of his vision, pressing in. The air had a heaviness, a thickness. He wanted to get away from it. It was unpleasant, though Tolan didn't know why it felt like that.

He turned, heading back toward his parents' room. The room had been turned over, everything sorted through, the wardrobe tossed and broken. Even the bed had been torn apart. Someone had come here looking for something.

He made his way toward what had been his room. The room was nothing like what it once had been. There were stacks of stone. Buckets of water. Wind swirled around it all. A flame danced in one corner. In the center was a strange pool of silvery liquid he felt as if he'd seen before.

Tolan backed up and when he did, he felt as if he ran into something.

A barrier.

He felt his way along the barrier, trying to get out.

He'd felt a barrier like this before, but where?

He continued to work his way around the barrier, straining as he struggled to get free of it.

There was nothing he could detect about how to get free from this barrier.

As he made his way through the house, the barrier surrounded him, preventing him from going anywhere but within the house.

"Mother! Father!"

There came no answer. Only an emptiness.

The longer he searched through the house, the more the darkness he saw all around him seemed to swallow everything. Shadows moved at the edges of his vision, and they seemed to grow thicker the longer he turned and looked. There was something here that he thought he was meant to find, but what?

He spun again, hoping for the sense of movement, and he was confined again. The barrier trapped him, squeezing in upon him. The more he fought, the more he felt as if he were trapped.

There was no way to escape.

Tolan hurried through the house. There was only one

place he could move, and that was to the workroom at the back of the house. It was the only part that remained open.

When he threw the door open, blinding white light welcomed him.

Tolan stood at the edge of the doorway, and it felt as if there was something significant about it, but he hesitated to cross over that threshold. If he did, what did it mean? Would he be trapped outside the home?

The barrier continued to press, pushing him further and further away.

He recognized the energy of the barrier. With sudden understanding, he knew this came from the Grand Inquisitor.

All along, he had thought the key to getting past her barrier involved sliding underneath it. He had feared attempting to power through it, afraid of what might happen if he were to do so, not wanting to draw that attention.

Tolan stood in place, fixed, refusing to yield and move away. He focused on a shaping. Would it even work within his mind, trapped as he was?

Power built within him.

With all the practice he'd done over the last month, he recognized the shaping. He wrapped earth and fire, combining the two. The power surged, and he pushed it upon the barrier, but it still wasn't enough. Her magic overpowered him, forcing him back. He was forced into the bright white light. With each step backward, he felt as if something were fading, some part of *him* were fading. If he allowed himself to slide back, he would be lost.

Her spirit shaping.

Tolan knew with sudden certainty that was what it was, but how could he avoid her shaping him? He put everything he could into resisting. Fire and earth weren't enough, but would he be able to summon water and wind?

He'd failed so far, but that didn't mean he would fail now. And now he had a greater need than ever before.

He reached for that power deep within him. It was the same power he drew upon when calling to earth and fire. It was there. He'd had access to it through the Keystone, an ability to reach for that power, but he'd never done so without the bondar.

The stirring of power came to him.

It came slowly, building with intensity, and the longer it came, the more Tolan recognized it. Having worked with water and wind at the Keystone gave him a sense of what it should feel like, and he continued to focus on it, drawing upon that power, calling to it.

Would it answer him?

All he needed was a surge of a connection. All he needed was a fluttering of familiarity. If that came, he knew how to use it.

A stirring came from deep within him. It reminded him of the warmth he'd felt from his mother's touch. It was like a kiss upon his cheek. The summer breeze. The wind tousling her hair. That power surged within him and

Tolan reached for it, summoning the wind, adding it to his shaping.

It left water, but could he reach for water?

A memory of the day his parents disappeared came to him, the hot tears running down his cheeks, and with that memory, he added the power of water to his shaping.

Tolan pushed, combining all four elements together as he forced his way against the barrier. There was a moment where he felt as if he had succeeded. In that moment, he halted the progress of the barrier as it pushed upon him, preventing himself from sliding backward even another step.

And then he was pushed back once more.

Tolan pushed back against the barrier, trying to force his way through it, battering it with the element powers, but his inexperience shaping water and wind didn't grant him the connection to those elements he needed. The shaping wasn't strong enough.

He wasn't strong enough.

It began to unravel. As it did, the barrier continued to force him back, sliding against him, and he slipped further out into the bright white light.

There was emptiness there.

Tolan struggled. He wanted to be anywhere but at emptiness.

Spirit. He had to protect himself with spirit, but how?

He didn't have a connection to spirit, but he believed he'd somehow been protected by it over the years. Somehow, he had managed to avoid getting spirit-shaped, until now.

The only thing that had changed was the physical touch.

He needed to fight. He needed to be strong.

More than that, he needed to find some way of accessing spirit, but he didn't know it.

Or did he?

What had he done with fire? He had protected himself, creating a barrier that had deflected her shaping. He had turned it inward, forcing it so she would not know what he had done.

Tolan started with fire. As he added it, he twisted it, inverting the shaping so it would focus upon him. He turned to earth, adding that element, doing the same thing as he created another barrier, layering it upon himself. The shaping continued to build, wrapping around him, and he inverted it much like he had with the other. Next came wind. Though he didn't know how to use it quite the way he did the others, Tolan wrapped that around him, trying to tie it off, twisting it inward. It was more difficult to wrangle, and it seemed to flutter away, almost like if he tried to pull on it too long, it would dissipate, and he realized he didn't need to force it. All he needed to do was direct where he wanted the shaping, and the connection to the wind would do the rest. Lastly, he added water. Water was healing. Water was restorative. Water was life. Water could also be death. Tolan had felt that when he had nearly drowned while Master Marcella had attempted to forge a connection between him and water, one they both thought he didn't have otherwise.

With the last wrapped around him, he felt a deeper stirring. All of the elements were aligned, and strangely, they were contrasting. Fire and earth shouldn't be stacked in that way, but neither should water and wind. Somehow, the connection allowed him to secure it. He took a step, pushing against the barrier. That step allowed him to take another. And then another. As he did, he forced his way forward, free from the bright light.

Tolan took another step. The barrier began to bulge.

For a moment, he began to think he would succeed.

And maybe he would. It was possible that shaping like this would free him, but then he was forced back once more.

This was all in his mind. He knew it was, and knew it couldn't be real, but at the same time, it *felt* real. It was terrifying, and if he were continually forced backward, he feared he would be dragged into whatever shaping Master Irina intended to use on him.

He needed to fortify the barrier, but his shaping wasn't enough.

Could there be another way to do so?

The elementals.

Tolan had enough of a connection to them to at least think he might be able to succeed. If it worked, if he were able to use the elementals, maybe he would be able to prevent Master Irina from overpowering him.

Which elemental would he focus on first?

Fire. He knew hyza, and he added hyza to his shaping, augmenting what he had done. It took a moment, but slowly—almost painfully—the connection to that elemental flowed into him.

From there, he added jinnar. He didn't need to draw upon the strongest of elementals, only those that would give him an opportunity to fortify his barrier.

Next came wind. He didn't have as much experience with shaping wind, having only spent some time with the wind elementals, thinking of ara while at the Keystone, but he was able to draw upon this, calling to it.

Lastly was water. They were many water elementals, but the one that came to his mind was the one tied to the mist, the spray that had splashed in his face when he had nearly drowned, that of masyn.

It surged, and with it, additional power flowed through him.

He took a step.

The barrier tried to force him back, and Tolan realized that trying to step through the barrier wasn't going to work. He needed something else. He needed a sharper way to puncture the barrier. He needed to force his way. There was no method of sliding beneath it. And attempting to bulge it gave the Grand Inquisitor an opportunity to resist. He didn't want her to have such an opportunity.

Tolan pressed, focusing his shaping to a point. He forced it forward and slammed it into the barrier.

There was no reason that should work. But then, there

was no reason *any* of this should work. It seemed as if his shaping was effective, allowing him to stay free of whatever it was the Grand Inquisitor was doing to him.

He continued to push power into his shaping, honing it into a tight point. It drove like a wedge into the shaping she was trying to press upon him.

The barrier began to fail.

As it did, he became aware of renewed attempts to fight, every attempt to thrash against what he had done, but Tolan resisted. With his shaping honed to a point, he was able to continue to push against what she was doing.

With it sharpened to a point like that, Tolan took a step forward.

The barrier separated.

It did so slowly, parting on either side of the sharpened shaping.

Tolan slammed that wedge again and again against the barrier. He needed to get free. This was his opportunity.

As he hammered, the barrier continued to fail under the onslaught of his shaping.

And then it shattered.

Tolan staggered forward. He half expected to come stumbling out of darkness, but instead of darkness, he stumbled into light.

For a moment, he thought he'd made a mistake and had been redirected, forcing him into the strange bright white light that the Grand Inquisitor had wanted him to go into, but as he stepped forward, warmth flowed over him, reverberating within him, echoing with his connection to the elements—and the elementals.

It was a sense unlike anything he'd ever felt, and he closed his eyes, breathing it in.

Power flowed into him.

The possibility that it was spirit. He wasn't combining any of the elements and didn't think he was tapping into any new power.

Yet, whatever he was doing allowed him to reach some new power.

The only explanation he had was that it was spirit.

Tolan drew that power inward and wrapped it around him, adding to the other elements he already had wrapped around his mind. He had no connection to an elemental, but with this one, it seemed as if he didn't need one. The summoning he'd used for the elementals flowed through him and echoed within his mind.

He held onto this power, reveling in it, feeling as if he could do anything.

It was unlike anything he'd ever imagined. It was the kind of power he could see protecting all the people he cared about. It was the kind of power he understood could be used to destroy. And it was the kind of power he knew to fear.

He released it.

It eased away, but a residual remained, circling a part of him. He let go of his other shapings, knowing he had no choice, his strength fading. Even in his mind—or this vision or dream or whatever it was—there were limits to shaping, much like there were limits in the outside world.

As the power retreated, he clung to it, hoping he could protect himself for just a moment longer. The moment he lost control, he worried Master Irina would find a way to harm him.

He needed to keep her from spirit shaping him, but his strength failed.

Tolan strained to hang onto his shaping, clinging to it, but it slipped away.

Water first. Then wind. Earth followed, though more slowly, and with a strange rumbling sense that rolled through his entire body. Finally, fire. It burned within him, almost as if he could grab at it, but then it began to fade, dissipating, and the longer he attempted to grasp it, the more it left him.

Shaping power departed him. It left him shaking, empty, tired.

A strange thought came to him: Why should he be tired within a dream?

And then that thought began to fade. As everything went black, there was a flash of white light, and he awoke.

TOLAN LOOKED AROUND AND SAW HE WAS IN THE SAME room he'd been in, the Inquisition no longer over as he had believed during his vision. He was trapped, stuck in this place—wherever it was—forced to be a part of whatever the Inquisitors were doing to him. His entire body ached and his head throbbed, leaving him feeling as if he had been out too late drinking in the taverns.

He pushed off the floor and realized he wasn't alone.

Master Irina lay across from him. She didn't move. He scooted back away from her.

As he did, he watched to see if she was still breathing. Her breaths came regularly, her chest rising and falling steadily, and he wasn't sure whether to be relieved or not. It might be easier if she wasn't.

But then, if something had happened to her, he would be the one blamed. In that case, it was better to have her still living. He was already in trouble with the Inquisitors.

If Master Irina ended up dead, there would be no one left to believe him.

As he watched her, he rubbed his knuckle against the side of his temple. His head throbbed, and he was hopeful he could relieve some of the pressure but touching the side of his head left it aching. Lights flashed behind his eyes and he took a deep breath, trying to clear his mind.

Seeing Master Irina like that made him wonder if perhaps what he'd seen in the vision had been real. That shocked him, especially as what he'd experienced had seemed too impossible to believe, yet what other explanation was there for the fact she was lying motionless on the ground?

His shaping had attacked her.

Tolan crawled over to the corner of the room where the barrier was. As he reached for it, he found it missing. He reached through, grabbing his cloak, stuffing the bondars into his pocket, and reaching for his pouch. He was surprised to find his books were still inside.

The only benefit to having these was the opportunity to continue to study the runes that marked each of the elementals, even though he thought he had fully memorized them at this point. He had spent enough time with them.

When he crawled back to the chair, Master Irina still hadn't moved.

He didn't know whether that was a good thing or not. It was possible her lack of movement meant she was far more injured than he knew. And if she was, what would the other Inquisitors do to him?

They would blame him.

Tolan nudged her with his foot. She moaned, but she didn't get up.

He made his way to the door, expecting it to be locked, but it pushed open.

He frowned. Had the barrier that had been around everything—including his belongings—also surrounded the door?

He peeked out into the hallway.

There was no movement. Nothing.

He made his way back to the chair. He could leave, but if he did, it was far more likely the Inquisitors would search him out again. At least here, he could wait and see what Master Irina might do once she awoke. How much of what had happened within his mind would she remember? How much of that had been real—and how much of it had been nothing more than a vision?

He didn't have to wait for long. She began to moan again and sat up slowly, leaning back on her hands, looking around the room before her gaze settled on him. There wasn't the same laziness within her gaze as there normally was.

"Ethar?"

"Yes?"

"What did you do?"

"I didn't do anything."

"You did... something."

Tolan met her gaze, and he wondered whether she would be able to identify what he'd done. For that matter, Tolan wondered if he would be able to identify what he had done. As far as he knew, the only thing he'd done was resist her barrier.

And what would she say if he told her?

Why should he be afraid? He'd fought off a spirit attack and had managed to survive.

There was value in that, and perhaps she might acknowledge it.

"You were trying to shape my mind," he said.

"I was not."

"I felt the effect."

"No. I've been trying to *release* your mind."

"Release it from what?"

"From the trappings you have holding it."

"What trappings?"

"Whatever trappings your parents and the Draasin Lord placed upon it. It seems they also placed some sort of protection. It is interesting," she said, getting to her feet. She was unsteady for a moment before managing to hold herself upright. She looked around the room before her gaze settled on him again, seemingly noticing the cloak and the pouch. "What do you think you're doing?"

"I think you've held me long enough."

"I am the Grand Inquisitor. I will decide how long you are held."

"You have accused me time and again of something I have no part of. And I'm done with it. It's time for me to return to my classes." He started to stand but she wrapped him in a shaping, forcing him down.

Tolan reacted, and the same shaping he'd performed inside the vision, the wedge that had carved through her barrier, formed, and he slammed through the shaping she was trying to wrap around him. It cut through it, and she staggered back a step.

He didn't think he had reached for the bondar, but now they were close to him, it was possible he had. He was tired and weakened after everything he'd been through and didn't think he would have enough strength to fight her off if it came down to it. Besides, he didn't have the same level of knowledge as Master Irina to oppose her in any realistic way.

"I just want to return to my studies."

"Do you think you can?"

He met her gaze, and as he did, the door opened. The Grand Master stood within it. He wasn't a large man, but he was imposing, and power radiated from him. It was shaping power, a combination of each of the elements, all swirling together, forming a powerful shaping.

How was he feeling that?

He was usually aware of shaping, but never aware of particular elements being used within a shaping. This was different, and as he paid attention to it, he could feel the nature of the elements within the shaping.

What had happened within that vision?

His parents had been there, and he had seen bondars being made, and he had seen the way the shaping had been used to create them. He could remember those shapings almost as if he had that knowledge stored within his mind.

It was much like the book he'd read through with Master Minden.

What had he seen in that vision?

His parents had given him a warning, but what sort of warning was it?

"What is taking place here?" the Grand Master asked.

"Shaper Ethar has decided the Inquisition is over," the Grand Inquisitor said.

"Is it?"

The Grand Inquisitor looked at him. "We have held him for nearly thirty days."

"Much longer than you agreed to, I seem to recall."

"You are not one of the Inquisitors," the Grand Inquisitor said, shooting a look in his direction.

"Must I be an Inquisitor to recognize the aberrancy within this? We both know this is highly unusual."

"Everything about this is highly unusual," she said.

"Including your response. I doubt a student shaper would be able to withstand an Inquisition for as long as this if he wasn't telling the truth. It's time for this to be over."

"I am the Grand—"

"I am the Grand Master of the Academy. You have one of my students, and it's time this is over."

The Grand Master nodded to Tolan and motioned for him to follow.

Tolan breathed out a sigh of relief and followed the Grand Master. They made their way along a narrow hallway. Several other Inquisitors were standing there, watching, and the Grand Master ignored them, continuing to lead Tolan past them.

When they reached the end of the hall, a narrow staircase headed upward. Tolan trailed behind the Grand Master up the stairs and around the corner before realizing they were once again on the main level of the Academy. He hadn't known where he was, but there apparently was some sort of lower level to the Academy, a series of cells, and now he was out of it, the Grand Master paused, turning to him.

"You will find there will be many questions asked of you."

"I'm sure of that," Tolan said.

"You will also begin to question yourself. You will wonder what you did to deserve the Inquisition. There was a time when many shapers faced an Inquisition, and it wasn't nearly as uncommon. The Grand Inquisitor seems to recall those days far too fondly."

The Grand Master hesitated, looking along the hall. At the end of it, the Grand Inquisitor appeared, and she stood for a moment before disappearing. There was a part of Tolan that feared she would grab him again and force him into another Inquisition. If she did, he wondered if he would ever be able to escape it.

"She fears what she doesn't understand," he said.

"Why would she fear me?"

"Because she doesn't understand you," he said.

"What is there to understand?"

"The nature of your shaping is different. She noticed that the very first time she met you. And it troubled her. She doesn't understand why you should have different shaping, only that it isn't anything like what most within the Academy have."

"That was why she brought me down there?"

"No. She brought you there because she wonders whether you are a part of what is taking place all around Terndahl."

"What is taking place around Terndahl?"

The Grand Master looked at him for a moment, studying him, and then shook his head. "I don't think I should share that with you, Shaper Ethar. You have been involved in enough as it is. If I reveal more to you, we run the risk of you getting involved in additional activities you should not. It's better this way."

"Thank you," Tolan said.

"If only I were able to rescue you sooner. I tried, but as she said, I don't have any influence when it comes to an Inquisition. It's something of a marvel she allowed me to bring you with me as it is." He patted Tolan on the shoulder. "Go and get some rest. At this point, I think you need it."

Tolan watched him disappear down the hallway. He took a deep breath and looked around the main level of the Academy. It had been so long since he'd been here, so long since he had been out of that room, anywhere but in that darkened space, surrounded by the walls and the shaping power the Grand Inquisitor possessed. Although he was tired, he didn't want to return to his room. Not yet.

Going back meant answering questions. He wasn't sure he was ready for the questions he'd get, and more than that, he wasn't sure he was ready to face the people who would be asking them. There would be Wallace and Jonas and Ferrah. And then there would be the others, those who may or may not have been questioned about him, but those who would have already made up their mind about his guilt.

He started off, pausing at the library for a moment, glancing inside and seeing Master Minden making her way along the rows of shelves. She hesitated, almost as if aware that he was there, and turned slightly toward the doorway. He caught a momentary flash of her milky white eyes, but then she continued onward.

That had to have been imagined. There was no way Master Minden would be able to detect him from this far out. There would come a time when he would return to the library, when he would see what else he could learn about spirit now he'd had that strange connection within the vision, but now wasn't the time.

What he needed was to get away.

He headed out of the Academy building and reached the grounds outside. From here, the sun shone down on him, a gentle breeze gusted, reminding him of the visions, and he let out a sigh, allowing himself to relax. Now he was here, he felt as if he finally could relax.

Tolan made his way toward the distant park. He wandered through the trees, letting his connection to earth stretch out, feeling the way the roots of the trees twined together. Farther from him, near the center of the park, was the pond. He found himself drawn toward it, compelled to make his way toward that body of water, and when he stepped up to the shore, there was a sense of peace.

He focused on the water. Could he shape it?

He didn't have a bondar, but maybe he didn't need it. In the vision, he'd been able to reach water, connecting to it, and had used that to layer upon his mind. Right now, all he wanted was some way of layering a protection upon him, a relaxing sweep of healing power, though that might be too much to ask.

The connection to water came to him quickly.

It was familiar. He did what he'd done in his vision, reaching for that deep part of him, connecting to the sense of moisture in his mouth, the blood in his veins, and feeling power swell up from deep within him. As he did, he reached for the water, pulling it into a spiral.

It reacted, spinning slowly in place. The spiral rotated around and around, and then he held it, spinning it out, forming a platform.

These were all shapings he had been forced to try during his water shaping sessions, but never had he been able to do them. He went through a few other water shapings, each of them increasingly complex, and when he neared the end of the series of water shaping that he'd never managed to do before, he took a step back, breathing out.

As his breath left his lips, he connected to the wind. The stirring from deep within him reverberated with the wind, echoing with it, and he sent a soft swirling breeze twisting around him.

He could shape.

The power came from within him and not from the elementals, and yet... When it had come down to it, when he had needed to protect himself, to use shaping to defend his mind, he had called upon both his connection to shaping—and the elementals.

Could it be that he somehow had a way of using both?

He stood at the shore of the pond for a long time, feeling the caress of the wind, the earth beneath his boots, the warmth of the sun, and even the soft murmuring of water as it headed toward the pond. It was the reason this place had been built, a way for student shapers to connect to the elements, and he understood it in a way he had never understood it before.

Tolan lost track of how long he stood there. The sound of voices in the distance tore him from his reverie and he drifted toward the trees, hiding within them, wishing he had some shaping that could mask him. There was a way of hiding within a shaping, but it was one he didn't know.

He remained hidden as the students made their way through, unaware of his presence. They were all first-level students, and he recognized them because Velthan walked among them, talking loudly, shaping building from him, but also from the others.

The last thing he wanted was to encounter Velthan as the first person upon leaving the Inquisition.

Tolan drifted back through the trees, heading out of the park in a different direction, and wound through the streets. There was an energy here, a vibrancy, and he had been aware of it before. As he walked, he realized he could feel it from everyone around him. Every so often, he paused to watch some of the carts roll past or to listen to the shop owners shouting at people making their way through, trying to cajole them into coming into their stores. At one building, the sound of music drifted out, a combination of strings and a flute and a sweet voice that hung above it all. The song tugged at him, pulling upon some hidden part of him. He stood in the doorway for a while, listening and saying nothing. Several others made their way past him, heading into the tavern and grabbing drinks, but Tolan wanted nothing to do with that. All he wanted was to listen to the music.

During a break in the music, he tore himself away and continued to wander through the city. That same energy surrounded him.

The longer he went, the tenser he began to feel. He would have to return to his room eventually, and he knew he was avoiding it. Returning meant facing questions. Questions meant explaining what had happened, though others would already know. Tolan hadn't decided how much he wanted to share with others, but as he went, he decided it didn't matter. Let people think the Grand Inquisitor had questioned him about his involvement with the Draasin Lord. He had come out of the Inquisition without any consequences. That should be answer enough for his guilt.

Only, he knew all too well that regardless of whether he actually was, they would think him guilty.

He reached the edge of the city, and he looked out toward the forest along the rolling road that led into Amitan. Every so often, he would glance up, feeling shaping high above, and he would listen to the passing of others upon the Shapers Path. Blooms of power reverberated, various shapers working throughout the city, and he finally found himself drawn back toward the Academy. It was near dark when he reached the doors, pausing for a moment before heading inside. He walked slowly, pleasantly surprised that the hallways were mostly empty. The few people here didn't glance in his direction. If they did, would they stop and stare?

The doors to the library were thrown open, and he paused. The desks inside the library were empty, no students sitting around them. Master Kelly and Master Minden sat up on the dais, and Tolan took a deep breath before heading inside. He walked slowly toward the back of the library, reaching into his pouch and withdrawing the books. When he neared the dais, he slid the books across to Master Minden.

She looked up. There was a tingling sensation he

attributed to a shaping, and then it faded. "You are done with these?"

"I figured I should give them back to you before anything else happens to me."

"What else do you anticipate happening to you, Shaper Ethar?"

"I was brought in for an Inquisition."

"So I heard."

"These books raised particular questions with the Grand Inquisitor."

"Why would these raise any questions with the Grand inquisitor?"

Tolan shrugged. "She accused me of siding with the Draasin Lord." There was no point in denying the accusations against him, and Master Minden didn't seem as if she cared.

"Seeing as how you no longer face the Inquisition, I presume you have been deemed reliable?"

"I don't side with the Draasin Lord."

"No. I would never have suspected you did. Had the Grand Inquisitor only come to me, I would have shared with her that you had borrowed these volumes from the library under my purview."

"I appreciate that, but I don't think she was interested in whether or not I was actually guilty of her accusations."

"That's unfortunate."

Tolan shrugged. "I'm not sure that matters."

"Why wouldn't it matter?"

"She's the Grand Inquisitor. She is the one who

Selected me. And she gets to decide what role the Grand Inquisitor plays."

Master Minden stared at him for a moment, her gaze lingering. "Did you discover anything?"

A small smile spread across his face. "I think so."

"And what is that?"

"That I no longer need these books."

She laughed softly. "I suppose you have had them for long enough. There are other volumes we have at your disposal, Shaper Ethar. I have not returned the rest."

He smiled to himself. "I would like the opportunity to continue reading them if the invitation remains."

"It does. I am not so harsh as an Inquisitor. I understand you didn't have a hand in the events the Grand Inquisitor would accuse you of. Then again, seeing as how she didn't come to me, I wasn't able to vouch for you."

"Thank you."

"What is that thanks for?"

"I think something in the book your ancestor wrote helped me understand something about myself."

"Is that right? A thousand-year-old book helped you understand something?"

"I thought that was the point of these books."

"For the most part, but some of these are old enough that we wonder what we can learn from them. Many have questioned the benefit of some of the older works. I'm pleased to hear you aren't one of them."

Tolan breathed out and smiled. "I've been avoiding returning to the student section," he admitted.

"You fear what your friends will say?"

"I worry what sort of spirit shaping was placed upon them," he said.

"There is no spirit shaping that can't be removed." She settled her hands on the desk and leaned forward. "Even the most potent spirit shaping can be unraveled. It may take time, and it may be difficult, but if you're patient and you have that time, anyone can eventually make their way through a spirit shaping." Her eyes seemed to clear for a moment, though Tolan knew that had to be his imagination. She leaned back, drawing her notebook back in front of her, and nodded. "If you don't fear your friends, then do you fear those who you aren't as friendly with?"

"I think I did, but strangely, a walk through the city brought me a certain peace."

"In this place, many who are sensitive to such things can find that peace."

"Sensitive to what things?"

"Why, to spirit. To that which binds us all together." She glanced down at her book. Lifting up a pen, she began writing. "Get some rest, Shaper Ethar. It sounds as if you need it."

He headed out of the library, his steps slowing the farther he got. When he reached the stairs, he took them one at a time, making his way up them, his heart speeding up and a nervous nausea beginning to burrow in the pit of his stomach.

It was foolish for him to feel this way. He had wanted nothing more than to escape the Inquisition. Every day the Inquisitors came, he had hoped to get away from them, to find a measure of peace, and every day he had failed. Now he was out, now he was free, he would dread going to his room?

What was the worst they could do or say to him?

Tolan stood tall when he reached the second-level floor. There was a steady murmur of voices in the common area. He started through it, keeping his focus on the far end of the hallway, the area behind the common area, and ignored the way the voices died off with his return. He reached his doorway before anyone started talking again. When he stepped inside, there was an excited chaos.

Ferrah was here, as were Jonas and Wallace. All were flipping through notebooks, presumably studying.

It took a moment for them to look up.

"Tolan?" Ferrah asked. She jumped out of the bed, racing toward him, throwing her arms around him.

He sank into her embrace, thankful for it.

"What happened to you?" she asked.

"An Inquisition."

A strange expression crawled across her face, and she frowned. "Why so long?"

Wallace sat with his back to the wall, watching Tolan and saying very little. It was fitting, and Tolan wondered what he must be thinking. The Inquisitors would have come to him, asking about Tolan, and then Wallace would have shared with him the fact Tolan had wanted to make a bondar. What did Wallace think about that?

And there was Jonas. He sat quietly, leaning forward, his elbows resting on his thighs, his brow clouded. Had he grown so distant with Tolan that he no longer even wanted to speak to him?

"I don't know."

"You don't know why they had you?" Ferrah asked.

Tolan took a deep breath, glancing from Ferrah to Jonas before looking at Wallace for a brief moment. "They accused me of serving the Draasin Lord."

Jonas gasped. "What?"

"Apparently, there has been enough strangeness since my arrival at the Academy that they accused me of serving the Draasin Lord."

"Why not accuse me?" Jonas asked. "Or Ferrah. Or Draln. Or any one of the second-level students who have been here the entire time you were here?" He glanced from Ferrah to Tolan. "I thought it was all about the bondars. With the rumors going around, and the shaping you made before you disappeared, I thought you were stealing them."

"I never stole a bondar, Jonas."

"You were able to shape much better than what I remember you being able to do. Something happened."

"Something happened," Tolan said. He held his hands out, and with a quick shaping of fire, he caused the flame to swirl, and then he settled it down, turning into smoke, and then into sparks that dissipated into the air. "They held me so long, I began to understand my shaping."

"You *what?*" Jonas asked.

Tolan shrugged. "I had nothing but time, and when you're bored, you begin to experiment. At least, I did."

Jonas glanced at his pocket. "That wasn't with a bondar?"

"Not with the bondar." Tolan took a seat on his bed, thankful it was still his bed. He was tired. He should have returned earlier in the day, and now he was here, back around Ferrah and seeing the way Jonas welcomed him back, he wondered if perhaps he had made a mistake in delaying his return.

"I'm sorry I put you through all of that," he said. He didn't look up, not wanting to meet any of their eyes, but realized he owed it to them. It would have been his fault the Inquisitors would have come to them. "I don't know what they put you through, but I'm sorry." He looked at Wallace, meeting his gaze. The other man nodded before turning his attention back to his books. Tolan glanced over to Jonas, and he only shook his head.

"You're the one apologizing to us?"

"It's my fault, and you were subjected to the Great Mother only knows what. I don't even know if they spirit-shaped you, and I doubt you would know, either."

Jonas frowned. "Why would they have spirit-shaped us?"

"Because the Grand Inquisitor was trying to pressure me to admit I was working with the Draasin Lord. I think she wanted to have others ready for the possibility."

"Tolan," Ferrah said, taking a seat on the bed next to him, "we didn't talk to any of the Inquisitors."

"You didn't what?"

She shook her head. "None of the Inquisitors came to us."

"What do you mean? The Grand Inquisitor said she had come to you. She knew..." The fact they didn't remember told him they had been spirit-shaped. And a shaping like that would have taken all memories.

"Did you know I was at an Inquisition?"

"Of course," Ferrah said. "You were seen dragged through the halls by Inquisitors."

That was odd. Why would the Grand Inquisitor try to spirit shape his friends to make it so they didn't remember getting questioned?

Unless they *hadn't* been questioned.

If they hadn't been questioned, how would the Grand Inquisitor have known some of the things she had known?

"Did anyone come to question you?"

"The only person who came to us was the Grand Master," Ferrah said. "He wanted to understand why the Grand Inquisitor would have been interested in you. He didn't tell us anything other than that you would be released soon. That was over a month ago."

Tolan leaned back. There was something he'd missed. Why would the Grand Master have come to his friends? And why would the Grand Inquisitor make it seem as if it had been her?

Maybe he *had* been spirit-shaped. As much as he had believed he had avoided it, it was possible he had been.

Voices approached the doorway, and Jonas looked over. "You'd better be ready to answer questions, Tolan."

He sat up. It seemed as if he wasn't going to be able to get any rest. It was better to get this over with now than to drag it out. With a sigh, he headed out toward the common area.

19

ALL TOLAN WANTED WAS FOR EVERYTHING TO GET BACK TO a semblance of normalcy, but unfortunately, there didn't seem to be a normalcy. His return was greeted by the excitement he'd expected, the stirring voices of everyone else all clamoring to find out what he'd done to be subjected to an Inquisition. It didn't matter to some that he'd been sent back. There were plenty who believed him guilty only because he'd been subjected to an Inquisition in the first place.

Tolan made a point of trying to stay in the background as much as possible. That was easy enough, as he had never really wanted to draw attention to himself before, and now he certainly didn't want the attention of most people. He stayed off to the side, or the back of his classes, and made a point of not speaking too loudly or saying anything that might be controversial. It was easier that way.

Classes continued to go relatively well. That was the strange and unexpected consequence of the Inquisition. Tolan had a command over his shaping that he'd not before. With that, he was far better able to handle the rigors of his classes.

The first one he returned to was the fire-shaping classroom. Master Sartan had nodded to him, saying nothing, and Tolan had demonstrated the shaping they were asked to do. He hadn't even attempted to reach for his bondar, though he still carried it with him. It was much the same in the earth class, where Master Shorav had looked at him askance for longer than Master Sartan, but he welcomed Tolan back without much else to say. The shaping Tolan managed was far more complicated than any he had attempted before. He still hadn't gone after a bondar.

By the end of the week after his return, as he was heading toward the wind-shaping classroom, Tolan thought life could get back to what it had been. He was allowing himself to get back into the routine, and the more he did, the more he felt as if he were a part of the Academy once again. There had been no further sign of Master Irina, and if she was still out for him, searching for something to blame on him, she hadn't come forward. There hadn't been any evidence of any of the other Inquisitors, either. And, thankfully, there were none of the so-called strange events that had occurred ever since Tolan had arrived at the Academy.

He sat at the back of the classroom in the wind shaping session, the first of the two elements he'd never effectively shaped in the classroom before. Master Rorn paced along the front of the room, his back to the others, and he was making shapes in the air with a shaping.

The one big change was that Tolan no longer sat next to Jonas. As much as Jonas had welcomed him back—and he had—Jonas still showed some reluctance to be fully associated with Tolan. He didn't even blame his friend for it. Were the situations reversed, would he have done anything different? Never mind the fact he knew he would.

Tolan took a space at the back and watched as the rest of the class filed in. Every so often, someone would glance over at him, and there were looks upon faces that left him wondering what they were thinking. It did no good to spend too much time worrying about it.

"Today we'll discuss the shaping involved in hovering," Master Rorn said, his back still to the classroom. "This is a more complicated shaping, though not nearly as complex as traveling on wind. Many of you have gained some competence in performing various shapings we've attempted, but very few of you have much control." He turned back around, his gaze sweeping around the class-room. He paused at Draln, his gaze lingering, and then moved on to Jonas. Both of the men were accomplished wind shapers. When he reached Tolan, his gaze lingered the longest, staring at him, a shaping building that Tolan could feel exploding out from him. There was a heavy component of wind within it, but there was something more than just wind. Was it earth? It seemed to be.

The shaping swept toward him, and Tolan resisted the urge to oppose it. He doubted Master Rorn would attack him with a shaping in the front of the class.

When it washed over him, there was a tingling across his skin, a reminder of the shaping he often felt from Master Minden. It wasn't uncomfortable, just there.

"As I was saying, many of you have some ability, but very few of you have any control. The key part of this shaping is mastering a level of control. Once you master control, that will allow you to hover and then you will be able to take the next step, which is a little more complicated."

He demonstrated the shaping. As he did, Tolan could feel the way wind whipped around Master Rorn, lifting him into the air. It held him up, allowing him to float, and he maintained the shaping for a moment, then two, then a little longer. He released it, lowering himself back to the floor gently. Through it all, there was no other disruption around the room. That might be the most impressive part of the shaping. He had such control over it that he was able to lift himself into the air without disrupting anything else.

"In this shaping, you must channel the element, and you must force it out from you, releasing the wind slowly."

There were chuckles around the room and Master Rorn surveyed the others.

"Do you find it amusing? Is the wind not powerful enough of an element for you?"

Power began to build, the force of a gale whipping around, pushing everyone back. It lasted for a moment before fading. It surprised Tolan that Master Rorn would find it necessary to demonstrate the power of the wind. There were very few people at the Academy who doubted its strength.

"As I said, this will be a complicated shaping, but it's one you must demonstrate in order to continue your studies."

The master shapers rarely let the students know which of the shapings would be critical for passing beyond their level, but it seemed as if Master Rorn had no intention of hiding the fact this shaping was one of the more important ones. What was it that made hovering with the wind so critical?

Maybe it was nothing more than the control required in order to do it. That would be difficult enough, and considering Tolan's record of shaping, he wasn't sure he would be able to have that kind of control.

"You may begin to practice," Rorn said, pulling out the tray of bondars. "I will be making my way through the classroom and working with you."

One by one, students in need of bondars went to the front of the class, taking one from the tray. Tolan hesitated. Should he grab one? It was expected of him, but he also wasn't sure whether he even needed one. He had continued to demonstrate a connection to all of the elements. With that connection, he didn't think he needed a bondar.

Would it raise questions if he didn't take one? He didn't want to draw attention to the fact something about him had changed, and there were certainly plenty of people in the class who knew he needed bondars for his shaping. Many probably expected him to take one.

Tolan got out of his seat and went to the tray. As he reached for one, Master Rorn looked at him sternly. "I expect that bondar to be returned, Shaper Ethar."

"Of course, Master Rorn. I've always returned the bondar at the end of class."

Master Rorn cocked his head to the side, watching him. "Always?"

Tolan nodded quickly. "I'll make sure I get it back to you."

He hurried back to his table, ignoring the pointed stares of a few of the students who had sat near enough to the front of the room to have overheard. Taking a seat, he stared at the bondar. Had it really gotten to the point where even the master shapers now accused him of the same things as the Inquisitors? He hadn't seen anything like that from Master Sartan or Master Shorav, but maybe they hadn't been quite as forward with it. Both would have more reason than Master Rorn to have accused him in such a way, especially as he had bondars of both of the elements in his possession. Neither had made an accusation like that.

He sighed, focusing on the bondar. He could think about the shaping, and perhaps he would practice it, but it might be easier—and better—if he did so outside of class and outside of the prying eyes of students who now had certain expectations of him.

His mind went back to the vision he'd had of the creation of the bondar. The wind bondar was different than the others, mostly in its thin, almost spindly appearance. It trailed in a wide circle, giving it something of a delicateness, enough that Tolan and the other students had always been fearful of damaging it. He couldn't imagine stuffing the wind bondar into his pocket, though the withering would probably withstand the jostling. It might seem delicate, but it really was far stronger than it appeared.

The runes along the side were familiar. Tolan had spent long periods of time reviewing them, documenting them, and was fully aware of what the runes were and which element they represented. On the wind bondar, there were over a dozen various runes.

At least on the outside.

The thought from his vision came to him, and he began to wonder if perhaps there were more runes marked inside the bondar. That was part of its creation. The metal within the interior of the bondar, hidden from view, had also taken on shapes of runes. He couldn't remember whether they were elemental runes or whether they were simply runes that marked the elements. He had a sense there were differences between the two, though not quite what those differences were.

He pulled upon the wind, feeling that stirring deep within him, and there came a soft fluttering around his hands. It was a faint shaping, and Tolan was careful not to pull on too much power and let it flow into the bondar. As he did, he tried to pay attention to what he felt as he drew upon power through the bondar.

There was nothing.

Maybe that was the wrong approach. He didn't want to draw power through the bondar. He wanted to push his shaping into it and wanted to see what he might be able to uncover from within the bondar itself.

As he shaped, he pushed that connection to wind into the bondar. It resisted, but he continued to push, a little bit more and more.

The resistance continued to build and Tolan released his connection, fearful that if he pushed too hard, he might damage the bondar. Maybe wind wasn't necessary to understand the shaping involved. What if he attempted earth?

He summoned his connection to earth and began to push it into the withering, but much like it had with wind, there was a resistance.

That wasn't the key.

Could it be water? Wind and water were opposites, counters with the elements, and so it didn't seem as if it would make sense for it to be water, but perhaps it was. He drew upon water, finding it easier than he remembered, and sent that connection into the withering. It flowed slowly, but it also met resistance.

Rather than forcing it, Tolan retreated, drawing back from his connection to it, and decided to try fire last.

Maybe he should have tried fire first, as fire and wind were complementary, though not quite as complementary as earth and wind. He pushed on fire, and because he had a greater connection to fire, his shaping went more rapidly. As it met resistance, he again retreated, withdrawing before damaging the withering.

That wasn't the key.

How was he to understand how the shaping was made?

Unless each of these elements wasn't the one he needed to use.

Could it be spirit?

Tolan didn't have any way of connecting to spirit. He still thought he might have reached spirit in his vision but had no idea what he'd done or whether he could repeat it. Even if he could repeat it, he didn't have enough control. He would be far too likely to damage the withering if he approached with spirit.

He sat back, staring at the withering. There were answers within it, but it seemed as if he wouldn't be able to reach them.

"Shaper Ethar. Do you intend to work, or will you be contemplating how to rescue the bondar from my classroom?"

Tolan looked up and met Master Rorn's eyes. Others in the classroom laughed nervously and heat began to rise in him, starting in his neck and working up toward his face. "I will be shaping, and then I will be returning the bondar, Master Rorn. Thank you for your concern."

He turned his attention back to the withering, ignoring the muttering around him. Tolan set the withering down, ignoring it, too. He focused on wind, the shaping Master Rorn had demonstrated. He could see it within his mind and recognized what was involved.

There was a release of wind as he had said, but it was a controlled release, and it needed to be not only from beneath him, but on all sides, holding him in place. He was tempted to attempt the shaping but decided against it. If he did, all he would do would be to bring attention to the fact he might not need the withering.

Instead, he sat and watched others in the class. Jonas had little difficulty with hovering. He demonstrated it over and again, lifting himself in the air before settling back down. Draln did the same, hovering in place before floating around the classroom, completely controlled, disrupting nothing, no differently than Master Rorn had done.

Master Rorn looked upon Draln with approval. Ferrah had some success and remained in place as the shaping held her in the air. They were the only three who did so without a withering. Others were using the bondar, holding it as they attempted their shapings, and many students were able to lift themselves, though some did so far more rapidly than others. Master Rorn made his way around the class, preventing students from slamming into the ceiling overhead. Occasionally, he had to bring them back down when they hovered too high and feared releasing it. He made his way around the desks, murmuring something to each student before moving on.

When he reached Tolan, he stared down at the withering. "You refuse to even try?"

"I'm not a skilled wind shaper," Tolan muttered.

"There is no shame in admitting your deficiencies, but all students must attempt to shape in class. I would like to see your attempt."

Tolan squeezed his eyes shut and reached for the withering. He had to be careful. He began shaping, pulling upon the stirring of wind within him, and released it. It came out as a trickle, barely more than that, and he listed off his seat. He floated in the air, and compensated for the movement, preventing himself from sliding too far off to the side. He began to shift again, and he compensated again.

Opening his eyes, he saw Master Rorn watching him. It seemed as if there was a pressure upon him, a shaping, and he realized Master Rorn was attempting to force him down.

Tolan clenched his jaw. It reminded him too much of what Master Irina had done during the Inquisition. Much like her, he was trying to use a band of shaping to drop him, to force him to his will.

Tolan added earth to his shaping, and he honed it to an edge, carving through the shaping trying to hold him down. When it sliced through Master Rorn's shaping, Tolan went shooting up.

There were gasps in the classroom, but Tolan quickly

320 | D.K. HOLMBERG

adjusted, shifting the nature of the wind shaping. He released just a little, enough that he would be able to keep from slamming into the ceiling, and then began to lower. He dropped slower and slower until he was hovering right in front of Master Rorn. He held the withering tightly in his hand, and Master Rorn grabbed it from him.

Tolan maintained the shaping for a moment. Master Rorn's eyes widened slightly, and Tolan let go of his shaping.

"At least you've tried," Master Rorn said.

He turned and headed back to the front of the classroom, leaving Tolan staring at his back. He took a seat, not looking up or at anyone else in the classroom.

Master Rorn set the withering down on Tolan's desk.

And it was possible he had been going about it all wrong. He had assumed it was using the elements within the withering to release that power, but what if it hadn't been the elements at all, but the elementals?

If it was the elementals, then there was a risk of something much more.

Tolan pushed the withering aside and simply sat, staring at his hands.

He felt empty. It was strange for him to feel that way, considering he had spent all of his time wanting nothing more than to be able to reach for shaping. He'd wanted this. Wanted to be able to reach for the wind, to manage to shape more than just fire, and now it was fire and earth and wind and water. There was hope for even spirit.

Despite his success, why did he feel this way?

He returned the withering to the front of the class, setting it on the tray, catching Master Rorn's eye. He wasn't going to have Master Rorn accused him of stealing it. The wind shaper stared at him for a moment, saying nothing.

Tolan turned away, returning to his seat, and sat there silently.

After a while, Master Rorn made his way back to the front of the classroom and began to speak, going through his lecture on the various elementals. Tolan barely paid any attention. There was no point. He was able to recite everything Master Rorn was saying and could even correct some of the inaccuracies. And there *were* inaccuracies, something that hadn't bothered him before, but now it did.

When the class was finally over, Tolan shuffled out, not wanting to talk to anyone. What would he say, anyway? There wasn't anything to speak about, other than to acknowledge the fact he'd been singled out.

He reached the main level of the Academy and headed back outside. Once there, he noticed that clouds covered the sky. He hurried off to the park, wanting solitude, and managed to avoid students who were making their way to the same location.

He took a seat near the pond, on the far side where students rarely went. He reached for the various elements, shaping them, and continued to walk through the various shapings he had been taught since coming to the Academy. Why not practice if he had nothing else to do?

Footsteps behind him caused him to turn around and look up.

"I thought I might find you here," Ferrah said.

"You don't want to be seen with me."

"Why would you say that?"

"You heard Master Rorn."

"That's one master."

"Master Sartan and Master Shorav will be the same. I don't doubt Master Wassa will be, too. It might be best for you to stay away from me for a little while."

"I get to decide what's best for me, Tolan."

"I know that. It's just—"

"It's just that you're trying to push people away." She fell silent for a moment, and Tolan didn't say anything to break the silence. What was there to say, anyway? "What was that back there?"

"What was what?" Tolan asked.

"That shaping. What was it?"

"It was nothing."

"It was more than nothing. You were holding yourself in the air far better than you should have been able to do. What were you doing?"

"I was shaping."

"I'm aware you were shaping, I'm just trying to get a sense of what sort of shaping you're doing."

"I think it was a frustrated one."

"You didn't need to react quite so strongly when Master Rorn was doing that."

Tolan shot her a look. "I get to decide what's best for me, Ferrah."

"Not when you're being foolish about it."

He breathed out. It wasn't that he wanted to get away from Ferrah. He was happy to have her sitting with him. It was more that he wished he could do something a little differently than he had.

"What really happened to you during your Inquisition?"

"Nothing they didn't want to happen to me," he said.

"You've changed. You would never have snapped at a master shaper before, and to Master Rorn, of all people?"

"He was antagonizing me."

"Did you consider the possibility he was doing so to see what reaction he might get out of you?"

"Then he got exactly what he wanted."

"Maybe he did, but is that what you wanted? Do you want to continue to draw attention for things like that? Or do you want to continue your studies at the Academy?"

He sighed again. "Since coming here, all I've ever wanted was to understand how to shape and feel as if I were a part of something. And for some reason, I just don't. It's been so many different things. Not only my inability to shape when I first got here, but everything that's transpired since then."

"Only because you allow it to set you apart."

"I'm not sure that's it. I think I was set apart from the very beginning." It was the reason Master Irina had been willing to accept him as a Selection. Had she wanted him to fail?

What purpose would there be in wanting that for him? Unless she already had known about Master Daniels and was trying to draw him out.

There were so many different things that raced through his head, and all he wanted to do was sit here and practice shaping, working on the various techniques he had learned, trying to understand how his ability was so different than others'.

"I'm going to continue my studies," he said. "I'll do my best to avoid angering any more of the master shapers."

Ferrah flashed a smile at him. "It shouldn't be difficult. I thought if anyone would irritate you, it would be Master Sartan, but the two of you have gotten along quite well."

"Only because I was able to reach for fire from the very beginning," he said.

"And now you can reach each of the elements. Without a bondar." She watched him, saying nothing for a moment. "I observed you for a little while before coming. I saw you shaping. That was something else you weren't able to do before your Inquisition. What did they do to you?"

"They might have unlocked something within me," Tolan said. He focused on his various connections to the elements, feeling fire, then earth, then wind and water. Each of them flowed deep within him, a connection that he could reach and claim. "I still don't know if they were successful in spirit shaping me."

"You can't spirit shape an ability to reach the element bonds."

"What if they unlocked something?"

"Then it was already there."

Memories of the vision and battling with Master Irina came back to him. He had fought her, resisting the barrier she had attempted to push around him, and in doing so, he had managed to connect to each of the element bonds, discovering a way of shaping he hadn't known before. If only he could reach for spirit, then perhaps he wouldn't have to fear a spirit shaping upon him. As it was, he still didn't know if she was using a spirit shaping on him.

"I can see in your eyes there's something more you haven't said, and I won't push it. Just know I'm here if you need me. I'm willing to help you." She laid back, resting on her elbows and looking up at the sky. "Great Mother. I'm not even able to shape all four of the elements quite that well."

"Maybe you need to be subjected to an Inquisition."

Her eyes widened. "I think I'd prefer to continue working on my own, thank you very much. I can work with you, Tolan. I might not have all the answers, but we're more alike than you realize."

"How is that?"

"Because Par is along the edge of Terndahl. You might not see it from Ephra, but most of those within Terndahl view Par as some backward place. And maybe we are, but it was still home to me. I'd hoped I could better understand that home by coming to the Academy. I still hope that."

"What did you hope to learn about Par at the Academy?"

"I wanted to better understand the markings. Some of the ancient ruins have writings upon them that has significance, but even the people who study such things haven't been able to fully understand them. I was hopeful I could learn something here, that I could gain an opportunity to work with the librarians and hopefully uncover something that would enable me to better understand my homeland."

"I'm sorry I kept you from that."

"You haven't kept me from it. You enabled me to ask different questions. Because of you, I've begun to see that perhaps the questions I have about Par aren't the only ones that need to be asked." She glanced over at him, smiling. "Then again, I'm not sure I necessarily want to be caught up in some of the things you've done. To think I'd face disciples of the Draasin Lord as a first-level student!"

"That was part of the accusations against me," Tolan admitted. He looked away, staring at the sky. "They accused me of being a part of some of the oddities that had been taking place ever since my arrival."

"There have been strange things that have occurred since we came to the Academy."

"There have, but they aren't my fault."

"I wasn't saying that. I was just suggesting maybe we need to begin looking for the reason behind all of the strangeness. I don't remember the search into the Convergence the same way you do, but first we had a shaper who attempted to dig into a deep place of power within the Academy, and then we had the disciples attacking before your Master Daniels was trying to do something with the Keystone."

"And that's after what happened at the waste," Tolan said.

"I'd forgotten about that. You and Jonas were also attacked when you went back for the Selection. I don't remember so many stories of attacks. The last time there were this many, the Draasin Lord had been active. As far as I knew, the Draasin Lord has been suppressed and the threat gone."

"What if he's making an attempt to return?"

"Why would he make an attempt to return? Why now?"

Tolan didn't have any answers. It was all speculation, anyway. Nothing really was able to be connected, and if it was, he certainly didn't have a part in it.

"Maybe rather than spending my time trying to dig into that sort of thing, I need to focus on my studies. With everything else that's happened, that's probably the best."

"Is that what you want to do?"

Tolan threw his hands in the air and shrugged. "I don't even know what I want. I've already told you what I thought I was doing with my shaping, but now, even that is different. Somehow, I'm now connected in a way I wasn't before. I welcome that, but at the same time, I'm not sure what it means. And I worry because of everything that's happened, the master shapers are going to be more like Master Rorn."

"All they need is time, Tolan."

He forced a smile, wishing that were true, but he had enough experience in Ephra to know that time didn't necessarily mend all things. Regardless of what Ferrah wanted for him, it was possible he would remain a pariah in the Academy.

And was that what he wanted?

20

The second-level rooms were boisterous and loud. Tolan approached the top of the stairs, stepping into the common room. The moment he did, everything died down. The sound of voices all around him quieted and he looked around, taking the survey of the people within.

At one table, Draln sat with three other students. A sneer crossed his face upon seeing Tolan. He leaned into Riley, whispering something into her ear, and she laughed.

At another table, Peter and Dion whispered silently. Tolan had half a mind to shape the wind so he could listen, but even if he did, he doubted he'd like what he heard. Others watched him, and he knew they would say something once he left.

Why was he even here?

It was bad enough that Master Rorn had treated him the way he had. Now, as expected, students were watching him.

He turned around, heading back down the stairs. Voices picked back up and he heard a distinct thread, with one phrase piercing the others.

Draasin Lord.

They accused him of serving the Draasin Lord.

It was much like he had feared, and even though he'd finished his Inquisition and had returned, supposedly able to return to classes, now he would have to deal with this.

How long would it linger?

If his time in Ephra taught him anything, it would be too long.

He reached the main level of the Academy, and even some of the upper-level students looked over at him, something in their gaze judging him. Tolan decided he didn't want to remain here.

He wanted to be anywhere but within the Academy walls.

He passed the library. Master Minden worked at the shelves, slotting books back into place, and she glanced over. He imagined her shaping as she studied him, though with her filmy eyes, she shouldn't be able to see him.

Tolan hurried out into the streets, focusing on the sense of shaping. There was power bursting all around him. It was that way in the city often. He had become increasingly attuned, a sign of whatever had happened to him during the Inquisition. He supposed he should be thankful for it, as without it, he would have less awareness of what was taking place around him.

As he turned a corner, he came face to face with Velthan and three of the first-level students.

Velthan grinned at him. "Ethar. They finally released you?"

"I'm not in the mood, Velthan," he said.

"No? You're too busy serving the Draasin Lord?" He said it loud enough so the others with him could hear. Velthan leaned forward, smiling as he looked at Tolan. "I always knew you did. Ever since your parents ran off and—"

A shaping built from Tolan and he pushed Velthan back.

He didn't use much force, and yet the other man was taken aback by it, stumbling. When the shaping departed, he staggered forward so he landed on one knee. He looked up at Tolan, anger clouding his eyes.

"Like I said, I always knew."

"And I said I'm not in the mood."

Tolan spun away from him, heading off into the city. That was just what he needed. Now in addition to the second-level students spreading rumors about him, he would have Velthan and these first-level students spreading even more.

When would it end?

Maybe it wouldn't. Could that be the lesson? Maybe that was the point of Master Irina holding him as long as she had. Regardless of whatever he might say, the damage was done. Any argument about his involvement was moot. He was tried and convicted.

He reached the edge of the city, and once there, he headed into the trees. It wasn't long before Tolan found himself in the park far outside the city, knowing it no longer mattered what the Inquisitors thought. If they found him here, it wouldn't make a difference.

Leaving the forest with a pulse of wind, the shaping lifting him up and over the wall, he made his way toward the center of the park. Everything was more peaceful here. There was quiet, and though he had the presence of earth and wind and fire and water, it didn't feel dangerous.

Strangely, ever since uncovering his connection to the element bonds, he had felt less in control than when he'd he thought he was only shaping the elementals. At least with the elementals, there was shape and function, but with these shapings, there was the sense he was out of control.

He wandered until he reached the center of the clearing where the Keystone once had stood. He took a seat, his hands pressing on either side of him. It was peaceful here, calm, quiet. There was a sense of comfort in being here that he welcomed.

It was much easier to come here than to return to the Academy. At least here, he didn't have to worry about others interfering when he attempted to practice.

He focused on fire, flipping through shaping after shaping, building one power after another. It came steadily, a surge of shaped magic, his control over it much more than it ever had been. He focused on the lessons he'd been through, his mind racing through the notes he'd taken over the last year, thinking of everything Master Sartan had wanted him to do. All of the shaping flowed out of him.

Moving on to earth, he worked through what he remembered of his lessons there as well. Sitting as he was, connected to earth—and in this place—he felt as if there were no restrictions to his ability to reach earth. Shaping after shaping flowed out of him until he was done with everything Master Shorav had taught.

He did the same with wind and then water.

It was tiring working through those shapings, but he rested, dozing off and then waking up to shape again. The position of the sun was all the notice he had that time was passing.

He could stay here. Continue to shape, practicing, and not return to the Academy.

Only... was that what he wanted?

There was still so much he could learn. There were things he had yet to uncover, lessons he still needed. And he was convinced there was some part of him that would eventually reach for spirit.

It had happened in his vision. Tolan was certain of that, though he didn't know what he'd done. Attempts to repeat it outside of the vision had failed. There was some key aspect of that shaping he had yet to uncover.

Somehow, that shaping was more powerful than almost any of the others he had done.

After resting and then waking again, Tolan sat,

focusing on fire. As he did, he added a touch of saa, mixing in the elemental. Flames danced, the fire swirling around him more brightly than before. He held onto saa, shifting to hyza, pushing forth the shaping he needed but focusing on that elemental as well. Both remained. Hyza made a circle around him, working its way around the park. No longer afraid he would somehow unleash the elementals, he made no effort to stop hyza. Releasing his control over it was easy and allowed him to focus on more elementals. He thought of esalash, the smoke elemental swirling, racing along the walls of the park.

Tolan sat back, watching as the elementals roamed. There was nothing about them that suggested they were harmful. They could be dangerous, but the same could be said about shaping in general. It wasn't unique to the elementals. And the longer he had been around them, shaping his connection to them, the more he had begun to believe they had no interest in harming him.

If only he had some way of communicating with them. He felt as if he had the beginnings of a possibility, but every time he tried, there was no response. He didn't believe the elementals were mindless creatures. There was some intellect to them. He felt certain of that.

Tolan shifted to the earth elementals, thinking of jinnar. It was the earth elemental he went to first, and rock began to rumble, forming the shape of the elemental. Tolan looked up at it, fatigue making him drowsy. "I wish you could talk to me."

He'd come a long way from when he had feared jinnar

during an attack at the Academy. Now he sat here, summoning the shape of the elemental, wishing to communicate with it?

Even if such a thing were possible, Tolan didn't know he should want to do so.

The ground rumbled, almost as if jinnar were trying to speak to him. Tolan smiled to himself. Maybe the earth elemental was trying to speak to them, and if it was, what would it have to say? He might summon the elemental, but he also suppressed it, forcing the elemental back down into the bond. He had no idea what that entailed, other than there seemed to be discomfort for the elemental when he did it.

Holding on to the connection again, he shifted, moving to wind and ara. It was a powerful wind elemental, and the first one that came to mind. As he held onto that connection, wind whistled around him. A face came into view, translucent and almost imagined. He smiled at the wind elemental. "You're all tied into the bonds, and I don't even know why."

He looked around. Hyza was wandering along the inside of the wall, the form increasingly more solid the longer he had it released. There was something very much foxlike about it, though there were still flames coursing within it.

Saa remained a flame, though it twisted, fluttering through the inside of the park, never causing damage. And they never threatened him.

Why had he not given much thought to that before?

Because of what he'd been taught. The fear had always been that the elementals were the domain of the Draasin Lord. Everything he'd ever heard was that the Draasin Lord wanted to release the elementals and control them. Seeing them like this, he had no interest in the elementals being controlled, but he wondered if perhaps they shouldn't be free.

Why shouldn't they? They were creatures, and they had power, and they belonged to this world. More than anything else, he felt that deeply.

He was too tired to focus on another elemental, so he rested, drifting once again.

When he awoke, he did so to a darkening sky. He looked around, jolted into alertness as he felt a tremor of fear about what had happened and where he was before finally remembering he was in the park. He was alone.

But not alone.

Jinnar sat watching over him. Hyza sat on the other side. There was a sense of ara flowing around him. Saa had to be somewhere, especially if the others were here. Tolan smiled. "I wish this place didn't hold you."

It was a troubling thought. A dangerous one. Thoughts like that involved him siding with the Draasin Lord.

And maybe the rumors about him were true. He had claimed he didn't serve the Draasin Lord, but if he was going to talk about freeing the elementals, what other answer was there?

He glanced at the sky, deciding by the time he returned to the Academy, it would be late enough that he should be able to sneak in. It would be much like what he had once done when he had first come to this place, and it would raise questions, but did those questions even matter?

He needed to stay in the Academy to continue his studies. He wanted to understand the element bonds. And as he looked at the elementals, he realized he wanted something more. He wanted to understand the elementals.

Where else would he be able to learn that but at the Academy?

It meant he would be forced to deal with the taunting. He would be forced to deal with all of the comments about his connection to the Draasin Lord. And he would be forced to withstand the unwanted attention from the master shapers.

Tolan could handle that. He *would* handle that.

He got to his feet. Jinnar and hyza did the same, and he had a sense of ara swirling around him, welcoming him.

When he left the park, he knew some connection to them would fade and the elementals would disappear. And maybe that was okay. He could return. This would be where he would come to pursue his own studies. It didn't have to be at the Academy all the time.

With that resolution in mind, he reached the wall and looked around. Jinnar and hyza and ara all waited. Saa flickered, giving faint light that danced around the inside of the clearing.

Tolan climbed up to the top of the wall and watched to

see whether the elementals would disappear or not, but they remained solid. Present.

And then he jumped over the wall.

As he headed back to the Academy, a feeling of relief washed through him. It was good to have come to a decision, even if it would be difficult. Then again, how difficult could it be? He lived so much of his life dealing with people making comments about him that a few more wouldn't harm him. He'd grown accustomed to it and dealing with that at the Academy would not be his preference, but it was a price he was willing to pay in order to continue his work and to continue understanding what that work meant for him.

At the edge of the forest leading into the city, Tolan paused, stretching out his connection to earth sensing, feeling all of the interconnectedness within Amitan. Maybe that was all he had felt when he had wandered through the city before, though he didn't think that it was. There had to have been something else. Maybe that had been spirit, and he had shaped it in some way he was unaware of.

And yet, Tolan didn't think so.

Starting down the hillside, the sense of shaping echoed all around.

After taking a dozen steps out of the forest, he paused.

There was something different about the shaping.

He glanced up at the Shapers Path, suddenly fearful of what might be up there. There had been rumors of disciples near the city. Could they be somewhere nearby? If they were, the fact he was out of the city, out in the park, would be difficult for others to overlook.

He raced into the city. Once he was there, he continued to feel shapings building.

One particularly strong shaping exploded at the corner of the city, back in the direction he'd come.

Tolan skittered to a stop.

Why would there have been a shaping like that?

The earth rumbled. That was not an earth shaping. That was an elemental.

Jinnar.

No.

He launched himself into the air, using wind and fire, searching for one of the Shapers Paths. In the darkness, they glowed faintly, something he wasn't aware of until standing upon it. He had only traveled upon the Shapers Path in the daylight, never at night, and never when he feared for an elemental making its way into the city.

He saw it in the distance.

It was jinnar, but moving alongside jinnar came hyza, prowling along the stone, the fire elemental walking alongside an earth elemental, neither of them where they should be.

Tolan's heart lurched. This was his fault. He had summoned the elementals but hadn't suppressed them again.

And now they were heading into the city.

Tolan raced along the Shapers Path, hurrying toward the elementals. He wanted to get near enough that he could try to speak to them, to warn them away. As he ran, he could feel something stirring within him. It was similar to the stirring he felt when he was shaping, but this came from a different place, a sense of nervousness, but a worry as well.

They were emotions, but they weren't his.

Tolan stopped, staring down at the city, his gaze fixed on the elementals, unable to tear it away.

He was detecting *their* emotions.

That couldn't be, could it?

You need to leave the city.

He sent the connection the same way he had before, uncertain whether it would work or not, but when he did, there came a pause. The elementals hesitated, stopping within the street. If anyone would wander out of the nearby buildings, they would get quite the shock.

Amitan isn't safe for you. You can remain in the park, and—

Tolan didn't get a chance to finish. A shaping built, slamming into jinnar.

The earth rumbled, and he felt the anger within the earth elemental. It was agitation… and fear.

The earth elemental didn't want to return. It wanted to stay out of the bond. And somehow Tolan was aware of that.

Trackers must have appeared, but where were they? It wasn't surprising they would respond so quickly. There were enough rumors about the possibility of elementals that he knew they would be on the lookout for this sort of thing.

Which was even more reason to have been careful.

What had he been thinking by leaving the elementals out in the park? The Keystone had been moved, so there was not anything to contain them as there had been. Now the elementals were able to roam freely—and it seemed they did.

Another shaping built and Tolan looked over, surprised by the suddenness of it.

It was one he recognized.

Not Trackers, but Inquisitors.

It surprised him that they would be the ones responsible for the elementals, but with their ongoing presence within the Academy, he didn't have any reason to think they'd do anything else.

Movement caught his attention.

Hyza raced between the buildings, darting quickly, no longer glowing with the same heat as it had before. Still, Tolan could feel it through his connection to fire, a sense that made little sense to him other than the fact he had been the one who had summoned the fire elemental. What of ara? He couldn't see the wind elemental, but he could feel the heavy gusting of wind and knew the elemental had to be here.

Please. I don't want anything to harm you. Return to the park. I will come back to you.

Hyza stopped, looking up, and there was a flash of red

in its eyes before it turned and raced back through the city, heading toward the trees.

Tolan let out a relieved sigh. At least hyza would get away. Jinnar continued to rumble, the sense of earth thundering, and he continued to send the request to the elemental, hoping it would return.

The Trackers—or Inquisitors, he wasn't sure—appeared. They were little more than outlines against the night, their dark cloaks making them difficult to see. Tolan prayed he remained hidden.

Shapings slammed into jinnar one after another, a steady onslaught of power that built, crashing into the elemental. There came a heavy and painful rumbling, like that of thunder and a storm crashing nearby, and then jinnar exploded, returning to the earth bond. Before it did, Tolan felt the pain, a strange sense of caring, almost as if the elemental was ripped from where it should be and forced someplace it was not meant to be.

That had to be imagined, didn't it?

He scanned for ara. As the wind elemental, it might be more difficult to find. And yet, the constant breeze had a source.

Tolan hurried toward the source. He found ara near the center of the city, making its way toward the Academy.

All three elementals had been following him.

But they hadn't been a threat. He was certain of that.

Two Inquisitors appeared on either side of ara. Power built from them, trapping the elemental in between.

As they did, he became aware of the pain from the elemental again.

He wasn't going to be the reason another elemental suffered.

Tolan crouched down on the Shapers Path and focused on smoke. All he needed was for a cloud to obscure ara, giving the elemental a chance to move away, to dissipate.

And he didn't want to summon another elemental. He thought he could call upon esalash and create the necessary smoke, but doing so would place that elemental in danger, too.

The shaping involved was difficult, and he had tried it on a small scale while in the park but never on a larger scale like this.

He had to try. More than that, he had the bondar. He slipped his hand into his pocket, gripping the furios, and focused on the shaping, pushing outward, letting that power flow from him. As it did, as he began to rise, he quashed it, squeezing it down so that smoke began to fill the space between the shapers, obscuring their attack.

Tolan held the shaping. There was a shout and another attempt to clear the smoke, a shaping of fire that drew upon his smoke, but Tolan was holding onto the furios, and drawing power through the bondar gave him a greater connection than the shapers had.

Go. Please return to the park. I will come for you. I don't want you to suffer the same way jinnar suffered.

He remained motionless on the Shapers Path, fearful that either ara had been trapped by the shapers or had decided to ignore him, but there came a fluttering and a swirling of wind. A brief flash of a translucent face appeared before him, and then it gusted off toward the north and the park.

Tolan rolled over, looking up at the sky. He continued to hold onto the shaping, but the strength in it was already beginning to fade. He needed to hurry off before the Inquisitors realized he'd been responsible for the shaping.

He raced along the Shapers Path, and when he reached a point near the Academy, he jumped, pushing off the Path with a shaping of wind and fire and landing in the courtyard. He paused, listening to the sounds of the night. There were other shapings, dozens of them, all searching for the elementals. He had seen no sign of saa and had to hope the fire elemental had remained where it was, not risking itself the same way the other three had.

Other distant shapings came, and they felt different, reminding him of what he had felt when he was drawn into the city in the first place.

Could they be disciples of the Draasin Lord?

If they were, he needed to get back inside. He'd made enough mistakes with running out and exposing himself with shapings that he had no interest in doing it again.

When he got inside the Academy, he was thankful there was no one inside.

He raced up the stairs and for a moment, he thought he felt a shaping, but that sense faded.

When he reached the second-level quarters, he headed through the common area slowly, but it was empty. He hurried back to his room, still feeling the nagging sense a shaping was building behind him, but any time he looked, there was nothing.

When he flopped down onto his bed, he stared up at the ceiling. His mind was racing.

He had denied to the Inquisitors that he served the Draasin Lord, and yet what had he just done?

What if he *was* the traitor?

Everything had started when he'd come to the Academy. And there *had* been a shaping over his mind, though he didn't know what it meant. It was possible he did serve the Draasin Lord, especially considering his view of the elementals.

Those thoughts stayed with him while he drifted, never falling fully asleep. There was always the sense of a shaping near him, and while it never built heavily enough to fear what it was doing, the fact he felt it throughout his sleep left him unsettled.

And mixed with it was the sense of elementals. They darted through his dreams, most calling to him, but occasionally, he felt a twinge of pain and a reminder of what he had detected when jinnar had been ripped out of this world and forced back into the bond. Each time he did, he awoke with a start, and it took a long time to fall back asleep.

21

THE WATER-SHAPING CLASS WAS BETTER THAN WIND shaping had been, and Tolan hadn't felt quite as harassed as he had with Master Rorn. Master Wassa was still stern with him, more so than he had been before, including looking at him askance when he had asked a particular question. Perhaps that had something to do with the fact Tolan had never shown much in the way of water shaping ability before and his questioning raised alarms for Master Wassa. Tolan couldn't help but think there was something more to it, possibly related to the fact Tolan had been involved with the upper-level students who had been injured during his first few months at the Academy, bringing them to Master Wassa for healing.

As he made his way through the Academy, he nearly collided with Master Aela. Spirit-shaping classes weren't nearly as frequent as the others, mostly because the ability to shape spirit wasn't something any of the earlier students ever demonstrated.

Seeing her now left him nervous. After what had happened with the elementals and his role in freeing them —and opposing the Inquisitors—he didn't want to be around any spirit shaper.

"Shaper Ethar. I hadn't realized you were released from your Inquisition."

Tolan blinked, looking her over. Master Aela was a small woman, dark of hair and with a round face. She had a slight frame, almost as if she would have been a wind shaper if she weren't a spirit shaper. She wore robes of white and had a silver belt buckle around them.

He wasn't quite sure how to respond. None of the other master shapers had been quite as forthright with their questioning about his Inquisition. She was the first one to have asked him a direct question.

"I've been out of it for about a week now," he said.

"A week? That means you were held for..." She frowned, and her mouth pressed in a tight line. "Much longer than anyone should have been held. Certainly, a student shaper should not have been held in an Inquisition quite so long as you. They must have felt as if they weren't able to obtain quite what they had intended."

Tolan considered whether he would say something about why he had been held in the Inquisition but decided against it. It would only draw more attention to the fact he had been accused of serving the Draasin Lord.

"I'm glad to see you back among the second-level

students."

"You are?"

"We need all the shapers in the Academy we can. Otherwise we run the risk of not having the necessary support to deal with the threat of the Draasin Lord. The continued attacks outside the city have certainly got those of us within the Academy nervous."

"What sort of attacks?"

"Nothing that students need to be concerned about. I shouldn't have said anything. I will see you in class soon." A shaping built from her but didn't seem directed anywhere.

"Do we have another spirit class coming up?"

"Seeing as how you're a second-level student now, you have them weekly."

"I've missed that many?" But then, it wasn't like he'd missed having any exposure to spirit. He'd been around spirit shapers exclusively over the last few weeks.

"We can get you caught up. If you would like, I have some time now."

Tolan wanted to say no. With what had happened, and how he had been responsible for the elementals, he *should* say no. Still, he'd committed himself to the Academy, to mastering shaping. In order to do that, he needed to be capable of everything that he could. Even if it involved spending time with the spirit shaper. Besides, it would draw attention away from him.

"If you don't have the time, we can find another time."

"It's not that, it's just that after the Inquisition, I'm a

little leery of spirit shaping." At least he could be honest with that.

"Ah. This will be nothing like an Inquisition. While the shaping sometimes takes a similar form, the technique in learning is much different." She turned and guided him along the hallway.

Tolan followed, heading toward the stairs and up to the platform that would lead into the spirit tower. As he did the last time he was here, he looked around, surveying the space, noting the markings. There were runes here, and he didn't know he had seen them quite as clearly before, but there was no mistaking them now.

With a shaping of wind and fire, she launched herself toward the tower. Tolan paused and decided to use a wind shaping, wondering whether he would be able to hover with it. He summoned the wind, pushing it through him, holding himself in place, and then pushed. He hadn't attempted this shaping since the last time he was in the wind classroom, though doing it without the withering was surprisingly easier. He didn't have to worry about having such an explosion of power.

When he landed in the spirit hall, he looked around. It felt as if it had been ages since he had been here last, though not much had changed. Not that much ever changed in the various classrooms, but this one was different. Unlike many of the other classrooms, Master Aela didn't have a desk at one end of the room. A small table rested in the center, a place where she would stand and speak to students who sat around her. There weren't workspaces like within the other classrooms, though there wasn't the same need, either.

As Tolan circled the room, he noticed a rune worked into the floor.

He paused, moving more slowly as he walked around, and wondered why he had never seen it before. It wasn't as if this rune was difficult to see. It was there, on display, but the table obscured it, and likely the presence of other students had done the same.

"You're admiring the pattern," she said.

"The rune, yes. It's similar to the one down in the main part of the tower."

She cocked her head at him and a shaping built from her. Instinctively, Tolan wrapped himself in fire, inverting it as he had with Master Irina, pressing the heat within himself. Her shaping struck his barrier and slipped around it.

He watched for any sign of recognition of what he had done, but there didn't appear to be any. Either she didn't detect it or she gave no sign of detecting it.

"Very few students pay much attention to runes."

"I understand they have a connection to the element bonds and are powerful," Tolan said.

"They are, or at least, they can be when used by the right person. But then, if you are aware of runes, then you already know this."

"I doubt I'd be able to identify too many of the particular runes."

"Many have studied runes over the years, looking for

meaning within the shapes. Very few have ever come to understanding anything about them, though there are some who invest considerable time in such things."

"I've been told students aren't allowed to study them."

"No. Study of that type of power is generally restricted to those who have knowledge of the element bonds, in order to ensure nothing more dangerous ensues. You can understand that if it weren't restricted, a power like that could cause considerable difficulty."

"How?"

"Using a power like that could lead to a disruption in the element bond. With the right sort of disruption, it could unleash the elementals."

"I didn't realize these runes were tied to the elementals."

She frowned. "I shouldn't be speaking of such things with you, Shaper Ethar. We are here to discuss your connection to spirit and to see if there is anything you could gain from having some additional instruction."

"When do shapers generally find a connection to spirit?"

"If there *is* a connection to spirit, the shaper usually develops it after they have begun to master each of the element bonds."

"Usually?"

"As with everything with shaping, there are exceptions. Some are born to spirit, the same way some are born to each of the other elements. There are some who manage to use that connection to make them quite a bit stronger."

"I didn't realize some were born to an element."

"Have you never had a connection to a specific element?"

"I was able to sense earth first, I suppose."

"Yes. Sensing would often precede shaping."

"I was a fire shaper first."

"Now, that is odd."

"Sort of like me," he said.

She chuckled. "Each of us has our own unique features. The Great Mother would ask we embrace that uniqueness."

"I find it difficult to embrace the things that have made me different over the years."

"And that is why you should embrace it, Shaper Ethar. Perhaps in time you will gain a greater understanding of your connection to the elements and understand your uniqueness is the way the Great Mother wanted you to be."

Tolan took a seat, crossing his legs and looking at the stand in the middle of the room. Master Aela stood in front of it, resting her hands on either side of it, a shaping building.

As it built, Tolan realized there was a swirling energy rotating around him.

He replaced his barrier, holding it in front of him, using the connection to fire as he inverted it, protecting himself. As he did, he had a sense that the shaping struck the barrier, forcing it down. Master Aela watched him, saying nothing as she did.

"Master Aela?"

"We are going to work on your connection to spirit, Shaper Ethar," she said.

"What are you doing?"

"I am helping you to connect to spirit."

Her shaping continued to build, and as it did, Tolan recognized it.

A barrier.

It was the same sort of barrier he'd faced in the Inquisition. Just as he had at that time, he pushed against it, though this was different. Stronger.

He got to his feet and tried to take a step away, but he was held in place. He struck an invisible wall and was pushed backward.

"Master Aela?" he said again.

"Just relax, Shaper Ethar. I will have all I need soon enough."

"Have all of what?"

"What you are hiding in your mind."

"I'm not hiding anything."

Master Aela smiled, and it was almost disarming. Tolan's heart began to pound, and it seemed to do so in response to the power of the shaping she was building. If he didn't do anything, whatever she was layering upon him would overwhelm him.

With a surge of understanding, he realized the shaping she used upon him was strengthened by the rune.

Great Mother!

Had the Grand Inquisitor had access to a rune when

354 | D.K. HOLMBERG

she was shaping spirit with him?

He didn't think so. Even if she had, it might not have been nearly as effective. He was in the spirit tower, a place constructed for shapings like this, and standing before a master shaper of spirit.

He added earth and wind and water quickly to his barrier, using it to wrap around himself, but even that would not hold. Tolan could feel the effect, could feel the way it was resisting him, and as much as he wanted to continue to fight, he was already growing weak.

But he had his bondars.

It was different than the last time, when he had faced Master Irina. He had been helpless then, and he hadn't had the bondars or anything with him that would have allowed him to shape more strongly. With those, he had to believe he could overpower her shaping, but how was he going to do that?

Tolan reached for the furios, pulling it from his pocket and squeezing it. He drew fire through it, adding it to his barrier. For a moment, it solidified, strengthened, and he reached for the earth bondar, holding on to it as he focused on his shaping, forcing it outward.

Power surged, and the two of them were strengthened, but even with those two bondars, he could already feel himself fading, the additional power he thought he could command not nearly enough when faced with a shaper of skill who was augmented by the rune placed in the center of the room.

"I have often wondered what you have hidden within

your mind, Shaper Ethar. I have attempted to extract it but doing so has been difficult. You have been surrounded by those who have attempted to protect you. It was easy enough to learn you were the traitor but understanding the protection has been more difficult."

"Who has protected me?"

"Who indeed?"

Her shaping pressed inward and she took a step toward him, unhindered by the power of her shaping.

Tolan pushed outward, trying to force himself away from her, and his hands struck the barrier. He dropped the earth bondar and tried to reach for it, but she got to it first, lifting it and glancing over at it.

"An interesting trinket. I'm surprised you managed to acquire a golan and furios, though perhaps you are far more resourceful than I had anticipated."

"What are you doing?"

"You are the key."

"The key for what?"

"For finding the Draasin Lord."

"I don't serve him. I told Master Irina the same thing, and regardless of what you might claim, I don't serve him."

"You may not remember that you serve him, yet you do. That is what I need to extract." She took another step. Her shaping pressed up against his hand and he dropped the furios.

Power washed away from him. She picked it up, sliding it into her pocket.

She had him feeling more helpless than he had even when facing Master Irina. Her power was greater. It was the rune, but now she had the bondars, he would have no way of escaping.

The shaping continued to press inward, collapsing his barrier with each step she took. She smiled at him, and he fought, but he wasn't able to overpower her.

He stood there. As she stepped closer, his hands were forced up toward his chest, folded inward at the elbow, until he was pressing his palms against his chest.

She stood directly across from him. Her shaping was incredible. There was something about it that he recognized, the heat and pain he thought he had seen in his vision.

"It will be far less painful if you don't resist," she said.

"Why?" he asked.

"Why what?"

"Why are you doing this to me? I've told you I don't serve the Draasin Lord."

"Did you know the Draasin Lord was a student here?"

The change in conversation was jarring, and Tolan nodded. "I've heard that."

"And he was a powerful shaper. Many who speak of him often neglect to report that, almost as if they fear that sharing his prowess would bring him back, but there is no shame in acknowledging the fact he was capable. Competent. And there is much we can learn from the Draasin Lord, but at the same time, we must protect the Academy. That is the role of the Inquisitors."

His breath caught. She was an Inquisitor. He should have expected it, considering the fact she had the ability to shape spirit so strongly. How could she be anything other than an Inquisitor?

And yet, he would have expected an Inquisitor to serve more openly, not hiding the fact of their service the way she did.

"The Grand Inquisitor already questioned me. There was nothing she tried to uncover," he said.

"The Grand Inquisitor is a fool," she said, waving her hand dismissively. "She believes the role of the Inquisitors is different, and if it were up to her, she would take us backward along a different pathway, one we have evolved beyond. Now we have established ourselves, the Inquisitors must be strengthened."

Was that what this was about? Had he somehow gotten into the middle of a battle between the Inquisitors?

If he had, there would be no way to win.

Her shaping pressed down upon him. "Once I find what you know, once I remove the threat of the Draasin Lord, I will be named Grand Inquisitor."

Tolan attempted to shape, but he was barely hanging on as it was. He tried adding an augmentation, trying to use a connection to the elementals, but as tired as he was from forcing her back, even that was too much. He couldn't reach the elementals. Though he strained for them, struggling to grab hold of what he could of that power, he was unable to focus well enough to call to them.

She leaned forward and her shaping continued to

build, swirling around him. "I can see why you would have been so difficult for the Grand Inquisitor. Unfortunately for her, she has not discovered several of the techniques I have uncovered."

"What techniques are those?"

She smiled at him. "Techniques that involve invoking the runes of power placed all around my tower."

Tolan squeezed his hands against his chest. As he did, his fingers fumbled through his shirt, and he came across something unexpected.

The ring he'd found in his home. His mother's ring.

He had a memory of it, a memory from the shaping of it, and whether that was real or not, he wondered. If it was real, if it was a bondar, could he use it?

Tolan squeezed his hand around it. It seemed impossible to believe a tiny ring would be able to help him, but what else did he have?

Tolan focused on the ring, thinking about the power he wanted to summon, imagining the various element bonds, all swirling, giving him increased power and a connection to the elements. If he could reach that, he could free himself. All he needed was enough force to push back against Master Aela.

Nothing seemed to work.

It had to be a bondar. He'd seen its making in his visions and knew that it had to be, but how was he going to effectively use it?

Nothing came to him. There were no answers despite his desire to find them.

He sighed, thinking back through his march through the city, the connections he'd felt. He thought about the way he had felt when his parents had been in his vision. He thought about the glowing power he'd connected to when he'd been there, the only power that had allowed him to stop Master Irina.

As he did, power began to build within him.

It was a deep, enormous, and it reverberated. It seemed to start from someplace buried within him. As it burbled forward, it exploded through the ring, but then it exploded outward, coalescing in the pattern all around him.

The rune.

Not just the rune, but the *spirit* rune.

He pushed, letting the shaping pour out from him, and when it did, it slammed into Master Aela.

She staggered back, her eyes going wide.

Tolan took a step away, but another shaping began to circle around him.

This shaping seemed to come from a different direction and he spun, realizing he and Master Aela weren't here alone. There were other Inquisitors within the room. Three at least, but could there be more?

As their shaping attached itself to him, he pushed upon them, holding onto that deep connection he had before—that of spirit or the element bonds or something.

It exploded away from him, forcing the shapers back.

He was freed.

Tolan turned, racing to the edge of the platform, and he jumped.

He didn't think about what he was doing, and poured power out, using that to allow himself to drop to the ground.

When he landed, he was immediately surrounded by other Inquisitors.

Could the Grand Inquisitor be a part of this?

And here he thought he had been freed, but that had been nothing but an illusion.

He focused on shaping, pushing backward, forcing the Inquisitors away from him.

There were too many. Seven Inquisitors filled the space of the spirit tower. Even with the bondar, he wasn't going to be successful.

Tolan forced his shaping outward, adding fire and earth and water and wind. It combined with that power he was drawing from somewhere deep within himself, and all reverberated, exploding outward.

There was an opening and Tolan took it, racing down the stairs.

At the bottom of the stairs, the Grand Inquisitor approached. She was with the Grand Master.

He glanced over his shoulder. Other shaping was building behind him, and it was incredible, enough power that he didn't know whether he would be able to ignore it.

"Shaper Ethar," the Grand Master said, hollering down the hall, his voice carrying on his shaping.

Tolan hesitated but turned away, heading out into the city.

Out on the street, he paused, looking around. What was he doing? He was running from the Academy.

No. He was running from a *shaping*. Whatever they intended to do, he knew it meant something dangerous.

He raced through the streets. As he did, he felt shaping all around him. Some of the shaping was incredibly powerful and seemed to chase him. Tolan was tempted to jump to the Shapers Path, but all that would do would be to carry him away from the city.

He needed a chance to regroup. To figure out what the Inquisitors were doing to him, and what they intended. He couldn't do that without returning to the Academy.

He reached the edge of the city, having run faster than he thought himself capable, and in the distance rose the forest. Out there was the Keystone, and the possibility of the elementals he once had known. It was gone, but the park might be a reasonable place to hide.

Tolan hurried away, darting toward the trees. Shapings continued to build and he glanced up, realizing there were shapers on the Shapers Path following him into the trees and the forest. He had to stay ahead of them. Once he reached the park at the center of the forest, he could jump the wall, use the power within there to hide himself, and then...

Then he would have to decide what was next.

At this point, it might simply be leaving the Academy.

What other options did he have? He was now an outcast, and he had abandoned what he had set out to do.

A shaper approached, and Tolan spun.

It was the Grand Master.

"Shaper Ethar. What are you doing?"

Tolan breathed out, looking around. Where were the Inquisitors?

"I... I don't know. Master Aela attacked me, and I..."

"Aela attacked you?" The Grand Master asked.

"She was using the spirit shaping. She had anchored it to a rune within the spirit tower. She seems to think I have some way of reaching the Draasin Lord, but I've already told the Grand Inquisitor I don't."

"Are you certain of that?" the Grand Master asked.

"I don't know anything different than anyone else knows about the Draasin Lord. I don't want to be a part of this anymore."

"Why don't you come with me, Shaper Ethar. We can get this all sorted out."

He was close to the park and the former location of the Keystone. It wouldn't take long, and once he was there, he could hide, take a moment to regroup, and then he could decide what he wanted to do. Right now, he wasn't sure what he wanted.

"Shaper Ethar. You need to return. Don't waste your opportunity at the Academy like this."

More than anything else, that got to him. He took a deep breath and went with the Grand Master.

22

AS THEY NEARED THE GRAND MASTER'S ROOMS, HE HEARD A voice behind him. It was Master Aela, and she was calling after the Grand Master. Tolan didn't know what she was after, but there was a sense of agitation in her voice.

"Go inside and have a seat," he said.

Tolan tried to look back, but the Grand Master blocked his view, and Tolan didn't try to push. He climbed the stairs and had reached the door when a shaping slithered out from the Grand Master, pressing into the door and unlocking it. Tolan glanced back, but the Grand Master had already begun to approach Master Aela. She was trying to look past him, but she couldn't, which surprised Tolan, as the Grand Master was not a tall man.

Pressing the door open, Tolan entered and closed it behind him. The room was cluttered, with various items stacked along shelves, dozens of books crammed in the bookshelves, and various artifacts resting along the floor.

At the center of the room was a large stone chalice, and a silvery liquid inside reminding him of the Convergence. He made a steady circuit of the room before taking a seat. He would wait for the Grand Master to return.

His heart still raced, and he worried about what would happen to him. He had opposed a master shaper, but more than that, there seem to be something going on with the Inquisitors. Given what he'd experienced with the Grand Inquisitor, Tolan wanted nothing to do with whatever disagreement they had.

When the door opened, he spun around, expecting to see the Grand Master, but it was not him. Instead, it was the Grand Inquisitor.

"You are causing quite the commotion, Shaper Ethar."

He scrambled to his feet. "I haven't been causing anything."

"I think you have. You were observed while shaping outside the city."

"Observed doing what?" he asked, his heart racing faster than he wanted it to. When he'd last been the park, he'd been shaping by himself, and if anyone had seen what he had been shaping, there was the potential someone would know he had been focusing on the elementals.

"You should have spent more time away from the city," she said.

"I don't know what you're talking about."

"Unfortunately, I'm quite certain you do, Shaper Ethar." A shaping built from her and Tolan reacted, slamming his barrier in place around him, using a combination of all the element bonds he could, but her shaping wasn't intended for him. It struck the door, pushing against it.

Why would she try to seal off the door?

"I'm afraid we don't have much time," she said.

"Grand Inquisitor?"

"Come," she said.

He tried to resist, but her shaping wrapped around him faster than he could react, and she headed to the back of the Grand Master's room. She reached a bookshelf where she tapped a series of shelves, and the wall slid apart almost as if shaped. She pushed him forward, sending him into the darkness behind it. She turned back around, pushing on something else, and the shelf slid back into place with the click. It plunged him into darkness.

A glowing orb was shaped into existence, and she set it to float in front of her. "Come with me, Shaper Ethar."

He followed her but wasn't sure he really had much of a choice. The tendril of a shaping remained wrapped around him, and after having fought off Master Aela, he didn't know if he had the strength necessary to resist.

The glowing orb guided the way, and at the end of the hallway—a hall that was hidden within the walls of the Academy—they intersected with a narrow staircase. She took the stairs, heading down, twisting in a spiraling fashion that seemed to follow the inside of the Academy, a slow spiral that wound deeper and deeper into the earth.

"Are you taking me to the Convergence?"

"You should never have seen the Convergence," she

said. "Your having that experience has created this problem."

"I don't understand," he said. "I'm not trying to cause problems, and I've told you over and over again that I don't serve the—"

"I know you said you don't serve the Draasin Lord, Shaper Ethar." She glanced back at him. "You held out far longer than I expected."

"I'm sorry. I wasn't trying to fight you."

"What makes you think you were fighting me?"

"What do you mean?"

"Do you believe I was the one attacking you during the Inquisition?"

"I saw you on the ground. I know what happened there."

"You saw what you needed to see, Shaper Ethar."

They continued down the stairs, and now curiosity piqued within him. Where was she bringing him? Was there something here that would help him understand?

Every time he thought they would stop, they continued to spiral downward and downward. Eventually, the stairs let out into a wide-open area. The air stunk, hung with a stench of mold and age and moisture. The sound of dripping came from somewhere distant, and he wondered how that would be possible, as deep as they seemed to be beneath the Academy.

The Grand Inquisitor stopped in front of a doorway. She pressed her hand upon it. A shaping built from her, and this time, Tolan knew with certainty it had to be spirit. It was pure, no other shapings mixed in, and it seemed to reverberate within him, a familiar sense.

How was he aware of that?

The door swung open.

Tolan stood behind her, watching, a fearful anxiety filling him. Could he have been wrong before? Could that not have been the Inquisition? Maybe they were bringing him to something new now.

"Where are you taking me?"

"There are tunnels all throughout Amitan. There's a reason Amitan was founded here."

"I thought it was the Convergence."

"The Convergence has given the Academy a certain power, but it has not always been here."

"How is that possible?"

"There is much you have yet to understand about shaping, Shaper Ethar."

She stepped inside a room and waited for him to follow. When he did, he found he was in a strange, arching tunnel. Water had flowed through here, though it didn't appear to be any longer, and everything around him spoke of shaped power.

Tolan glanced over at Master Irina, looking for some way of understanding what she was doing.

"A series of tunnels extends all throughout the city. That is the reason Amitan was placed here," she said.

"Because of the tunnels?"

"Because the tunnels interconnect between here and elsewhere."

"Where elsewhere?"

"You'll see."

They continued to make their way through the tunnels, and Tolan followed her. They walked for what seemed an hour, passing various branch points before finally, she motioned to a specific fork and guided him through. At the end of the tunnel was another door much like the one they had entered before. She created a shaping of spirit and the door opened. She walked him through, motioning for him to stay ahead of her.

Tolan didn't know whether to be afraid or curious, and both emotions warred within him as if to gain supremacy. He was nervous about what she was doing with him, but he was curious as to where she thought to bring him. More than that, he wondered if perhaps she intended to help him.

"Does the Grand Master know I'm here with you?"

"I hope not," she said, closing the door.

She left him.

He was alone, standing on a stairway much like the one that had led down into the tunnels in the first place, and he tried pushing on the door to open it, but it didn't open. He reached for his sense of shaping, that of what he thought to be spirit, but it didn't work. Even if it did, he wasn't sure he knew the proper shaping to open the door.

What choice did he have but to head up the stairs?

As he went, he felt a nervous tremble within him. There was something here, but what was it? Why would they have wanted him to go in this direction?

No answers came.

With each step, he felt a growing uncertainty.

At the top of the stairs, he reached the door.

He pushed on it, but it didn't open. He shaped, trying to open it, but again it didn't work.

Focusing on the ring and his sense of shaping deep within him, he gave the door another shove, and finally, it swung open.

Sunlight streamed in.

He didn't recognize anything around him, but there was lush greenery. A gentle breeze pulled on the air. A bright sun shone overhead.

He stepped forward carefully, separating from the darkness, and as he did, he pushed the door closed.

Sounds of wildlife around him seemed to call to him. Everything had a welcoming warmth, a comforting feeling, and Tolan wanted nothing more than to stay here, but he knew he couldn't.

Distantly, he became aware of a shaping.

There was nothing else around him, and he headed off, following the path of the shaping.

He paused, looking around, and couldn't help but feel as if he had been here before, but why? He didn't think he had, though there was something distinctly familiar about all of this.

As he headed forward, following the sense of the spirit shaping, he worried if perhaps the reason he felt as if he'd been here before was because he had.

What if all of this was a spirit shaping?

The Grand Master had left him in his room, and the Grand Inquisitor had come to him, guiding him. With a sudden fear, Tolan wondered if perhaps all of this was a mistake.

He reached toward the bondar, attempting to shape through it, but there was no reaction.

Where had she brought him?

Deeper into his mind again.

Tolan could feel the distant shaping.

Another step, and the power of the shaping continued to build.

He took another step, and everything blurred past him.

Now he knew this was shaped.

How had she spirit-shaped him so subtly?

He followed the shaping in the distance. It was growing stronger and stronger, a beacon.

Had the Grand Inquisitor known about that?

If she had, maybe he couldn't go this way. If this was what she wanted, he knew he needed to do anything but take that path.

And yet there was something strangely compelling about it calling him across the distance.

He approached and could feel the power continuing to build.

Tolan paused, focusing on that power.

If he went that way, he would be going where she wanted him to go.

But maybe that power was trying to help him, trying to draw him out of his shaping.

No. He needed to head back.

Which meant returning to the tunnels. Which meant returning back into the Academy. Which meant finding a way back to himself.

Tolan spun around, running away from the shaping he detected. He found the opening in the wall and raced down the stairs. At the bottom of the stairs at the doorway, he unleashed a shaping into the door, and it dissolved. Tolan ran, following his steps back to where he'd been, uncertain whether he could retrace his steps, but there was a familiarity, and he managed to make his way back to the initial door, and he sent another shaping of power into it. Once more, it dissolved. This time, when he raced up the stairs, his heart beating wildly in his chest, he could feel a resistance pressing upon him, as if some unseen force didn't want him to take this path.

Did that mean he *needed* to take this path?

Tolan no longer knew, but what he did know was that somewhere out here was his way back into his mind and back into reality.

And he needed to reach it.

He formed a wedge with his shaping, carving through the resistance, racing up the stairs, winding around the inside of the tower once again until he reached the back side of that bookshelf. She had tapped a series of sequences along it, and he thought about how she had done it before deciding it didn't matter.

He slammed power into the wall. Like the other doors, this one dissolved. He stepped out, and as he did, he real-

372 | D.K. HOLMBERG

ized his body was still sitting in a chair in the Grand Master's office.

Tolan raced toward it, falling forward, back into his body.

He opened his eyes, and Master Aela stood in front of him.

"How do I find the Draasin Lord?"

Tolan pulled upon a shaping and slammed it into her.

The suddenness of it startled her and he jumped to his feet, racing toward the door to the Grand Master's room, throwing it open and hurrying outside. The Grand Master lay motionless outside his office. Inquisitors lined the hallway.

Where was the Grand Inquisitor?

Tolan spun, hurrying toward the opposite end, when footsteps behind him caught his attention. He darted into the first open door.

The library.

His heart sank.

He threw the doors closed. In all the time he'd been here, the library doors were rarely closed, and he quickly shaped, sealing them closed.

He leaned on the doors, breathing heavily.

"Shaper Ethar. There is no shaping in the library."

Tolan turned around carefully and saw Master Minden watching him. Her eyes were narrowed and he knew he'd made a mistake. Not only had he shaped in the library, but he had *shaped* in the library. It was more than forbidden, it was impossible to do—and yet here he was, having used a shaping to seal himself inside.

"I'm sorry. The Inquisitors and Master Aela and—"

"Come with me," she said.

"Don't tell me you're going to betray me too," he said.

"Betray you? Shaper Ethar, I have done nothing but help you."

"They think I'm the traitor."

She looked back at him, the film over her eyes making it difficult to know what she saw. "Are you?"

Tolan took a deep breath. How could he lie to Master Minden? She'd been kind to him the entire time he was here. She was the only person he trusted.

"I don't know. I just wanted to learn. I can't help it that I don't see the elementals the same way as the master shapers."

She frowned. "Come along."

She guided him to the stairs leading up to the restricted section, and he followed her, glancing back at the dais. She was the only librarian here at this time, and he was thankful for that, though he wondered why Master Minden would be helping him—if that's what she was doing. It was possible she was betraying him the same as everyone else, but he would take the risk with her.

He'd never been up here and didn't have an opportunity to spend too much time looking, for she guided him into a narrow hallway with a ceiling so low, he had to duck down. It led through a tight stone section. At the end of it, she pushed open a doorway. Sunlight streamed in.

"Go, Shaper Ethar."

"Go where?"

"Go where you must. Find your way. Find yourself. Understand what happened and who you are. And when you do, perhaps then you can return."

"I don't understand."

The sense of shaping built all around him, slamming into the Academy.

Disciples.

Master Aela hadn't lied when she had said they were here. Disciples of the Draasin Lord were attacking the Academy? And Master Minden wanted him to leave?

"It's not safe for me to go," he said.

"On the contrary, Shaper Ethar, it is imperative you do."

"Because you think they're here because of me as well." His heart sank. "I'm not with the Draasin Lord. I'm not the traitor."

Master Minden smiled. She met his gaze with her milky white eyes, and she nodded. "I know you think that."

"Then why do I need to go with them?"

"Because they are here for you."

She pushed, and Tolan was forced outside of the Academy. The door closed behind him, sealing closed with another shaping. Seven shapers—disciples—landed on the Academy roof. He hadn't realized it, but she had let him out into the center of the Academy, and atop a tower he was surprised to realize was spirit. The other four towers surrounded it.

He tried to build a shaping, wrapping it around himself, prepared to do whatever it took to escape the disciples, and he had started to push outward when one of the disciples' faces caught his attention.

Time seemed to stop.

"Father?"

His father strode forward, taking his hand. "Tolan. There you are. It's time for us to go."

"Go where?"

"To complete your training."

EPILOGUE

THE WALK THROUGH THE FOREST TOOK LESS TIME THAN SHE had anticipated. The ground was hard, tamped down from footsteps made over repeated journeys back and forth between Amitan, creating an obvious path through the forest. Were it not for those footsteps, she doubted she would even be aware of where it would lead.

Every so often, she paused, focusing on the sounds of the forest, stretching outward with earth shapings, but nothing came. When she was satisfied there was nothing else, she let spirit shapings drift away from her as well. Those were far more tightly controlled. Spirit took considerable strength, and while she had talent with spirit, excessive strength was not a part of it. Hers was more a creativity and understanding of the benefits—and limitations—of spirit. Knowing those limitations allowed her to know her own limitations.

Satisfied, she continued onward, maintaining the

subtle shaping concealing her, masking her comings and goings from others. That was one of her greatest strengths, and a technique she had learned from her first mentor. It was a difficult skill, focusing the shaping upon oneself. Most believed it couldn't be done, and for most people, it couldn't be. Doing so was dangerous, and it risked burning off the ability to shape, but for those who knew how, such a shaping created potential. It allowed her to move without fear of others seeing her passing.

When she reached the stone wall, she rested her hands upon it. The protections remained. They were ancient, formed well over a thousand years ago by shapers who understood the elements and the elementals differently than shapers of today. There was power in that knowledge, and unfortunately, far too many people believed those ancient shapers were ignorant. They failed to understand the nature of how shaping had changed and evolved.

There were times when she wished it hadn't evolved *quite* so dramatically. There were times when she wished shapers of today understood and appreciated that power more the way they once had, but unfortunately, pride often got in the way of recognizing the differences.

She climbed up along the wall, boosting herself with a shaping of earth, and stood atop it. As she stood there, she sent out a summons. Power radiated from her, pressing outward, reaching into the earth, stretching beyond and into the bonds.

As she focused, she listened.

Many viewed the element bonds as something shapers were meant to tap into. While that was partly the case, that power had been twisted over the years, as many things twist over time. Men became fearful of others with power, and they forced that power into the one place where they thought they understood it. In doing so, they changed the very nature of the world, often in ways they could never understand.

The element bonds were unsettled these days. They were agitated, and it didn't surprise her the so-called master shapers did not notice it. Were they more attuned to the elements they shaped, perhaps they would be, but instead, all they focused on was power, attempting to draw that out, unmindful the very source they pulled it from rebelled against them.

Probing deeper, she focused upon the lost powers within the bonds. It was there, buried and waiting.

There was the sense of the various elementals working within the bonds. As she focused, she could reach to them, calling to them. Summoning them and freeing them from the bonds was not her ability, but she could use her connection to spirit to reach for them, to understand how they were trapped. She could feel the anxiety within them. And she detected something else, something unexpected.

Hope.

Why would there be hope within the elementals? Could have anything to do with all of the recent attacks? The disciples had continued to work, wanting to free the elementals from the bonds, understanding the suffering they'd faced, but they were limited in how quickly they could work. They required help to free the elementals from the bonds, needing those with the natural-born connection, something only those who had it from birth could provide.

It was difficult to detect it. Not all were capable of it, and those who were capable were incredibly valuable.

Patience. We will free you soon.

You must find him again.

The voice that came back to her was deep and booming, and it seemed to flow through her, practically burning her.

The Draasin Lord.

He is coming to you, she said. *He will need guidance and a direct connection.*

It will be provided. You must do what you can to ensure his safe arrival.

There is little I can do, but I will try. You know I need to remain here. Others work to solidify the bonds, to make the connection permanent. Once it is...

I know. You must stop it before it becomes permanent.

The voice became distant. Communicating in this way was difficult, even for one as powerful as the Draasin Lord. She released her spirit connection to the bonds, relaxing it, and hobbled away, making her way back to the forest. She maintained her shielding, hiding herself from those who would find her, and wandered her way through the streets back to the Academy, ignoring the Inquisitors she passed. They wanted to find a traitor, and they had, only they didn't fully understand. Eventually, they would.

It wasn't until she was back inside that she finally allowed herself to relax, releasing her shaping, as she took her place upon the dais.

Click now for book 4 of Elemental Academy: The Wind Rages

After discovering the Inquisitor's plot within the Academy, Tolan is offered a chance to go with his father and learn from the Draasin Lord. Doing so not only means turning against the Academy and everything he has come to know, but means the Inquisitors will succeed in their plan.

When the Grand Master comes to him asking a

dangerous favor, Tolan must make a choice that might bring him into direct contact with the Draasin Lord.

Everything he's been taught about the elementals and the Draasin Lord is wrong.

If he can stop Aela and the Inquisitors, he might be able to save the Academy, but the Draasin Lord has something else in mind for him.

ALSO BY D.K. HOLMBERG

Darkness Rising

Endless Night

Summoner's Bond

Seal of Light

The Elder Stones Saga

The Darkest Revenge

Shadows Within the Flame

Remnants of the Lost

The Coming Chaos

The Shadow Accords

Shadow Blessed

Shadow Cursed

Shadow Born

Shadow Lost

Shadow Cross

Shadow Found

The Collector Chronicles

Shadow Hunted

Shadow Games

Shadow Trapped

The Dark Ability

The Dark Ability

The Heartstone Blade

The Tower of Venass

Blood of the Watcher

The Shadowsteel Forge

The Guild Secret

Rise of the Elder

The Sighted Assassin

The Binders Game

The Forgotten

Assassin's End

The Dragonwalker

Dragon Bones

Dragon Blessed

Dragon Rise

Dragon Bond

Dragon Storm

Dragon Rider

Dragon Sight

The Teralin Sword

Soldier Son

Soldier Sword

Soldier Sworn